# ERA!

The years following the Great Depression in America were lean years, to put it mildly. That statement takes on an even deeper meaning when it applied to the migrant farm worker during that time period. Welfare was as scarce as hen's teeth and just about as hard to come by where they were concerned, and most of those families were too proud to accept help if it had been offered.

Such was the way of life in the Olfson family. Mr. Olfson had been known to say that if a man doesn't work, he doesn't eat. Their lives were lived at the bottom of the social ladder. And yet there was a magic to it that couldn't have been achieved had they been on a higher plane. There is a certain dignity to being on the bottom of the barrel looking up. When up is the only road one has to travel, the vision becomes clearer.

This is a story of how one such family survived those years and actually had fun doing it, at times.

This work is a piece of fiction. While inspired by the author's life and experiences, any resemblance to events or people, living or dead, is purely coincidental.

ISBN: 145-365-3880
EAN:  978-145-365-3883

Edited by Vicki Armstrong

Cover Art by Cathy Clayton

Acknowledgments
My eternal thanks go out to my husband, Bob, for his patience and good advice while I struggled with this story. And many thanks to my dear friend, Vicki Armstrong, without whom this book would never have reached the print stage!

## Chapter 1

A soft spray of rain is kissing the window overlooking a well ordered, colorful flower garden. I can just barely see the edge of it over the top of the wheel chair that is awaiting my time for the shower. I look forward to that every evening, after supper.

Steam, resembling white smoke, is floating lazily from my coffee cup. Memories of smoke rising from the top of a chimney attached to the side of a tar paper covered shack from long ago revive themselves. Those memories, you know, the ones you tuck away to bring comfort in the future when you might have need of them. This is one of those. It is my eighty first birthday.

I lift the cup and my mind wanders back through the years to those first vivid memories. I had kept them for just such a day as this. Those are the memories that surely set the pattern for how I saw life thereafter.

"What in the name of hell do you think we pay you people for?" Mr. Redgrave yelled those words right in Mama's face. "Everybody else has been in the field for an hour!"

Mama turned and started walking toward the field without comment. She was apparently not going to give him the satisfaction of an explanation.

Just then a flock of Canada geese flew over, in military file. They were so close to the ground I could see their piercing, black eyes as they looked down on us. Their distinctive voices rang out clearly in the crisp morning air. Mama paused, glanced up and muttered, "at least some of us creatures are still free."

"Don't get your ass on your shoulders either, you can be replaced," was Mr. Redgrave's comment as he turned smartly on his heels and strode toward the big house.

Mama looked at me and said, "stay in the yard and out of the way this morning." Then with a smile, as if satisfied with something she was thinking, she turned and walked toward the other women who were already pulling suckers from the tobacco plants.

The year was 1942, around the middle of July. Our World was at war, and even though it wasn't talked about much, the feeling of dread hung in the air like an unseen demon. It was December 8th and Pearl Harbor was a topic at every dinner table, even on the smallest farm.

The place where we lived had been a slave plantation in the past, one of just a few in North Carolina. It was called the Redgrave Farm when we were there. Being well after the civil war, there were no slaves at the time, though poor working conditions and low pay can be cruel masters to people of any color.

That's where Daddy left Mama and me when he joined the Civilian Conservation Corps, better known as the CCC. He rarely came home to visit. I missed him desperately.

Granddaddy had died of a stroke when Daddy was thirteen years old. That left Grandmother a widow with four boys to care for alone, without money or a formal education. Keeping the farm running and profitable had proven to be too much for her. So, she had sold out for what she could get and moved to this thousand acre plantation to work the fields with her boys.

Up until that time they had lived on the family farm, located on the banks of South Creek, near Aurora, North Carolina.

Having slaves to work the plantation had allowed the owners to operate it at a huge profit. After the civil war eliminated slavery, the landowners changed their work force to people they could get for the least amount of money. When we lived there, it was just known as the Redgrave Farm. It was worked by dirt poor white people like us, mostly.

I was too young to work the fields at that time, but Mama would occasionally put me to work weeding the crops with her. She said that was to get me accustomed to the life she expected I would probably be living in the future.

She had left me in the backyard of Mr. Redgrave's home with the other children that day, just as she had almost every morning since I could remember. The house stood facing the road at the front edge of that vast expansion of farm land.

We often played around the stocks where slaves had been shackled for unruly behavior in the not too distant past.

That morning found the group of farm worker's kids in the backyard near a mysterious, round concrete building. It was about six feet in circumference and had no windows. The floor, we had been told by our elders, stepped down about five inches to rough concrete which would cut our bare feet. The roof on the place came to a point at the top, kinda like a spire capping the steeple of a church, minus the cross. The hand-made door had something like railroad spikes driven through it from the outside, and we had been told the sharp ends stuck all the way through. We had been warned to stay away from it.

"They kept slaves in there," Walter announced. He sounded like he had some knowledge the rest of us were ignorant of. Looking straight at me he said, "if the black people didn't want to work, or cook, or anything, they would be put in there until they came around to the boss's way of thinking. The slaves would bang their fists against the nails sticking through the door until they were all bloody. They put little girls in there too when they got too big for their britches!"

By the time he had completed the oratory, he was towering over me. His fists were clenched and he was frowning. This behavior was not unusual. He had never made any attempt at liking me and tried bullying me at every opportunity. I supposed that was because I was the smallest and therefore the easiest mark. He said I was too much of a Mama's baby because I would tell Mama when he was mean to me. I stood my ground, stretching on tiptoe as tall as I could, chin up and chest out.

When Walter realized I wasn't going to cry, he stopped threatening, and the group's interest went back to the door on that building. It had been left ajar.

We were staring at it because none of us had seen it open before. I felt we had a vested interest in what was in there. After all, we played around that building daily and had never been allowed to see what was inside. We were a very inquisitive group of kids.

"Bet you won't go in there," Walter stated to no one in particular.

"Bet I will," replied Charlie, taking him up on it.

"Bet you won't."

"Bet I will."

"Well, why don't you then," Walter challenged, effectively ending the standoff.

"What you got?"

"A white marble."

"I'll bet my slingshot."

It was a deal.

Walter held the loot and we all ventured toward the door. Charlie pulled on it and it swung open with a loud, creaking noise. We leaned forward and peered into the dark space. The nauseating odor of sweat and blood, mixed with that of rotting wood stung my nose.

Charlie didn't look too happy about his decision, as a matter of fact, he looked downright sick.

"What's the matter scaredy cat?" queried the holder of the loot.

"Ain't got no shoes," Charlie stated and produced a bare foot for all to see. "I'll cut my feet."

"Here, take mine."

That did it. There were no more excuses. Charlie knew he was in danger of being terribly ridiculed by all us kids if he didn't go in there now. After all, a dare was a dare, and not to be taken lightly.

We watched with great interest as he sat down, slowly pulled the brogans onto his feet, and made his way over to the door.

Bunching together we waited with a sense of grave anticipation to see if Charlie would be accosted by the ghosts of slaves we thought might still be in the place. They certainly were, if all the stories we had heard were true.

As soon as Charlie stepped in, Walter swung the door shut and propped a four by four against it, effectively barring Charlie's exit.

No sooner than the door shut, Charlie started yelling. "There's something crawling on me. Let me out of here. I'll kill you, Walter Taylor! Open this door!"

About that time Mr. Redgrave came around the corner and gasped, "What are you doing, there are likely to be black widow spiders in there!" He yanked the four by four away, grabbed Charlie by the collar and pulled him out.

Turning to us he demanded, "Who shut him up in there?"

We just stood staring at him and said nothing.

"Okay, I'll let your folks take care of it when they come to the house for dinner," he stated.

Then he turned his attention to the door, locking it with a big, rusty looking key he carried on a chain around his waist.

Dinner came all too soon. We knew what would happen when our *folks* got there.

Mr. Redgrave wasted no time, quickly spilling the beans, as it were.

We were lined up in the back yard from the shortest to the tallest and told to go pick out our switches. Of course, being the shortest, I was first in line.

"Liz," Mama said, "if you bring me a little switch, you'll get two whippings, one with the little one you bring me and another with the one I pick out." We were learning about crime and punishment.

Charlie's mean eyes stared at us from his ugly head peeping around the corner of the house. He could be really bad when he took a notion. He giggled while our legs took on the red stripes of what we considered corporal punishment. Walter would get even with him later. At least that was what I hoped.

About two months after that Daddy came home for good. I was *so very* happy. His most recent job had been working with one of President Roosevelt's New Deal Projects on the Outer Banks of North Carolina. His job was terminated because funding for the projects had run out. The war was doing more for the economy than the projects, so they were left to die a natural death.

At that time, Pearl Harbor was still weighing heavy on everybody's mind. I was too little to understand, but I felt the uneasy dread that constantly permeated the atmosphere, just like the adults.

The *New Deal* was President Roosevelt's plan to restore the environment and to put poor people back to work. The CCC was its most popular project. Young men, and a few women, mostly white, enlisted voluntarily and were paid thirty dollars a month. The *boy's* were allowed to keep five dollars, and the remainder was sent home to each enlistee's family, or at least, that was the plan. Mama told me she never saw a dime, so what happened to the money sent home for us is anybody's guess.

The New Deal Projects were put in place, in part, as an effort to relieve the stress placed on poor folks by The Great Depression. Its plan was to use unemployed citizens to plant trees, build highways, bridges and public buildings. It did a wonderful job of reconstruction as it related to infrastructure needing attention in this country at the time.

Another one of their great achievements was the job they did to restore vegetation on the prairie lands after the Dust Bowl disaster of the 1930's.

One of the projects centered around reinforcing the Hatteras coast line with sand dunes, to help stabilize and protect structures on the Island. That's the one Daddy was assigned to when government funding ran out.

He talked a great deal about that Island. I remember him saying mosquitoes on the sound side weighed about ten pounds. The *boys,* he said, slept on the beach instead of in the *barracks* that had been constructed for them to live in, military style. A constant sea breeze helped keep the mosquitoes and other flying insects at bay along the shore line.

Mostly, the local people on the outer banks at the time had lived on the Island for generations. They left it only when forced to by weather such as a really bad storm. And it had to be *really* bad, like life or death! Their distinct English sounding brogue attested to the fact that they didn't spend much time on the mainland.

Mama was French on her father's side; American Indian on her mother's. Her skin, hair and high cheek bones were that of the Indian. Her big blue eyes those of the French persuasion. Her frame was small and delicate. She stood barely five feet tall and weighed no more than one-hundred pounds. But that was all that was frail about her.

She had a constitution of pure steel, a will of iron, or so it seemed to me.

Her beautiful, dark skinned, flawless face was seemingly created for the painter's brush. She was shy, never talking unless it was necessary, and never giving her opinion on any subject in public. She never spoke ill of anyone and made it clear she didn't gossip.

Mama was christened Elizabeth Bardo, and was generally referred to as *Miss Lizabeth.* She never had much of what the world considered valuable. That being said, what she did have was clean. I guess you could say she took cleanliness to the nth degree. Every Sunday she scrubbed the house we lived in from ceiling to floor with a mixture of Clorox and water, and or, lye soap. We could barely breathe in there with the door shut for a couple of days afterward, the odor was so strong. During that time, even the bugs avoided us. She made the lye soap herself, to wash clothes, scrub floors, etc. We purchased Octagon soap to wash ourselves with from the store in town.

I often watched her clean house with cracked and bleeding fingers. It must have been painful, but she never complained. It seems to me she was always working on, or cleaning, something. As a matter of fact, she never sat down unless the task allowed her to sit while doing it. For instance, she sat while eating or making our clothes on her prized treadle type Singer sewing machine she had inherited from her Mother. She also sat while reading her Bible for the few minutes a day she allowed for that. She told me it was of the utmost importance; to read the Bible every day.

"Liz," she would to say, "work hard, learn to take care of what you have, and don't covet what others have."

"What's covet, Mama?" I asked one day.

"That's what I get for talking to a child," Mama stated and walked away shaking her head.

They named me Liz after Mama, Daddy called me *Son*. I am the son he never had, and he treated me as much as he could as if I were a boy. My hair is blonde and my eyes blue like Daddy's side of the family. I'm small in stature like Mama's.

Daddy's name is Andy Olfson. I remember him being almost the exact opposite of Mama. She was a very devoted Christian lady who would tell you the truth if it killed you to hear it, and clung to every word in the Holy Bible. She fed and cared for every living creature that turned up at our door asking, saying that God would expect that of us. And it was apparent to everyone who knew her that she loved most everything God made.

On the other hand, Daddy would tell you what you wanted to hear most of the time, to avoid argument. He was more of the superficial type, except when it came to his religious beliefs, which were kind of unusual, to say the least.

I asked Mama once how the two of them got together. She stated with a smile, "I met him on the street one day; he asked me if I wanted him to walk home with me. I said yes, and we've been together ever since."

Daddy had a very unusual way of looking at life. He was outgoing, talkative, and never met a stranger. He was perpetually happy. Nothing, I mean nothing, ever bothered him. He never worried about where the next meal was coming from. He never worried about having an extra change of clothing, and didn't particularly care if they were clean. He apparently never worried about money, either. The only thing that concerned him was the moment at hand, the here and now. Tomorrow, to him did not exist. He was one of those rare souls that truly just enjoyed living day to day and hand to mouth.

Mama, on the other hand, quietly worried about most everything; always wanting to be certain we were going to eat next week, and so on. Her character was

impeccable and her days spent living as close as she could
to the Word of God.  She kept her family clean and her
house in order.

"It don't matter none what you accomplish in this
life, Elizabeth," Daddy often said. "You ain't gonna' take
nothin' with you when you go, and life don't last forever.
Don't worry yourself if the clothes has holes in them.  As
long as your nakedness is covered up, seems it don't matter
none to me."

He was an avid reader and enjoyed reading cowboy
and Indian stories. However, for some unknown reason as
far as I could see, he pretended to be illiterate. For instance,
when he went to the polls to vote, he usually declared he
couldn't read or write.  As a result, someone would offer to
mark the ballot for him.  Then he would spend the next two
hours talking about why he was a Democrat.

Daddy most assuredly loved my Mama.  I think that
was the reason she was able to keep him on the straight and
narrow, at least from the stand point of taking care of the
family.  He did what she told him to do most of the time.
He didn't seem to be able to figure out what to do on his
own.

Daddy was a five foot eight, one hundred sixty-five
pound, sturdy built, red headed, blue eyed Norseman.  Most
all of his kin folks had blue eyes and blonde or red hair.

He was a self proclaimed descendant of Eric the
Red.  We spent many long winter evenings sitting around a
red hot, pot bellied wood heater, listening to stories of
Viking conquests. Daddy's eyes would glitter in the glow
of the lamplight when he told his stories. His voice would
adopt an air of excitement.  His descriptions were so vivid I
could almost feel the heat of the battle.

I remember him telling me an extra gruesome story
once about a battle that was so bad it prompted Mama to
say, "Andy, don't tell her that stuff!"  Daddy just kept right
on talking as if he never heard her.

"War is hell, Son," he said. "The object of the battle is always the same; destroy your enemy. The Vikings were not hindered by no rules of engagement, to kill and plunder; they skipped unnecessary preparations and got right down to business. Their leaders fought right out in front of the regular warriors. If you ask me, I think that would help avoid wars today. That is, if we were to put the world leaders on the front line of the battle."

"If you start a fight Son, always be ready and willing to finish it, and know you can win before you start."

Those stories tended to bring to life for me a reality: You have to fight for what you want in this life, and nothing worth having comes easy.

We left Grandmother's house around the tenth of December, 1942. It was a cold day when Daddy decided to move us. The weather in eastern North Carolina is that way; it gets very cold a few weeks before Christmas, then usually warms up to shirtsleeve weather until near New Year's Day.

We moved quite a distance; to a tar paper covered shack at the back corner of a tobacco field in Beaufort County. The little farm was near Tranters Creek.

The tenant who had lived there before us had gone off to war, or so we were told, and had since returned *shell shocked*. Our boss man told us he had moved back in with his parents. Their names were King. We weren't told anything else about him or his family at that time.

It was early one Saturday morning when we moved in. Mama had completed cleaning the place to her satisfaction several days before, but the place still reeked of Clorox. When Daddy mentioned it, Mama said, "Well, at least we don't have to worry about bedbugs." She was a practical lady.

Upon arrival, we had gone directly to the front porch. Mama wanted to check on a stain she had poured a bleach solution on when we were there cleaning earlier in the week. It was a reddish-brown colored area about three feet across, appearing to be where someone had spilled a bucket of rust-colored paint that had dried into the porous wooden planks. Now listen up, my Mama detested anything that looked dirty.

"Andy," Mama said as she stood there, hands on her hips, staring at that stain. "I have got to get rid of that, it looks like blood to me."

"You're always seein' things that ain't there, Elizabeth," Daddy said. "It don't look like blood to me, but I guess you'll do what you want to about it anyway."

Mama proceeded to pour full strength bleach on the stain before we walked around to the back of the house to more closely inspect the open water well. It had a round brick lining rising up two feet above ground, and was built under a shabby little A-type roof structure. The galvanized steel top was encrusted with mold. There was a bucket covered with green, slimy moss, tied to a rope and wound around a pulley. It looked as if it hadn't been used in a long time. Mama looked down into it and said, "We will be drinking water from the pump. I can use this for washing clothes." There was a hand pump by the back door.

A thick wooded area lined two sides of the place, reaching to within twenty feet of the structure. The stark skeleton like limbs of the foliage deprived trees tended to deepen the hurtful loneliness that virtually permeated the atmosphere. A few healthy looking long leaf pines and towering cedars attempted to camouflage the empty feeling. They were unsuccessful. Tobacco fields reached out about a mile from the other two sides of the place for about a mile in each direction.

The yard had litter strewn everywhere. Two or three old car tires lay scattered around, exuding that peculiar odor rubber has when it is dry rotted. A fallen oak tree lay in contorted fashion at the edge of the woods.

"We'll clean this up tomorrow, it's getting late," Mama said, and we went inside.

The next day Mama went to work on that place like a mad woman. She was determined, it seemed, to make it as pretty as she could with practically nothing to work with. I remember watching her climb onto the top of her sewing machine that particular morning. She was using it as place to stand to hang the starched white curtains she had made from a cloth flour sack.

Etched on my memory is a picture of a thin little figure of a lady with a pouched out belly that looked grossly out of place. She was perched on tiptoes, reaching as high as her five foot frame could to hang her curtains. Her jet black hair hung straight down her slender back, almost to her tiny waist, as she struggled with hammer and nails.

That's where Bessie Mable was born on December seventeenth, 1942, a week after we moved in. It was an exceptionally cold day. Frost decorated the inside of the window pane. I was busy scraping another hole in it so I could see out when a black Model-T pulled up to the front door.

A tall stranger carrying a black satchel got out and came into the house. He was such an imposing figure, it left an impression on me. He went into the bedroom with Daddy, where Mama had disappeared a little earlier.

After a short while they came out and presented to me my little sister. Daddy put her in my arms and let me walk around the kitchen with her. Mama told me the man had brought her to us in the bag. I remember thinking I had something to play with. I called her Bet. I liked the sound of that better than the name they had given her. It was easier to say than Bessie Mable.

It didn't occur to me there was anything wrong with her. I didn't know the fact that she rarely cried was a problem, or why her pinched little face looked somehow old and wise. I knew I resented the fact that Mama paid so much attention to her. Daddy told me she was very weak and needed a lot of taking care of.

The old shack had three rooms: a kitchen, a living room and a bedroom which had a small part sectioned off for Bet and me to have a place to sleep. The walls throughout were plastered with age-darkened newspapers. At present you couldn't read any of the print, it was so smeared from having been washed with lye soap earlier in the week. There were four small windows, one looking out from the kitchen, two onto the front porch and one in my room.

It seems to me now that every morning at that place started out the same way. Daddy would get up well before daylight and start a fire in the wood cook stove. Mama would fix our breakfast of fried fat-back, black-strap molasses, and the best darned biscuits in the whole county.

Then she would pack us a dinner of whatever happened to be left from supper the night before in a four pound metal lard stand she kept for that purpose, and we would go to work. In the summer it was to the fields; in the winter to whatever work there was to be done.

Farm work started with the rising of the sun and ended when it was too dark, rainy or cold to continue; usually five and a half days a week.

It was dirty, hard work. I remember one day in particular when we had come home early because it was raining. Daddy had managed to track in some of the rich, black mud from the kitchen door to the table where he dropped into his chair and asked, "where's supper?"

Mama, the lady who scrubbed her floors at least weekly with Clorox water, was to have no part of that. "Andy", she stated, "please sweep that mud out and wash your feet."

To that Daddy replied, "can you not read the Bible, Elizabeth? It says man is made of the dirt of the earth, so what's wrong with gittin' a little of it on you?"

"Why is it that you always come up with a Bible quote when you want to excuse yourself from the rules that go along with proper living, Andy?" Mama asked.

Then she said with a chuckle, "just go on out back and clean your feet." He did.

Daddy didn't attend church much. He had his legitimate reasons for that. However, I remember he did read Mama's Bible from time to time. He could quote it as well as any preacher, doing so when the situation called for it.

Mama's work was never done. When she got home from working the fields, she cleaned Bet and me up, cooked supper, and as I remember it, fell into bed around ten or eleven o'clock each night. That was, more or less, the routine at our house.

On Saturday afternoons we would go to town if we needed to and had the money to spend. On Sunday Mama would wash our clothes and clean house while Daddy and I would go fishing or hunting.

A little black girl named Barbara lived about a mile down the road from that old shack. Her Mama worked the fields too. There were many days when her Mama and mine worked at the same place. That allowed Barbara and me to play together. It was during those times that we made mud pies and ran along the river bank chastising evil spirits, in which she had a deep seated belief. She described the demons that haunted her world to me in great detail. After that they haunted mine too.

Barbara's Mama, everybody called her Aunt Lillian, was the local fortune teller. I never saw her Daddy. She would go to the *white folk's* houses in the middle of the night and tell their fortune for a nickel.

She never came to our house; although she had a standing invitation. Mama had invited her to come visit us on more than one occasion and she had always responded with answers like: "No thank you, I gits a bad feeling when I goes near that place."

We visited their house when we could afford to ride the train to town. They lived close to the railroad crossing where the train would stop and pick us up.

Aunt Lillian would make us sweet tea, cooled with a bit of ice chipped from the block that resided in an ice box on her back porch, while we waited. We would all sit quietly out there in the cool shade of towering, fragrant Magnolia trees, sipping tea and listening for the train whistle. It was a rickety old porch, engulfed in the soulful sound of song birds in the evergreen thickets, and the unforgettable fragrance of the ever present honeysuckle.

Oh my, that train was an adventure for me. For Bet it seemed to be a horrible experience. She would cling to Mama and close her eyes as soon as she heard the whistle blow.

It was essentially a freight train; but it had one passenger car. Daddy would flag it down with his white handkerchief, and it would come to a stop with the passenger car where we were standing. Soon after we got on, an old black conductor would collect the little bit of change required for the trip. Usually, the only other passenger for this short ride was the engineer.

The conductor did double duty; collecting fares and feeding the firebox. The train ran on steam generated by coal power. The seats resembled green colored park benches which were bolted to the floor. They would sway slightly as the train lumbered along the tracks. There was an upside down glass water bottle with a spigot bolted to the wall, and little white, cone shaped paper cups to drink from. I would stand by the window and watch the trees go by. Mama would have her hands full with Bet the entire trip. She would cling to Mama and whimper occasionally, refusing to open her eyes. Our destination was always the train depot in Washington, North Carolina.

Right across from the station was Bill's Hot Dog Stand. They were the best hot dogs in the world (and still are). I declare I believe the chili is addictive. It is not chili in the true sense of the word, but rather a hot, spicy, yellow colored mixture of pure delight.

When we could afford it, a hot dog all the way with extra chili and a Pepsi was my treat, with any visit to town. And trust me; with the heat of that chili, the Pepsi *was* a necessity.

If we had enough money we would go see a movie at the Turnage Theater. I remember just before the movie started they would show clips from *the front*, meaning scenes from the front lines of World War II. That was our primary place for news about the War, as it was for most folks in those days. At the time television was non-existent, at least around our part of the State.

Our only other source of information was the radio, that, and word of mouth. One big problem with the radio was the batteries. They didn't last long and were very expensive and difficult to transport due to their size, being about as big as a car battery. And there was a shortage of them like everything else during the war years.

We would visit a small grocery store near the train station before going home, to buy provisions for the next week or so.

Many commodities were rationed. The rationed commodities included but were not limited to: sugar, tires, automobiles, fuel oil, coffee, gasoline, meat and processed foods. It was supposed to prevent wartime inflation and was the duty of The Office of Price Administration to enforce. Usually we didn't have enough money to buy what we needed anyway, so the rationing didn't mean much to us.

The flour was in cloth bags. Mama used them to make clothes for Bet and me, as well as curtains, pillow cases, sheets and diapers, etc. The cloth was white and had flowers that came in an array of pastel colors printed on the borders. Mama would get as many different colors as she could.

We would buy coffee, flour, dried beans, fat-back, lard, sugar, a can of molasses, a couple of cans of Carnation milk, and sometimes a can of Karo Syrup for me. Daddy would also buy enough kerosene to keep our lamp lit for the next week, and for starting fires.

If he had enough money left he would buy his favorite food, red hoop cheese. It was a part of Eastern North Carolina's heritage and tradition; found nowhere else in North America. It was a favorite of locals but was difficult to cut because it would crumble so easily. It was so popular around Washington during those times, however, that the local stores had purchased what they called a hoop cheese cutter. This expensive device resembled a turntable where the round cheese fit exactly. The cutter, which was a part of the turntable, was suspended above it. It could easily cut the exact amount of cheese the customer wanted to purchase.

The cheese was covered with red-colored wax to preserve it. Then it was boxed in round wooden containers for shipping to the stores. Daddy liked it so much he always bought all he could afford. It was sold by the pound.

We could usually catch a ride home with someone going that way. The train never seemed to be available when we were ready to go. If we couldn't hitch a ride, Daddy would heft the box of groceries onto his shoulders and we would start walking. I never remember walking the entire distance.

Mama would plant a row of collards and a few tomatoes and string beans in the spring. She would can enough of the tomatoes and beans to see us through the winter months.

She had been careful to keep collards growing all winter at Grandmother's house. The collards she had planted that year, of course, had been left behind, and it was too late to start another garden. We had a few dozen jars of canned tomatoes and beans left.

As usual, it took Daddy very little time to meet up with almost every male person in the community. And he soon struck up a friendship with local farmers that Mama didn't take kindly to, at all, I suspected. He threw in with a crowd who worked at a little more lucrative business at night. That would be the one that kept the revenuers busy. In a word it was called *bootlegging*; meaning the unlawful making of whiskey for sale to the public.

The big problem with bootlegging was that taxes were not being paid to Uncle Sam, plus, sometimes it was brewed under less than sanitary conditions. However, the less than sanitary conditions were probably offset by the fact that it was over a hundred-proof.

The lead contained in the stuff was considered to be the major problem, because most of the bootleggers used radiators from old cars as condensers.

Unlawful whiskey stills could usually be found in lean-tos or deserted shacks deep in the swamps that lined the rivers and creeks. Being close to a stream which could be used for the necessary water was also seen as a positive when looking for a place to set one up.

Mama tried to keep it a secret from me, but there are few secrets in a three room house. Life was hard and you kept your family fed any way you could. As for Daddy, I believe he did it just for the excitement of it, staying ahead of the law and all that.

Our routine was always the same when we arrived home in the evening. Mama would light the kerosene lamp and Daddy would build a fire in the wood burning cook stove. Then he'd get out the old blue enamel coffee pot and start the water to boil. He was always responsible for making the coffee. He used a handful of Luzianne with chicory to which he added a pinch of salt. Sometimes he would throw in a few egg shells if we had any. After he decided it was ready he would set it aside for a while to let it *settle*. Then he would pour our cups carefully to avoid the grounds that had settled to the bottom. He would fix his first cup with a piece of Hoop cheese softened in it. He would eat the cheese and throw the greasy coffee away; then he would proceed to drink coffee until the pot was empty.

After supper Daddy would play the radio and smoke his pipe. I remember the battery usually had to be heated up on the stove to get it charged enough to work. The night I'm thinking about we were listening to one of Roosevelt's *fireside chats*.

Mama had put Bet and me to bed around ten o'clock. Bet slept in a dresser drawer a lady had sold to Mama so she could make a little bed for her. I had a bed Daddy had built for me when I got big enough to have one of my own. President Roosevelt's voice was droning on from the radio, something about helping poor farmers, I think.

A half full, silvery moon peeped at me from behind the nearly naked limbs of a maple tree outside my window. I snuggled down between Mama's hand-made quilts and the feather mattress and fell asleep. In my dreams I relived the day's journey. I entertained myself that way, in my vivid dreams. It was almost like going to the movies. I would think about what I wanted to dream about just before drifting off to sleep and would almost always remember the dream upon awakening. Sometimes I would continue the same dream the next night, and so on, until the story had an end.

## Chapter 2

It was the middle of January, 1943. We were hunkered down for the winter in the still relatively new place. Making sure we had enough to eat was at the top of Mama's list of wants that winter, as it was every year.

Daddy said she didn't have to worry, but if it was her duty she could go ahead and do it. He didn't care as long as she didn't tell him about it. "I'll see to it that we have somethin' to eat," he said.

Hunger was not *usually* a problem for us, however, as we were country folks. The woods around us were full of birds, rabbits and squirrels; not to mention the rivers and creeks, which were brimming with seafood.

Sometimes though, Mama worried that she might not be able to keep Daddy motivated to go hunting for the free food. I remember hearing her say once: "If you don't go fishing today, the kids are going to be hungry and I'm going to take them and go to my sister's!" That was what it took that day to get Daddy moving in the right direction. She always seemed to know how to do that. I knew she was serious and so did Daddy. She had done it once. Daddy had turned over a new leaf for a week or two after that episode, so he knew she would leave him if it were necessary to keep her kids fed.

Wonderful memories of summer lay heavy on my mind that cold, winter day. It was a pleasant memory of there always being an abundance of wild strawberries and blackberries, in addition to the apple, peach and cherry trees. There was also sassafras and dog fennel tea for us to take when we were sick, and poke salad which grew in abundance along the railroad tracks for a tonic in the spring.

I didn't get sick often, which was lucky for me. Mama was a staunch believer in letting the kid get the disease and then have immunity to it. We didn't usually go to the doctor, either; we more or less knew we would live or die with whatever we had.

There was also a general practice in the community households of making all the kids in the house sleep with the one who had measles, whooping cough, or whatever the one kid had. The idea was to get it all over with at once.

Mama was one of the ladies who believed in the spring time dose of castor oil. She was certain her use of it was the reason I didn't get sick very often. That was debatable in my book for several reasons; one being my early discovery of Karo syrup and castor oil being of about the same consistency and color. Therefore, I took it upon myself to empty any new bottle of castor oil at the first opportunity, refilling it with syrup. After that I had no problem taking the *castor oil*.

Daddy was a good painter and the weather had been dry that winter, so he had done a lot of painting at the Boss's house to help with living expenses.

He and Mama had helped Mr. Josiah Williams, owner and boss man of this smaller farm where we had moved, clear some land for the right to cut wood to burn. Daddy had built a shed to dry the wood under.

They had borrowed a crosscut saw early that morning, and were cutting up the tree that had fallen in the back yard. I helped them stack it under the shed. It was already dried out, ready to use right away. It takes a long time for newly cut trees to dry enough to be good firewood. It took us about half the day to fill up the space under the shed.

Just after dawn the next morning, Daddy and I checked on his rabbit traps. It was bone chilling cold. Mama fussed at him for taking me out in that weather, but the only time he wouldn't let me go was when I was sick, and I was ridiculously healthy.

"She has to be tough to make it in the world we live in now, Elizabeth," he would say when Mama insisted he treat me like a girl. She couldn't deny that.

Rabbit meat tasted like chicken. I really liked it. Daddy never let me see him kill the rabbit, though. He'd always make me turn my head when he shot the prey. He said I wouldn't ever eat it again if I saw the little animal die. He was probably right. At least I would have to have been *really* hungry.

The old shack we lived in was rent free. Daddy had an agreement with Mr. Williams to plant and work the tobacco crop that next year for the privilege. He was also to help with work around the boss's house, and with the corn and cotton crops.

There were things we needed that we couldn't grow or make, so the little bit of extra money we got was a necessity, especially in the cold winter months.

As I remember, those winter days rapidly followed one another, each a near carbon copy of the previous. They represented a challenge to survival, until the winter was spent and spring finally arrived.

That late May morning, 1943, I awakened to the strong aroma of coffee brewing, and the comforting sound of Mama and Daddy talking in the kitchen.

I sat up and stared directly into a pair of black, beady little eyes. They were those of a dove, balancing on stick-like legs, staring back at me from my window sill.

"It's going to be a long day; we have tobacco plants to set out. Better get Liz up," Mama was saying. "I'll feed Bet."

Daddy came to get me, giving me a ride to the table on his broad, sturdy shoulders. He sat me down on the two Sears Catalogs that converted the kitchen chair to a highchair.

"Son", he said, "you got to help Mama and me with transplanting that tobacco today. And you can ride old Jim to the field if he'll let you." We both laughed at that.

When we moved there Mr. Williams had told Daddy he might have some trouble with the mules. Mr. Williams didn't like tractors, so we just had the two one horse-power mules, Jim and Jake, to work with.

Jim was the most confoundedly lazy mule east of the Mississippi. When he got tired he would sit right down on his haunches in the middle of a row and refuse to move. At that point, Daddy would calmly tie the reins to the plow handle, grab Jim by his ear and bite down, hard. Then he would look him in the eye and say, "Are you ready to pull this plow now, old boy?" Nine times out of ten that was all it took. Jim would show Daddy his teeth in a menacing manner; then decide he could get up and keep going after all.

On the other hand, Jake was better mannered, so Daddy used him a little more. But Daddy was determined that Jim would do his fair share.

The sun had yet to make its appearance over the horizon when we left for the plant bed. A misty haze hovered over head, shrouding everything in white. An ever present aroma of honeysuckle permeated the cool, damp air. The plant bed was on the farther side of the field, about a mile away. The wet shroud of fog seemed to require that we be quiet and listen to the silence as we made our way around the edge of the woods.

Daddy removed the stretchy, white cloth that protected the young plants from the pesky flea beetles. Then Mama tiptoed carefully through the young plants and placed her three legged stool in the center of the bed. From that vantage point she could pull the plants up without constantly bending over, which could cause a terrible backache by the end of a long day.

Daddy placed the little box Bet was sleeping in at the edge of the plant bed and told me to stay close and watch out for her. Five foot rattlers had been seen in that part of the field. There was an axe close by, just in case.

I found myself a convenient log and sat down to watch over her. I pulled the blanket up close around her face and made sure the mosquito netting was intact. The pesky things were still active at that time of the morning.

Mama was as quiet as usual. Daddy was keeping up a rather constant flow of chatter about everything going on in the area.

By mid-morning the air had heated up and felt quite hot for that time of year. The changeable Eastern North Carolina weather was up to its usual tricks. The veil of fog had lifted and the loneliness of the place was pressing in on me. After a while it seemed to take on a presence of its own, like a thing alive. The air felt too thick to breathe. Trees stood absolutely still in the heat of brilliant sunlight.

A few honey bees buzzed around the area, winging their way lazily from one honeysuckle plant to another. There was no wind at all. Everything except Daddy was deathly quiet in that little clearing where they were working. It felt to me as if the world was waiting with great anticipation for some unknown thing to happen.

I pulled Bet's box into the thin shade of a Silver Maple and watched the little animals around us to pass the time. There was a mama robin trying to teach her little brood how to find the big fat worms around the edge of the plant bed. She wasn't having much success because each time she pulled a worm out of the soft earth; the chicks took it out of her mouth. They just didn't seem interested in hunting on their own. I watched her walk out of sight with her unwilling little chicks in tow; tilting her head side to side, trying to get them to listen for worms. I wondered if this particular group would ever learn and asked Mama what she thought about it. "I don't have time to worry about the birds. I've got my own brood to think about," she said.

They were working with the plants, laying them neatly in a line, side by side, in a wooden container. It would make the job of transplanting easier that afternoon.

The lonely cry of a dove calling its mate came to my ear from somewhere away off in the distance. Occasionally a crow would wing its way overhead, questioning us with its plaintiff call, "*caw*", "*caw*", echoing into the silence. It seemed to me to be asking what we were doing in its domain.

My mind formed pictures from the fluffy white clouds floating between me and a deep blue sky. The one over there reminded me of Mama; a small, delicate little thing. The white trail of broken wisps reminded me of smoke rings from Daddy's pipe.

So the morning went until around twelve o'clock when Mama said, "It's time to eat."

Mama fed Bet and sat rocking her back and forth for a few minutes while Daddy and I ate the collard biscuits and baked sweet potatoes she had prepared for us. Then she tucked Bet back in her box and sat down to rest a minute.

While she rested, Daddy and I explored the edge of the woods. He pointed out a tree. Then he told me the story of the dogwood tree. What happened to it to make it the way it was, I mean.

"Son", he said, "when Christ was crucified, they used a dogwood tree. At that time it was a tall, straight tree. God put a curse on it 'cause it was used to kill his son. It would forever after be twisted and unfit to be used for a crucifixion. The stained place in the middle of its white flower represents the blood of Christ, the whiteness of its leaves His Purity. Always remember this story when you see a Dogwood tree." I did.

By the time Mama finished resting herself; Daddy was carefully watching the sky. "We had better hurry, it looks like rain," he said.

During the past thirty minutes, gray clouds had gathered on the horizon to our southwest. Daddy called that our *rain hole*.

Mama quickly scattered the leftover bread crumbs for the birds, picked Bet up and told me to come along. We were going to the stables to help Daddy get Jim hooked to the plow.

What remained of that day was spent transplanting. Daddy and Jim plowed the furrow. Mama walked behind them, using a peg to make a hole in the sweet smelling earth; then deftly dropping a plant into it. It was like magic to watch her work the field. That kind of work was all she had ever known, and she was very good at it. The black, fragrant smelling earth seemed to yield to her touch as if it knew and loved her.

Following close behind, screaming and whirling over our heads, was a flurry of snow white seagulls with black tipped wings. They made a beautiful contrast between me and the Carolina blue sky. Occasionally they would touch down when they spotted a worm or bug of interest in the soft, black dirt. Sometimes they would fight a gallant battle over an interesting specimen.

I watched with great interest as they settled momentarily on Jim's back. He tolerated it with a few flinches of his thick skin; then grew tired of their using him for transportation, and used his bushy tail to swat at them. They reacted to that by lifting up into the air for a few seconds, hanging suspended on a thermal wave, then settling down again. All the while they searched the ground from their perch for the worms they enjoyed so much.

Jim was in a pretty good mood, so the planting went smoothly until around three-thirty when thunder began to rumble in the distance. The clouds were getting thicker and darker. Jim kept trying to pull Daddy and the plow toward the shed.

"That does it", Daddy finally said, "animals know the weather better than we do. Better go on to the house."

By the time we got Jim to the shed, black clouds were billowing forth from the southwest. Fingers of hungry lightening streaked from cloud to cloud; like blind white death, seeking its' next victim. Thunder grumbled and echoed its message back into the blackness of the vast fuming cauldron, and the temperature dropped rapidly.

I was fascinated by those explosive storms that came up frequently without warning, and watched this one as it advanced over the tree tops at the edge of the field. Sitting on the bricks that served as a step up to the kitchen door, I felt relatively safe for the moment. The wind swirled around me and a blast of chilled air struck my face as I sat folded up with my chin resting on my knees. Chill bumps rose on my skinny bare arms.

"Liz," Mama's voice broke my concentration. It sounded a long way off. I would ignore it. Louder, "Liz," this time followed with, "come in and shut that door, now! This is not a time to play outside." Then to Daddy she shouted over the roar of the advancing storm, "do you think the crop will survive?"

"I don't know", he said. "Only God knows. If it don't we can replant. We got plenty of plants left, that is if hail don't git them."

A strange feeling came over me when I heard those words, not unlike cold fingers closing around my heart. I had felt that way before but didn't understand exactly what caused it. Perhaps it was the tone of Daddy's voice. It took me away from the excitement of the storm at hand.

A strong wind fought me as I struggled to pull the screen door open. Once inside I put my back to the wooden door, pushing it shut with some difficulty. I turned the hand-made latch to secure it, and went to sit on my bed to watch the storm in all its fury. I was awed by the unstoppable rage I saw in the thing. A streak of lightening followed by a rumble of thunder shook rain from the black, low hanging clouds. It poured over the tin roof like a waterfall, so loud it was almost impossible to hear anything else. I watched as time weakened tree limbs snapped in the wind, as easily as a smoker snaps a matchstick. Tall pines bent to grotesque shapes, swaying side to side, as if an invisible giant hand was moving among them.

Mama sat silently in the rocker holding Bet, who was terrified of storms, as well as most everything else. I climbed up on her other knee and buried my face on her shoulder. She gathered us up in her arms like a mother hen gathers her chicks, holding us safe against the terror of the threatening elements.

Daddy was busy trying to start a fire in the kitchen stove with wet wood. The wind had blown away the shed he had built to keep it dry. A match to the kerosene would light up a fire, which would quickly sputter and go out. He was cursing, I think, but we couldn't hear him plainly, the rain was drowning him out. That was a good thing, because Mama got very upset when he used words like I thought I was hearing.

Around five-thirty the rain abated and the storm passed, leaving us with a soft, soothing, pitter patter on the tin roof. The air had a chilled feel to it for May. Daddy had managed to build a fire and Mama was baking a molasses cake. I was so hungry I could almost taste the smell of it.

For as long as I could stay still, which was about fifteen minutes, I sat behind the cook stove feeling the warmth of the wood heat down to the marrow of my bones. By that time I was thoroughly warmed from the chill of the vicious summer storm that had just passed. They always made me feel cold, regardless of the season.

There was a pot of large lima beans boiling on the stove. Mama cooked those with a little flour, salt and pepper. That made a really good soup base. She was preparing to bake a pan of her big, fluffy biscuits to eat with them.

To my delight, she was making me a little flour-bread man with some of the biscuit dough, as she often did. She allowed me to roll the dough for the extremities.

Daddy turned the radio on. It was time for *The Inner Sanctum Mysteries.* That program was about as scary as it got in those days, on the radio anyway.

"Andy, do you think Liz ought to be listening to that program?" Mama called out.

"It don't scare her none", Daddy replied. Then turning he asked me, "does it son?"

I replied in the negative.

After the door stopped squeaking and the man had said his piece about the *inner sanctum*, I lost interest. I walked out on the porch to catch rain drops in my cupped hands as they trickled off the roof.

It was almost dark, although it was only six o'clock. Clouds heavy with rain still hovered in the lowering sky. I took a deep breath. Everything smelled so fresh and clean after a spring rain. Something about the look of wet trees, and their dark green leaves dripping with fresh rain water, brought with it a feeling of tranquility. A shaft of light fell on the porch from the lamp Mama had just lit. I could hear her singing, *Just as I Am,* while Daddy listened to the radio.

Suddenly a cool wind caressed the back of my neck. I imagined it to be someone's chilly hand. I could feel the hair rise on the back of my head. An unreasonable fear engulfed me. I was afraid to turn around. I backed up until I felt the door latch, pulled it open and ran to Daddy.

Pulling me up on his knee he asked, "What's wrong, son?" I told him I thought there was someone on the porch. He quickly put me down, reached up over the door, took down his squirrel gun and went to see.

Mama called after him, "I told you that program would scare her, there's nobody out there. Nobody ever comes around here!" She turned the radio off. Daddy spent the next twenty minutes pacing around the house to satisfy his curiosity before giving up.

"You like to dramatize everything," Mama said.

We went to bed around ten o'clock. It was still raining softly; otherwise it was deathly quiet. On nights like that in the woods, when clouds hang low in the sky, hiding all the heavenly elements, the pitch blackness envelopes everything like six feet of dirt over a grave might.

Then I heard it, someone was walking on the porch! Mama had heard it too, she got Daddy up and he went to the door. I listened with the sheet pulled up securely over my head. When Daddy opened the door, the sound stopped, starting up again when he closed it back.

Mama got up and lit the lamp. "Andy, she said, "I don't know what that is, but I do know I want to get away from this place. Whatever, or whoever that is, doesn't want us here."

To that Daddy replied, "You know we can't leave 'til the crop is in, Elizabeth. We made a deal with Mr.

Williams. If we leave him in a bind we can't git another place to stay this late in the year."

"Well, I'm not sleeping with the light off," Mama said. "So you better find a way for us to get enough kerosene."

After the rain stopped we didn't hear anything else. The lamp stayed lit the remainder of that night.

The next day was Saturday. Mama and Aunt Lillian had been asked to come to the boss's house and help Mrs. Williams with the spring cleaning. Daddy was to check the field and reset the plants if needed.

The Williams's house was a two story monstrosity built on a three acre plot that was set apart for that purpose. It was sectioned off from the farm land by pecan, dogwood, crepe myrtle and ancient Magnolia trees. They camouflaged the farm land from the eyes of people in the house.

It was a nice morning, so Barbara and I stayed outside to play with the peacocks and turkeys that roamed freely in the back yard. Even though they were not caged, they seemed to know the boundaries of home. When the turkeys got tired of being chased around the yard, they would turn on us and stand their ground. We knew better than chase them after that. They would fight back. The peacocks were a little more tolerant of a pair of frisky little girls. We set out to scare them into spreading their beautiful feathers and strutting about. They looked like they would topple over with the weight of it all. It was lots of fun.

Around noon, Mrs. Williams and Aunt Lillian fried chicken, baked biscuits and made sweet tea. Then we were called in for the dinner meal.

We were to eat in the kitchen. I guess Mrs. Williams had to keep a distance between the farm hands and her family. They would be eating their dinner with her in the formal dining room.

While we were eating, Mama, who had been her usual quiet self all morning, ventured to ask Aunt Lillian a question. "I've been meaning to ask you something", she started out. "I know you'll probably think I'm crazy, but thought you might help me figure it out, as you've lived around here a long time."

"Most all my life," answered Aunt Lillian.

"Last night, Andy and I heard something at the house that frightened us. It sounded like somebody walking on the porch, like a women in high heeled shoes maybe, but we never could see anybody. This morning I'm tempted to think it was our imagination."

Aunt Lillian stared at Mama, fork half way to her mouth for a full thirty seconds before answering her. Then she said, "I'm most scared to tell you somethin' I knows, Miss Lizabeth. But since you ask, I'll tell you this. Barbara and me was out there late one evenin', a while before you all moved in. We was looking for berries in that patch near your house when we hears somebody a'cryin'. I thinks it was somebody in trouble up there so I creeps up nearer the place and looked and I ain't seen nothin'. It was mighty late in the evenin', so might be it was a live somebody I couldn't see, but I don't think so. I tell you, that woman that come up missin' a while back, she dead. I knows it, and I knows she haunts that place. Her husband is that young soldier boy that come back from the war to find her missin'. They's the ones that lived in that place last, that King feller, and his purty wife."

"There now, I've said my piece and don't you tell a soul I told you," she continued. "I ain't supposed to know these things. I likes you and I wish you all hadn't ever moved in there."

"I wonder why Mrs. Williams didn't tell us about that?" Mama questioned out loud.

Miss Lillian said, "I wouldn't say nothin' bout it if I was you. The Williams's has their reasons."

We walked home slowly through the cool of the late spring day. The breeze was dying down and frogs were crying out for rain from the ditches. It seemed they did that every evening whether we needed it or not. The walk was quiet and uneventful. Mama carried Bet and I ran ahead, feeling the cool sand that made up the roadway squeezing up between my toes, happy to be going home.

Another long spring day had been spent working for just enough money to buy our next sack of flour and bucket of lard, when we made it to town again.

Mama put her little bit of change in the jar on the shelf above the kitchen stove. It would stay there until we got a chance to go for supplies.

Daddy had already built a fire for cooking supper. He seemed to know about when Mama would be getting home and was doing all he could to help her. They sat at the kitchen table and talked for a little while before Mama started cooking.

Then Daddy tuned the radio to *WCKY, Cincinnati Ohio,* and we listened to country music while beans boiled on the stove. I remember hearing Ernest Tubb singing *Walking the Floor over You,* followed by *Rainbow at Midnight*.

## Chapter 3

It was five o'clock that clear Sunday morning in June. Mama was already up, getting ready to wash our clothes. Daddy and I were going fishing on Tranter's Creek. I loved fishing and had happily helped Daddy dig up the fat, wiggly worms from the moist soil behind the well the evening before. They awaited their doom in the back yard, up next to the door, in a tin can half full of black dirt.

In addition to the worms, he had managed to capture a few crickets, in case we wanted to try for Bass. It was not easy to catch Bass with a cane pole, but it was possible.

After breakfast, Daddy drew wash water from the well. He filled the twelve gallon galvanized tub, and the heavy iron wash pot whose three legs presently rested on bricks. There was a small trench in the ground under the wash pot where he had built a fire. Mama threw a handful of flaked lye soap and a half cup of Clorox into the water.

She scrubbed the first load on a scrub-board until most of the dirt was out. By that time the water in the iron cauldron had reached a rolling boil. She threw in two sheets and several pieces of clothing, allowing them to boil for three or four minutes while she stirred with the paddle. Daddy had carved it from a pine tree limb for her. The end of it was broad like a boat paddle. He had smoothed it down with his knife so it wouldn't damage the clothes.

When the time was up, Mama lifted the clothes out of the boiling water and transferred them to the tub of rinse water. I watched as she struggled to squeeze as much water as she could from the sheets, and helped her hang them on the line. This process would be repeated until all the clothes were clean and hung out to dry.

When the first load was on the line, Daddy made sure there was a small pile of wood for Mama to use and decided she could do the rest herself. We were anxious to get on with our fishing trip. The laundry would take Mama most of the day, that and taking care of Bet. I'm certain she was glad to be rid of Daddy and me.

She called after us, "Andy, I have something to tell you about this evening when you get home. Something about this house that Miss Lillian told me yesterday. I wanted to think about it before I told you, but we need to talk, I'm worried."

"Okay," Daddy called back over his shoulder, "but I want to git to a fishin' spot before all the good places are taken up," and we were off.

We trudged carefully through the woods to the banks of Tranter's Creek, traversing the thick underbrush with a little difficulty. It was cool there under the shade of the big old trees.

Patterns of tree-filtered sunlight played softly with a dense marsh carpet. I kicked at dried leaves and laughed as they scattered away from my feet, swirling in a multicolored frenzy. Squirrels scampered across our path here and there. They would run up the trunks of trees and sit on a limb to stare at us as we passed under. Occasionally the ornery little rascals threw pecan shells at us.

We passed a briar patch where we would be picking berries for Mama's flour bread dumplings later on. All in all the woods were alive with the sounds and smells of wildlife and honeysuckle.

Before we reached the Creek, Daddy started looking for the bamboo patch that grew there. He could make the canes into disposable fishing poles. We had left our old

ones on the skiff the last time we went fishing and Daddy
was sure they would be gone. The wind would blow them
away if they weren't secured firmly, and it seemed he never
got around to that at the end of a long day of fishing.

Within ten minutes he found the bamboo, picked
out just the right canes and cut them to the length desired.
Then we sat down on the creek bank while he tied strings
onto the ends of the poles and attached little red corks
produced from somewhere deep in his overall pockets. The
corks would float until a fish pulled them under.

Daddy had his little wooden boat attached to a tree
root by a rope that reached out into the creek a bit. He
pulled the skiff close to the bank and we got in. It was a
rickety little thing and wasn't exactly watertight. Daddy
kept a can in it to bail water from time to time. As a matter
of fact, we had to bail water as soon as we got in.

There was no fear of us drowning if the boat sank,
though. Daddy and I swam like ducks, but the creek was
inhabited by water moccasins, as dangerous a snake as lives
in the river. It's an olive brown pit viper that inhabits the
rivers and swamps of the southeast U.S. It is akin to the
copperhead and sometimes confused with a harmless river
snake. They can be distinguished by their tell-tale brown
cross bands and a white mouth inside. Because of this they
are sometimes referred to as *cottonmouths*.

You can trust me on this, the last thing you want to
see in that water is one of those open white mouths aiming
at you. That was one of the many reasons it was unlikely a
person would survive if their boat sank on the part of the
creek where we were headed.

At half past six o'clock we pushed our little skiff
free of the landing and were on our way to catch some
sunfish, and maybe a few bass if we were lucky.

With us were the usual collard biscuits and corn
bread Mama had fried for us to nibble on, along with a jug

of water stowed in the bow. We would be drinking lots of that when the sun started bearing down like it was wont to do out there in the middle of the afternoon.

Usually at the hottest part of the day we would tie up under a tree whose branches hung out over the water a few feet, providing a little shade. Daddy would try to find a place where the thick gray moss swinging from the Cyprus trees wouldn't be right above our heads. That was in case there were ticks, and in some cases snakes hiding in it to fall on us.

Most of the time that's where we ate our dinner, listening to the off beat songs of frogs croaking;   watching turtles parade by on their half submerged logs heading down river.

Tranter's Creek empties into the Tar River along with other creeks that join in to ultimately combine forces with the broad Pamlico Sound. The tide was on its way out that morning, heading towards the Atlantic Ocean, which was about sixty five miles to the east, as a crow flies.

From the Pamlico River on down to the Outer Banks there are many sandbars. They are known as shifting shoals because they *move*. Daddy said that Blackbeard and his crew used those shifting shoals as a way of escaping the British Royal Navy, who at intervals tried to hunt them down. He said a white dolphin was reported to swim ahead of Blackbeard's ship to guide them around the sand bars.

I don't think one could say much about the Pamlico River or the Outer Banks without talking about Blackbeard, North Carolina's resident pirate. Daddy talked to me often about him, usually when we were on one of our fishing trips. Mama didn't like it when he told me those blood-curdling stories. Blackbeard supposedly had several aliases, i.e.: *Edward Teach*, *Edward Drummond* and *Thach*.

According to some stories, Governor Charles Eden, and the secretary of the colony Tobias Knight, helped

Blackbeard in his riotous ways for monetary gain. There are also stories that support other reasons for this *help*. Perhaps it had more to do with being *neighborly* than the sharing of loot.

Blackbeard was killed on a Saturday morning in November, 1718, near the old watering hole at Ocracoke Inlet. A certain Lt. Robert Maynard of His Majesty's Royal Navy slipped up on him and his crew that day. They disguised themselves in two small vessels, pretending to be innocent merchants. According to history, at that time, Blackbeard's crew had most of their ill gotten gains laid out on the sand while they prepared to transfer it to another ship.

When Daddy told that story, he never forgot to add that he thought there was some of that treasure left buried along the coast and along the river banks of Eastern North Carolina.

Blackbeard supposedly had a sister named Susanna White who lived on or near the old Grimes Plantation, close to Grimesland, North Carolina. The stories have it that he came to her house when he needed to rest or to recuperate from some injuries he had sustained in battle. Apparently he felt safe there.

When he was ready to leave the area, he would climb a tree on the banks of the Tar River where he could determine if the coast was clear. The settlement that would later become Washington could be seen clearly from that vantage point. The tree was called Old Tabletop; so named because of its flat top. It towered above all the other trees around.

Daddy showed me such a tree more than once on hunting trips near the Tar River, as he told and retold me the stories he had heard since his youth about *Sister Susie*. There were spikes driven into it and notches carved out to help with climbing. Its stump still stands there today.

But, I digress. That morning we were going up Tranter's Creek to Daddy's favorite fishing spot. We knew Mama would have the iron skillet on the stove filled with lard to fry the fish in as soon as we got home. She had a lot of faith in us, so we were determined to make her proud and bring home dinner.

That was our usual fare on a night when we had been fishing, if it wasn't raining too hard to catch anything that day. A light rain was good for fishing, but a *frog strangler* as Daddy put it, would be bad. The fish just didn't seem to be interested in eating then.

We paddled out into the water and turned west, following the Creek. We were headed toward a little tributary that turned off the main branch into a stream. It was so narrow you could almost spit on land from the center.

We passed other fishermen as we went along. They were, like us, bent on having fish for supper. Some of them wore broad-brimmed straw hats pulled low over their foreheads; some like Daddy were bareheaded. The boats were tied to old tree stumps and thick brush at the edge of the water. The fishermen were sitting with their bare feet dangling precariously close to the snake infested water, apparently half asleep, waiting for a bite.

For the most part, they were all dressed in similar fashion; ragged old pants with legs rolled up to their knees, sporting baggy shirts. They too were fishing with cane poles.

It was one of those lazy days on the creek. There were the ever present perky sounds coming from trees filled with bird's singing their little hearts out. At intervals the sound of gar jumping out of the water, then falling back with a soft splash would break up the bird's songs. Daddy said they were washing their tails.

Occasionally, one could hear the soothing sound of water slapping against the little skiff as it traveled under the bow, or washed up against the tree lined shore. Leaves drifted past us, riding the surface of the water.

Daddy knew about everybody within twenty miles by the time we had been at the new place three months. It didn't take him long to make his way around and introduce himself. As noted before, he was as outgoing a soul as God ever created. He knew no strangers.

Seeming to know everybody we passed that morning, he spoke politely, nodding his head in their general direction, as was expected of him, I suppose.

When we finally reached Daddy's favorite fishing spot, we found it had not been taken. In fact, we had the whole area to ourselves. Daddy told me to turn my head while he threaded a live, protesting worm, onto my hook. There was enough female in me to be quite squeamish about such things. Then we dropped our lines into the water to see what was there.

It was about twenty minutes before we got the first nibble. It was on Daddy's line. I watched the little red cork bob up and down a couple of times before I elbowed Daddy, as he was half asleep.

"Daddy, you got a fish!" I squealed in my most high pitched tone. I tried to tell him softly, so as not to disturb the other fish, but I always got *so* excited when we caught the first one.

All in all we got four robin, several bream, three catfish and one small Bass. The Bass came after Daddy carefully placed the last cricket on his hook. He was happy that we got at least one, because Mama liked those best. He and I preferred Sunfish.

Just before sunset, those rambunctious blood suckers better known as mosquitoes, arrived with a vengeance. It was time to go home. Daddy pulled the string of fish out of the water and looked at them with pride. Then he placed them carefully back in to trail behind the boat until we got back to the landing. It was closing in on dark by the time we got there.

Ancient Cyprus trees cast ghostly shadows onto the still dark waters. A snow white Egret sat on the opposite bank watching us hungrily as Daddy pulled the line in with our catch strung along it.

Fireflies, I called them lightening bugs, swarmed over the fast darkening banks, displaying their luminescent glow. To me they resembled twinkling stars, gently moving in beautiful circles, swaying in time to the soft breeze of a spring evening on the creek.

"I have a stop to make on the way home," Daddy announced. "You remember Uncle John?" I said *yes*. "We're going to stop by and say hello to him, we have a little business to attend to."

The business was about the whiskey being brewed in the still, hidden deep in the woods, about a mile from our place.

Daddy didn't have anything to do with the working of the still itself, as he had no money to put into it. But he knew everybody around the area and was a good source the moonshiners could use to deliver the stuff locally. And, Daddy had an excellent hiding place to age the whiskey until the patron came to get his order filled. He was paid a small token for the job.

I overheard Mama tell him once she didn't want him to be involved, but she couldn't deny that the little bit of money helped. Had she known Daddy was taking me to the site of the still, however, she would have been very angry. But that was not likely. When Daddy asked me to not tell something, a wild elephant couldn't have pulled it out of me. Besides, I loved to visit the place and knew Mama would have put a stop to it.

The fellow we called Uncle John was running the last of the corn whiskey that night, with the help of three of his trusted friends.

It took three or four men to run the thirty five gallon still efficiently; two or three to handle the brewing, and one sentry with a whistle or a bell to sound the alarm when they saw the law coming. That would be James.

Being discovered had not been a problem thus far with that still because it was so well hidden. They had even diffused the smoke from the burning wood through a long convoluted pipe so it wouldn't be easily seen.

John was standing with his back to us slowly feeding wood into the firebox.

"Hey there, Andy," he said without looking up, apparently recognizing Daddy's voice. "Hope you are ready to take this run, she'll be through by morning." Daddy answered in the affirmative.

Jason was stirring the mash, and Tom who had nothing to do at the moment, was standing to the side whistling softly. He stopped whistling to look us over carefully; then blew a long, deliberate stream of white smoke upward. I had noted before that he was the quiet one of the group, only saying what needed to be said, when it needed to be said.

Daddy made plans for picking up the liquor before daylight in the morning. He was busy showing off our catch when a long, low whistling sound pierced the relative calm. That was followed by the sound of a shotgun being discharged close by. It was the sentry, James.

One of the sentry's jobs was to draw any strange intruders away. If the sentry didn't recognize them, they were automatically thought to be the law.

Daddy put his hand over my mouth and whispered, "Shhh."

None of us moved or breathed for what seemed to be an endless amount of time. We could hear feet stomping around and another gunshot farther away as the intruders, whoever they were, followed the sentry away from the still. James knew the woods like the back of his hand and was good at his job. The shouts drifted slowly to the north and out of our hearing range.

"Sometimes I don't think it's worth it," Tom stated matter-of-factly as he tossed his half smoked cigarette to the ground, snuffing it out with a twist of his heel. Then he relieved Jason at the stirring.

Jason, who was as white as the proverbial bed sheet, sank gratefully to the ground. He had been released from jail just recently. Having been incarcerated for thirty days for being drunk and disorderly in public, he was not looking forward to another stint there any time soon.

Daddy and I left as soon as it was safe to do so and made a bee-line for home. When the soft, yellow lamplight's glow came into view from our kitchen window, Daddy said, "Better not tell your Mama about this for sure Son. She's not going to understand."

I agreed.

Mama was waiting in the kitchen, rocking Bet. Daddy cleaned the fish and started a fire while Mama kneaded the biscuit dough, keeping her eye on Bet. She sat quietly clinging to the side of her little box, on a chair by the table where Mama had deposited her.

I went to sit on the floor in my bedroom; propping my chin on the window sill to get a good view of the eastern sky above the trees. It was chock full of stars. The moon had not made its way above the tree tops, as of yet. It seemed to me there were a million little lights, winking at me, like sparkling diamonds in an upside down bowl, set against a velvet mat of pitch-black sky. It was breathtakingly beautiful, a beauty that could not be reproduced by a mere human being, not even verbally.

I listened contentedly as Daddy told Mama about the fishing trip. "A lot of people out there," he was saying, "but we got enough fish for our supper and that's enough for me. Some of them people are just greedy. They seem to want more than they can eat. We tried to leave some for another day, didn't we son?" he called to me.

"I have something to talk to you about," Mama said, when she could get a word in edgewise. "Miss Lillian told me yesterday she thinks the woman that disappeared before we moved into this place was murdered here. She thinks the sounds we hear on rainy nights are her ghost. What do you think?"

"I think that is one of the most stupid things I've heard of lately, that's what I think," Daddy stated.

"I don't know, Andy," Mama said as she dropped the first flour coated fish into the boiling grease, producing a loud sizzling sound. "You remember when you tried to scare me to death with those stories about ghosts. You repeated that verse in the Bible where King Saul went to see the witch of Endor and had Samuel's *shade* brought back from the dead. I believe that would be his ghost. You said Samuel had rebuked him for it. If there ain't no spirits coming back from the beyond, then where did that story come from? I think we now have our own ghost," she continued, "and we have a local fortune teller who might be able to shed some light on it. I've got a good mind to ask Miss Lillian if she'll come over here on the next rainy night, and see if she can make heads or tails of this walking we hear on the porch. Only thing is, I don't know if the Lord would approve."

"You'll do no such thing, Elizabeth," Daddy said. "She ain't so smart nohow. She couldn't even see far enough ahead to keep her husband from being caught and hung by that gang with the white sheets over their heads."

"Now Andy, you don't know that for sure. Sometimes I think you believe everything you hear," Mama said. "I understand her husband just disappeared."

"He went somewheres Elizabeth, nobody just ups and disappears," Daddy said.

Mama just kept on dropping the fish into the bubbling grease and didn't say anything more about it, which usually meant her mind was made up and the subject closed. I didn't understand about the white sheet thing, but I sure hoped Mama would get Miss Lillian over here. I loved playing with Barbara.

## Chapter 4

We had spent that hot Friday in mid-July, 1943, in the field. I was watching over Bet while Mama and Daddy cleared weeds away from the tobacco plants. The plants were still small, but wherever clothes rubbed against them, they left a stiff, nasty feel. By the end of the day their clothes were so stiff they would probably have stood alone.

"You don't have to wash them," Daddy said, laughing at Mama. "Just stand them in the corner tonight and I can jump in them in the morning."

Apparently Mama didn't think that too funny. A frown crept across her forehead. She ignored him.

Bet and I stayed in the shade, but it was hot there too. The wind had all but disappeared. My skin was already dark brown from sun exposure, although I was naturally very fair.

Feeling the need of companionship, I tried desperately to get Bet interested in something. She just stared at me while I did cartwheels and made funny faces at her. I felt responsible for her somehow, as if I should be able to make her happy. At last I pulled her out of the box and onto my lap. I pretended she was the pretty little doll I had never had. After a short time, the humid air got so hot I had to put her back in the cardboard box, where she would be cool enough.

We were really tired when we got home that evening. The heat and humidity had taken its toll. Mama washed Bet and helped me clean up, then bathed herself.

Daddy was procrastinating as usual. He always said he thought too much water was *weakening.* Mama told him that was just an excuse for not taking a bath, and that if he expected to sleep in the same bed she slept in that night, he should think about it. That did the trick. They only had one bed and the rough wood floor was mighty hard. Daddy didn't have to sleep on it many times, to my knowledge.

The summer days were long, and it was nine o'clock before supper was over and the dishes washed. Darkness had almost taken over when Mama flung the back door open with the intent of emptying the dish pan into the backyard. She almost drowned the man standing there, apparently about to knock.

Mama just seemed to freeze in her tracks, holding the half empty dish pan in her hands. She was staring, apparently astonished, at that hardened looking fellow well over six feet tall. He had black curly hair and a long bushy beard. The part of his face that could be seen was wrinkled, and he wasn't smiling. His eyes reminded me of Bet, sort of like *nobody's home*. He was wearing new looking work clothes; was barefoot and kinda slumped over.

It couldn't have been more than a few seconds, but in that length of time I made up my mind. I liked him. I couldn't help laughing at him standing there drenched with soapy dishwater.

Laughter seemed to break the ice and Mama stepped back. By that time Daddy was to the door inviting the man in with a big smile.

When we lived with Grandmother, we always had lots of visitors. Mama and Daddy made everybody welcome at our door, and had said they missed the company. I believe they would have been happy to see Jack the Ripper!

The man stood there quietly while Mama got a dish drying towel and handed it to him.

Still standing on the steps he said, "I'm Johnny King, I used to live here." Then he walked slowly through the door and stopped just inside, looking around as if he were expecting to see something.

Mama asked rather lamely, "What are you looking for?" I noticed she never mentioned that she had heard about him from Miss Lillian just recently.

"I was seeing what you all had done with the place."

There wasn't much to see. We owned a kitchen table, four stool chairs, one rocking chair, a wood cook stove and heater, a treadle type Singer sewing machine, two little hand made beds for Bet and me, and one for Mama and Daddy.

There were nails on the wall with our meager supply of clothes hanging on them. A trunk in the corner of Mama's bedroom held Bet's diapers and shirts, along with the bed linens, towels and wash clothes. There were just barely enough dishes and silverware for eating, a blue enamel coffee pot and a dishpan. Daddy said we didn't need anything else in the house; said it would tend to clutter things up.

"We got coffee on the stove if you want some," Daddy said. "I was just gittin' ready to drain the pot and set it up for tomorrow mornin'."

"Okay," Mr. Johnny said and took Mama's seat at the table. "I wanted to see the place, that's all. It's been a while."

"How long did you live here?" Daddy asked. "I heard that the man who lived here before we moved in went away to the war, and that's why the place was empty."

"That was me," Johnny answered. "My wife and I had lived here for a while before I went away. I was sent home early because they said I wasn't able to do my job anymore, I don't know why."

The curiosity of youth overwhelmed me at that point. I drew close to the stranger and stood staring up at him.

"Hey, little girl," he said, looking me straight in the eye. "Do you like living here?"

"Yes," I answered. Then I said, "Mama don't like it, but we don't have anywhere to go 'till the tobacco crop is in."

"Why don't your Mama like it?" he asked. Before I could answer, Mama told me to stop bothering the man and find me something to do. I started walking away just as he was saying, "Do you like candy?" I looked at Mama for the answer. Not seeing *no* in her eyes, I answered *yes*.

At that he produced a red-stripped candy cane from his shirt pocket. It was wet with dishwater. I took it, looked at it for a second and placed it on the edge of the table. I liked candy, but somewhere between the sticky, the wet and the soapy, I had lost my appetite.

Mama picked it up and said, "I'll put it away for a treat tomorrow." Then she walked me to my bed, listened to my *Lay Me Down to Sleep* prayer, and pulled the sheet up around my neck.

I listened from the cozy safety of my bed while they talked. Indeed, Mr. Johnny turned out to be the husband of the woman who had disappeared from this place. He had come home to find what he described as *blood stains* on the front porch. His wife wasn't there and was never seen again.

I was determined to stay awake and hear what was going on. However, the combination of a cool night wind blowing softly across my face through the screened window, and the fact that I was very tired prevailed. I fell asleep.

I got myself up the next morning, and upon arrival in the kitchen, discovered Mr. Johnny was still there.

Apparently he had stayed all night in Mama's chair at the table, and was at the moment, sleeping soundly with his head cradled on his arms.

Daddy was busy fixing coffee but he stopped to acknowledge my presence. Mama was getting ready to fix breakfast. She put her hand on the man's shoulder, shook him and called, "Johnny".

Mr. Johnny jumped like that bob cat we had seen once on the porch roof when we came home late from town and interrupted his snooze. He stared at Mama with wide open eyes and fear etched all over his face for the space of a few seconds. Then his expression slowly softened and he said, "I'm sorry, I was dreaming. I didn't mean to fall asleep here. I guess I was more tired than I thought."

Daddy looked at him questioningly and said, "It's alright; you can come over here and stay with us any time you want to. We like having somebody to talk to. Elizabeth will make you some breakfast."

At that Mama started to cook. She cast a look at him over her shoulder, and I could see she felt sorry for him for some reason. I just thought he looked funny. I'd never seen a man with a beard like that. He made me think of Daddy's description of Blackbeard.

"I can't stay," he said. "My Mother will be worried about me. I told her I was coming over here to see who had moved in, and that I wouldn't be gone long."

Mama looked relieved.

I asked him why he had come to see us. "Nobody ever comes here," I said.

"If I'm welcome I'll come often, I miss this place," Mr. Johnny said with a hurtful look on his face that I didn't understand.

After he left Mama asked, "Why do you think he came over here, Andy?"

"Who knows, Elizabeth," Daddy said, "he's probably lonely. He came straight back here from the war to see his wife, and found that stain on the front porch, which he thinks is her blood. That's enough to make a man feel crazy. Maybe he just wanted to see the place agin' like he said. You remember what we were told, that he came home *shell shocked*."

"Something about him makes me feel uneasy," Mama said, her face clouding over with that worried look I'd seen often lately.

"Don't worry about it. We have things to do other than talkin' about him this mornin'," was Daddy's reply.

It had started raining about daybreak so we wouldn't be going to the fields until it stopped. Daddy said he was going to hang a swing on the porch for me.

"You're not talking about *that* porch, are you?" Mama asked as she gestured toward the front of the house.

"She can't swing in the rain," Daddy said.

"Well, she can wait until it ain't raining," Mama said. "I don't want her on that porch! You can hang the swing on that low limb of the pecan tree in the back yard."

I stood there in silence, waiting to see who would win the discussion. Mama usually did, but Daddy was determined to put me a swing on the porch. I wasn't afraid of being on the porch during the day, but Mama had made sure I was afraid of it at night. She had forbid me to go out there after dark. I was frequently reminded of the footsteps we had heard. She always pulled the curtains across the windows and secured the front door latch well before the sun went down.

Daddy denied being *scared of ghosts* but I noted he never went out there after dark either. Right then it was a rainy day and I just wanted to swing.

Daddy had gone to the boss's house earlier that morning and secured a link of rusty old chain nobody was using, just for that purpose. I was ready to make use of it.

Without another word Daddy went to the front porch, threw the chain up over an exposed beam where there were no leaks at the moment, tied it to an old car tire and started swinging me on it. We were having so much fun that Mama soon got over being upset and came out to watch.

The last thing she had to say about it to me was: "You're not to be out here after dark." *I didn't have to be told that*, I thought.

I played on the swing under Mama's watchful eye most of the day as we couldn't work the fields in the rain. It had been pretty steady, so being on the porch was about as close to the yard as she would let me go. She said we would have to work all day next Saturday to make up for today because we needed the money. Daddy and I just enjoyed our reprieve from the fields.

Around six o'clock that evening, Mr. Johnny showed up again. He had a question about us going to church with him that next day. And he had brought me candy.

Mama and Daddy treated him like an old friend. They fed him supper, which he ate with the gusto of a hound dog. I shared my flour-bread man with him, and noted that he liked to soak his biscuit in the bean soup before eating it, just like I did.

Later on while Daddy listened to the radio, Mama washed my hair. Then she and Mr. Johnny tore the brown paper bag the candy came in into long strips, and curled my hair up with it.

"You shouldn't bring her candy, Johnny; it's expensive and hard to come by now with the rationing and all," Mama told him. "I know she likes it, but we ain't got the money for such things. I would rather you didn't give her stuff we can't afford. But we thank you anyway." Mama wasn't one for spoiling a child. I found that out early.

Mr. Johnny said he understood; then winked at me as if to say: *We'll find a way around that.*

"You have hair and eyes just like my Katie," he said. "You're almost as pretty too."

"Is Katie your little girl?" I asked.

"No, she was my wife," he said. At that point, a strange look came across his face. He got up suddenly, said a hurried goodbye and left.

"That man *is* strange," Mama stated flatly after he'd gone.

"He's harmless enough," Daddy stated absently, and went back to his coffee and pipe.

I fell asleep that night worrying with the knotted paper rolled up in my hair. I didn't particularly want curly hair, but Mama was determined that I should have it tomorrow. We were going to church with Mr. Johnny.

He had asked us to go as they were having a revival, and all the members were supposed to bring somebody. He hadn't been able to get a soul to go with him. Mama had agreed we would, and Daddy had reluctantly gone along with it.

"You know I like to fish on Sunday, and you have things to do too, Elizabeth," he said. "Besides, they will look down on us, you know that."

"These are not the same people, Andy, maybe they will be different." She had made up her mind. Her memory seemed to dim from a bad experience in a church in the past that Daddy was more than willing to bring up. It was a memory Mama put a stop to before he could finish the sentence he had started on the subject.

"You know the service doesn't start at night until about seven-thirty," Mama said. "I believe Johnny needs a friend and I've been wanting to find a good church somewhere anyway. We'll have plenty of time to do all the chores in the morning, and you and Liz can go fishing too. You'll be home by five o'clock, if you don't dawdle around like you usually do. Johnny said he'd be here around six-thirty."

Well, that was that, Mama had decided. She had inherited her stubborn streak from her Indian ancestry, Daddy said. There was no need to protest.

The first night of revival was to be tomorrow night. Daddy and I were to leave on our fishing trip by daybreak in the morning; Mama was to get the laundry done by dinner time.

Sunday morning turned out to be a beautiful, Carolina blue sky day. My most pressing problem at that moment was the paper strips tied up in my hair. I hated the ugly things and wanted them out before we went fishing.

Mama refused. "Absolutely not," she said. "You will keep them in until we get ready for church, and that's that. Your hair is as straight as a stick and you're too young to wear it in a bun, so you'll wear it curled up if you go fishing with your Daddy this day. You know that damp air on the water makes any curl fall right out."

I knew when I was whipped, so I kept my mouth shut after that and went on. Daddy didn't help the situation any. He laughed at me and said we'd probably not catch a live fish, because I'd scare them to death if they saw me first. I was not a happy urchin, and promised myself I would cut all my hair off the next time I got hold of the scissors.

We turned right from our mooring place, traveling toward Washington; then took another right into the Tar River, heading toward Grimesland.

Daddy pointed in the direction of Old Tabletop, Blackbeard's look-out tree. I was reminded not to forget that he had traveled these waters and probably hidden treasure somewhere around here.

Tar River was much wider than Tranter's Creek. We followed it for about two miles; then paddled in close to the shore to see what we could catch.

A blazing sun beat down on us unmercifully. My dress was sticking to me like glue, and not a breeze was stirring anywhere. The fishing wasn't as good as it had been last week, either. When it was this hot, Daddy said, the fish tended to stay down deep where the water was cooler.

Since the fishing was so poor we decided to go ashore for a while. Daddy tied the skiff to a protruding stump and we scrambled onto the bank. We could get a breath of cool air in the shade of the trees that lined the river.

We finally found the log Daddy was looking for and sat down. For a few minutes the usual rustling of tree leaves and the muted sounds of small animals milling about were all we heard. Daddy was whistling softly like he did sometimes when we were alone in the woods. There seemed to be no reason for talking, and Daddy was never quite silent.

Suddenly the thundering sound of a shotgun exploded in our ears. Daddy jumped up and shouted, "Hey, watch out where you're shootin', you're gonna kill somebody!"

"OH God!" a voice yelled back and a face appeared around an old cypress tree trunk with a terrified look on it.

"Sorry, Andy, I didn't know you all were there!" It was Jason from the liquor still. Dangling from his belt were two dead rabbits.

I found myself staring at them. Their huge, bulging eyes were still wide open. They were hanging by their necks on a rope slung around Jason's belt. I had seen dead rabbits before, but something about the way those rabbits looked made me feel sick.

When Jason had gone, Daddy started talking about animals. He had apparently seen the look on my face.

"Son," he said, "I never let you see me kill the food we eat, but you've been huntin' with me when I killed 'em. The fact that we kill things to eat ain't bad. How we go about it can be. The Lord lets us kill to eat. There's a place in the Bible that tells us we can eat just about any animal, as long as we ask the Lord to bless it. But we need to have respect for the animals we kill. There's a right way and a wrong way to do everythin'."

"Don't ever feel you are better or worse than the creatures we eat. I want you to know somethin' about them, so sit here quietly and listen for a while. Don't say a word until I tell you to. I want you to listen to the animals. They have their way of communicatin' with us."

We sat there for what seemed to me to be hours. Actually it was probably about thirty minutes. I began to hear sounds like I had not heard them before. Two doves settled on a low lying limb across from us. They seemed to be talking to each other.

"They're talking about the weather," Daddy whispered and smiled at me. "They're sayin' it's a hot day."

While we sat there, several squirrels and a couple of rabbits turned up to stare at us. At one point Daddy slowly reached out his hand to a rabbit. The rabbit actually came and put his wet, shiny nose right against Daddy's fingers.

"If you're not afraid of them and don't think yourself above them they know it, Son. Always remember we are not a superior animal, just a different kind. They

were all created by God before He created us and He
looked after them then. Now He expects us to take care of
them for Him. That doesn't make us better than them. It
just makes us their caretakers."

By that time it was around two o'clock in the hot
summer afternoon. Daddy said we had better take the fish
we had and head home because Mama would want us to be
ready to leave for church by six-thirty. Then he visibly
shivered.

Mama was waiting impatiently when we got there.
After helping me take a bath that suited her, she started in
on my hair. I wished I had gotten to the scissors before she
got to my head. I became even more determined to cut it
all off at the first opportunity.

Then she got her iron and sat it on the stove for
about ten minutes, to press the clothes with. It was awfully
hot in the house because of the fire, but Daddy and I knew
better than to say anything. Mama was going to iron, and
that was that. Before we got home she had sprinkled our
best clothes with water, and rolled them up in a ball to keep
them moist until time to iron. They sat in an orderly pile on
the kitchen table.

Daddy only had one pair of overalls and one shirt
that were anywhere close to being decent. Mama did her
best to make them look alright. She had patched the big
hole in the shirt. She was ever so careful to make our
clothes look as good as they could, and was very
meticulous about ironing out all the wrinkles.

It took about thirty minutes of that hot afternoon
for the ironing, with Daddy keeping the fire burning and
Mama heating the iron and pressing the clothes. I
remember her wetting her finger on her tongue and
touching the sole plate of the iron occasionally to make
sure it was not too hot.

All in all, she spent a lot of time getting us ready. It was making Daddy more and more nervous. If there was one thing he hated it was *dressing up,* as he called it. He said that the Lord certainly didn't mean for him to be all cleaned and polished just to go to church.

"I can talk to God anytime I want to, Elizabeth," he said to Mama, "I don't need to go through all this mess to do that. If people can't read the Bible then there's a need, maybe, to go listen to a preacher. I can read. I don't need that!"

Mama simply ignored his protests and just kept on getting us ready until Mr. Johnny and the truck arrived.

It was an old Ford and didn't sound like it would make it if the church were very far away. I remember Mama looking at it with some dismay.

By the time we had all crowded into the cab it seemed unlikely that the thing could struggle up to the top of the slight incline in the road, with the extra weight. But somehow it did, and we drove toward one of Daddy's most dreaded destinations.

It was a tight fit in there to say the least. I sat between Mama and Mr. Johnny. Bet sat on Mama's lap, looking oblivious to everything as usual, and Daddy was crammed in between Mama and the door.

And so, we bounced along from one rut to another over the sandy back road, hitting a bump that would jar your teeth every now and then. A tire blew out about half a mile from the church. Daddy helped Mr. Johnny fix it with the comment, "I'm glad we started early."

We finally arrived, miraculously in one piece, at the proper church house. We had passed two before we arrived at the right one. There were many churches around, this being in the Bible belt of the south. It sat facing the road in the shadow of several large pine trees, fronting a heavily wooded piece of land behind and on both sides of it. The

steeple reached a stately height above the porch roof. I had
seen many churches with steeples, but never one with the
steeple on the porch. I asked Mama about it and she just
said, *hush*.

We pulled up in the churchyard and Mr. Johnny
found a place to park among the five or six cars and trucks
there. It was seven-twenty. All but the stragglers had
arrived.

Several small groups of people stood around the
yard talking about the weather, the crops, and the price of
commodities. A few were even talking about the evangelist
who had been selected to preach that first night of revival.
He was new to the community and people were curious
about him. From conversations I was hearing, there
seemed to be a few people from other churches here to
support him.

Standing in a little alcove just inside the church
door was the aforementioned preacher. He was a tall, gray
haired, elderly gentleman dressed in a black suit and tie.
That was a sight to behold for most of the people in
attendance, as they were mostly dressed in overalls with
colored shirts. Those were their Sunday best.

He was shaking hands with all that entered the door.
When Daddy reached out to shake his hand the preacher
hesitated, looking at Daddy's dirty hands from where he
had changed the tire. Daddy quickly withdrew his hand
and we walked in. I felt bad for Daddy but was too naive to
put a name to the feeling.

I was beginning to understand what Daddy meant
by, *we're not like them*. As I looked around that church, at
the way people were dressed, and compared it to our
tattered clothes, I realized we were not dressed properly. I
felt sadly out of place.

We sat down on the back row of pews with Mr.
Johnny, who was also being ignored, but didn't seem to

mind. His Mama came over and spoke, but not another soul seemed to notice us. They would look our way; smile and go on to someone they knew better and start talking. I supposed that those church people were the neighbors Daddy must have missed when he was making his rounds in the neighborhood.

When the preacher started his sermon, the people stopped talking to listen, and I felt better for some reason. I remember the preacher saying something about the Lord taking care of *his* needs in this life because *he* was a son of the Almighty God. And, when *he* needed something, God always made sure he got it.

I remember wondering why we had to work so hard for everything we got and he got his for free, until the donation plate for the preacher came around. Daddy put a dime in it. I knew that was all he had. I remembered the story he had told me about the widow's mite, and wondered if people would get back according to what they put in.

I must say it was an impressive sermon, though. The preacher practically walked on the back of the front row of pews, which were empty. He hollered at us, told us we were all sinners, and how absolutely worthless we were. Then he shot out a volley or two while looking straight at Daddy about cleanliness being next to Godliness. In general he informed us that we all needed to be saved, and that *saving* would be by Grace and not by deeds alone.

"This could be your last night on this earth!" he shouted. "Do you want to burn in hell fire forever because you're too proud to come to this altar tonight, not being willing to bow your knees before God?" The rafters overhead shook with the sound of his voice.

Several of the ladies started shouting and praising God. It was an awesome sight, I must confess. I didn't understand, but I did feel like something important was happening that didn't particularly involve me.

After a while things calmed down and the preacher invited everybody to the altar. There were no takers. He looked up at the ceiling, in an apparent sign to God that he was washing his hands of this unholy group, and went to sit on his chair behind the pulpit.

Then a deacon came up to announce the evangelist for tomorrow night. He asked everyone to stand and say a prayer for the departing one, which we all did.

At that time the donation plate was passed around again, for something the church wanted to do. We got up and silently withdrew, having no more money to contribute. Nobody noticed us leaving, except Mr. Johnny, who got up and followed us out.

Nothing was said about us leaving early until we were inside the truck. Then Mr. Johnny said, "I think we should have stayed at least until the end of the service."

"I don't think I should have," Daddy said. "I'm just glad to git out of there!"

"Why?" Mr. Johnny asked.

"For one thing," Daddy said, "I don't think the preacher should take money from the people."

"Why do you feel that way?" Mr. Johnny asked.

"I've read in the Bible that when Jesus sent his disciples out to preach the gospel, He gave them power over unclean spirits and the ability to heal. Preachers claim to be followin' the example left by Jesus, don't they? They were to take nothin' with them for the journey. He told them to find a house in the neighborhood and stay there until the preachin' was done in that town. They were not to go house to house. If the people did not listen, he should dust his feet off upon departin', and it would be better for Sodom and Gomorrah than for that place at the Day of Judgment. I don't remember Him sayin' nothin' about a collection plate for the preacher. And I didn't see nobody git healed, either," Daddy said.

"But it say's a worker is worthy of his hire," Mr. Johnny said. "It takes money to travel around."

"Is he doin' it for God or himself?" Daddy asked. "It looks like he's doin' it for himself to me if he takes money for it. If he's doin' it for God, and he has faith that God will take care of him, why does he need money from the people? God will take care of His own. I agree with him that the Bible says that, and I believe it."

The conversation continued when we got home. Mr. Johnny followed us into the house where it heated up. He told Daddy he didn't think he'd read anything of the sort in the Bible.

Daddy took Mama's Bible down from the shelf over the kitchen stove and looked it up in the Book of Mark. He also read that when you pray you should shut yourself up in your own closet and pray to the Father who is in secret, and that He would reward you openly. He said that you shouldn't pray where you could be seen by everybody; that he thought doing that was kind of like showing off that you are a Christian. He said he thought you should show off your Christianity by what you do and how you live your life, not by what you say.

Finally, Mr. Johnny stated that maybe he should start reading the Bible for himself, and stop relying so much on the preachers.

Daddy told him he thought that a good idea.

Mama's last and only word on the subject was: "I think it's a good idea to go to church to be with people who also believe in God."

Nobody challenged her on that!

Mama fried the fish and Daddy made coffee. After we ate, he and Mr. Johnny smoked and kept on talking well into the night. I fell asleep to the sound of their voices.

I awoke around two o'clock in a cold sweat from a frequently repeated nightmare. Mama had told me they were caused by the ghostly sound of someone walking on the porch we had been hearing. The house was very quiet. I went to the kitchen to see if Mr. Johnny was still there, but he wasn't. I pulled Bet's bed close to me and fell asleep with my arm across her little body, for her safety and my own.

### Chapter 5

Mr. Johnny was a regular visitor by the end of July, 1943. He fit right in with the family. He never tried to get Daddy to go to church with him again, and went fishing with us often on Sunday.

One day Mama asked Daddy if he had noticed we hadn't heard that *ghost* walking on the porch very often since Mr. Johnny had been coming around the house.

"Well, maybe that's because it ain't rained much at night since he's been comin'," Daddy said, laughing. "Anyhow, I believe it's somebody that don't want us here that's very much alive, Elizabeth."

"Either way I think we ought to tell Johnny about it," Mama said. "He used to live here; maybe he has some ideas on the subject."

"I don't think we ought to tell him. He might think it's his wife's ghost or something like that," Daddy said. "Remember, he thought that stain on the porch was her blood."

"We have that in common," was Mama's final comment.

After that conversation died down, Daddy and I went to the barn and picked out a couple of hoes.   I watched as he sharpened them for the day's work.   It was a rather cool day for late July.  The trees were still displaying some of what Daddy referred to as Ireland's forty shades of green.  Usually by now they had a tired, dull hue from the excessive heat of long summer days in the southland. Perfectly shaped, tiny pink rambling roses grew in wild profusion, cascading playfully along the broken wooden fence around the barn yard.  They effectively camouflaged the mule droppings that presented a hazard as we traversed the landscape to feed Jim and Jake before going to the fields.

My mind was on Mr. Johnny's visit the day before. He had suggested we go to town this coming Saturday with him. He said he had business to take care of and we wouldn't have to pay to ride the train. The only problem was that he would be there all day. He could pick us up around six o'clock in the evening at the grocery store to come home. Mama said she'd like that and thanked him.

For the next week I almost worried Mama to death asking her how many more days before we could go to town with Mr. Johnny. I especially loved to go with him because if it wasn't raining he would allow me to ride in the back of his pickup truck. He would place a bale of hay up next to the cab and I would sit on it and ride to town in style.

Saturday finally arrived and Mr. Johnny picked us up around nine o'clock. It wasn't raining so I was given my seat in the back. The sun was beating down on me and would have been unbearable if it had not been for the wind blowing around the cab. Mama had pulled my hair back into a ponytail and secured it with a twine string. The long, straight strands swirling around my face shimmered in the sunlight like fine spun gold, or so Mr. Johnny had said to me.

It would be a nice long ride because Mr. Johnny had business to attend to in Grimesland before we went on to Washington. We backtracked and went the long way around. That suited me just fine. I *really* liked to ride in the back of that truck.

A plume of dust curled up behind us as the rickety old Ford made its way toward Grimesland over the heavily rutted back roads. We passed corn, tobacco, and cotton fields where people were bent low, stoic and sweating through their heavy labor. I waved and smiled at everybody, and occasionally someone would wave back.

Highway 264 (33 now) from Grimesland to Chocowinity was paved with concrete. Between the slabs of concrete, cracks had developed and had been filled with a coal tar product. This tar would expand and make a soft mound when the temperature got to around eighty-five degrees in the shade. Then the tar would get soft and pliable.

Sometimes after visiting family in Grimesland on a Saturday afternoon, we would walk back to Chocowinity where we could catch a ride home. During those long walks, I would torment Mama by pulling up the black, gooey tar. It made pretty good chewing gum, but it also made my teeth black. I wasn't bothered about that, but it seemed to infuriate Mama.

There were wooden poles supporting wires carrying the meager supply of electric power to the few homes along that roadway. Occasionally when the linemen worked on them, they would drop those pretty blue glass insulators from the cross bars at the top of the pole, and wouldn't take time to come down and retrieve them. I had a stack of those that I had saved up. I kept them with the robin's eggs I had taken from a nest in a tall bush in our back yard, near the outhouse. Mama tanned my backside for that one, but said the mama robin wouldn't take them back after I had handled them anyway, so she let me keep them.

Mr. Johnny finally finished his business in Grimesland and we drove the few miles to Chocowinity, then turned north onto Highway 17 toward Washington. The bumps smoothed out a bit, but the truck would still bounce when it hit the repairs to the roadway. I wrapped my long skinny fingers around the wire holding the bale of hay together, to keep from being thrown from my perch, when we occasionally hit one of those bumps.

The trip didn't seem to take long that Saturday. Just before being bounced around one time too many on my seat, we passed over the bridge that separates the Pamlico from the Tar River at the edge of town. Looking to the west, I could see where the bend in the River turned toward Tranter's Creek. Several people were fishing along the shoreline on that side. A dark, foreboding, mirror image of trees lining the edge of the river in the deep blue water caught my attention momentarily.

To my right, the Pamlico River literally sparkled. Rays of sunlight played with tiny ripples on the water. It was *so* brilliant I had to shade my eyes as it actually hurt. Shrimp and crab boats clung to their tethers along the docks that lined the waterfront. I knew that was where Daddy and I would wind up sometime that day. Daddy loved the water almost as much as he loved to mingle with those boat captains. He felt himself to be one of them. He sold white lightening to a number of them when they were in town.

Mr. Johnny let us off on Main Street. We went to Bill's; bought hot dogs, and took them out to the waterfront where there was a place to sit and watch people on the River while we ate. Then Daddy and I walked with Mama and Bet to her sister Kathleen's house to visit. Along Water Street we passed houses that still sported cannon balls from the civil war imbedded in their walls, and breathed in that peculiar odor of fish that was being sold along the river.

Some call the little island in the middle of the Pamlico, across from town, Castle Island, others call it Queen's Island, depending on which story you believe about the place. I couldn't help but think how forlorn it looked in the bright morning sun that day.

One story about that island told by the locals goes like this: It was inhabited by women of ill repute. That lasted until the wives of some of the men who frequented the place went over there one night and burned the house that stood there to the ground.

Mama had been known to say that was just an ugly rumor. It was so named, she said, for the smoke stacks that appeared to be the turrets of a castle rising up from an old cannery that once occupied the space. I liked the story about the rude ladies myself.

Some time after that, goats were placed over there by some concerned citizens who used them to keep the place mowed. At the time, kids were allowed to play on the little Island. It wasn't long, however, before the goats disappeared. I always thought the alligators that make their way up the river at times were the culprits. A local oyster bar owner had shot one over there once. He was *big,* well over twelve feet long. The owner had stuffed it and hung it over the front door of his establishment. It made a good conversation piece for his customers.

As we walked along Water Street, Daddy kept up a string of chatter about the day ahead. Mama's lone comment was that she was just happy to be spending the day with her sister.

After seeing Mama happily talking with Aunt Kathleen, Daddy and I made our way back to the waterfront, and straight to the boat he was interested in visiting.

Captain Worthy welcomed us aboard. His deep bass voice matched his six foot, five inch, two hundred fifty pound weather hardened body to a "T". Life as a fisherman over the years had darkened and wrinkled the skin on his face. The unmerciful southern sun, along with the constant pressure all fisherman face on their long trips off shore, had taken its toll. Daddy said he looked at least ten years older than he actually was. That was what life on a fishing boat did for you, Mama said.

He seemed genuinely happy to see Daddy and pulled up a barrel for me to sit on near the railing, so I could watch the action on the river while they talked. After ten minutes or so, Captain Worthy pulled out the liquor jar from the crate next to his chair. They proceeded to pass it back and forth between the two of them.

After a while he and Daddy started singing songs like: *Ninety Nine Bottles of Beer on the Wall,* and *Sixteen Men on a Dead Man's Chest.* They drained every drop of whiskey from that bottle within a short period of time. It was good they held their liquor well; otherwise they would have been flat on their faces. As it was, they were just happy.

I traveled everywhere with Daddy, so I knew the songs well. I sang with them until they sang themselves sober, and I sang myself hoarse. Then Captain Worthy made us a big pot of strong coffee, and told Daddy he had better drink a lot of it so Mama wouldn't know what he had been up to. It was so strong he offered to water mine down, but Daddy told him I could probably drink it stronger than they could, and we all laughed at the thought of that.

Along about one o'clock, Daddy said he had to be getting back to Mama and Bet pretty soon as the Movie Matinee started at two, and it was to be Roy Rogers and Dale Evans. They were my favorite movie stars. Even Mama was fond of cowboy and Indian movies. Daddy said he didn't know why Mama liked those shows so much because the Indians almost always lost. At that Mama would say something like: *It's just a movie, after all, Andy.*

I wasn't happy to leave the docks. I loved watching the working fishing boats. I especially liked to watch the ladies hike up their skirts and travel timidly toward a boat that featured the seafood they wanted. It seemed to me they were having trouble holding onto their dignity, as they carefully made their way through discarded clam shells and crab carcasses. I couldn't help but laugh as I watched. I tried to do it quietly as Daddy took a dim view of my laughing at people.

Daddy got real serious just before we left. "Cap'n Worthy," he said "I been thinkin' about somethin' for a long time and I think now is the time to bring it up to you. I won't blame you a bit if you don't like the idea, but I'm in hopes you will. I've been told a hundred times in my life that Blackbeard hid some of his treasure along the shore up the Tar a'ways. I been meanin' to git somebody I could trust to go with me to see if we could find somethin'. I'd like it to be just you and me. You know you can't trust a lot of people with somethin' like this. Are you willing to give her a try? I don't think it's safe to go alone on a trip like this; somebody needs to be on the lookout, while the other does the digging. You might get your head knocked off while you're busy with the shovel."

Captain Worthy's weather aged skin above his eyebrows wrinkled even more, and his eyes narrowed to a point resembling a cat's eye when he is on the prowl.

"You know that wouldn't be an easy trip. Might be something to the story that's been told about how the old boy left a curse on the treasure he buried. I've no doubt that he hid something along that river somewhere, but how to go about getting it out of that snake infested swamp is another story. The gold, or whatever he buried there, might just not be worth the trouble. And anyway, what makes you think you might know about where that stuff is, Andy?" Captain Worthy asked.

"You'll think I'm crazy if I tell you, but I can see you ain't goin' if I don't, so here it is. I've been havin' the same dream about every night for the past couple of years, and feel it has somethin' to do with treasure being buried up the Tar River. Anyhow, I kinda believe in followin' up on dreams like that. I've thought about it a long time. Now I'm ready to do somethin' about it. Are you interested or not?"

It seemed he was.

Then the discussion began in earnest. Should they go at night where they would have the cover of darkness, or during the day? If they went during the day there was the chance they would be seen, and whoever owned that part of the swamp might claim the treasure.

On the other hand, at night there was the problem of rattlesnakes, water moccasins, mosquitoes, spiders and God only knows what else that you couldn't see until it was too late. And perhaps the light from a lantern would bring more attention than if they just went out there during the day. Finally, they hit on a plan. They would go during the day and check the territory out first. Perhaps Sunday after next would be a good time.

Captain Worthy didn't own a car; not that he didn't have enough money to own one had he wanted it, he just, for all practical purposes, lived on his boat. He did have a friend in town he could borrow a car from, however. He would pick Daddy up early that Sunday morning at the bend in the road, where they couldn't be seen from our house. Daddy was not going to tell Mama about this trip. Captain Worthy and I understood the wisdom in that. They would go to the landing and travel in Daddy's skiff with their fishing poles in plain view to avoid undue attention.

As soon as we were out of earshot of Captain Worthy, I started right in with, "Can I go Daddy?"

"We'll have to see, Son," he said, "It's a mighty dangerous business, and in no case will you tell your Mama, you hear?" I felt indignant; he should have known I wouldn't.

It took about half the way to Aunt Kathleen's house to get Daddy to agree that I could go. I believe he finally understood that I might accidently let the cat out of the bag, and Mama wouldn't let either of us go if he said no.

We went to the movies and Daddy bought us some popcorn. It was my favorite treat, but we couldn't always afford it. Daddy seemed to be in a generous mood, for some reason.

The Matinee lasted an hour and a half. That was about as long as I could be still. Mama seemed to be enjoying sitting for a while in a relatively cool place. Bet just slept, even through the loud gunshots. She never flinched.

We stayed through the cartoons and the final newsreel about the war at the end of the movie; then made our way back to the grocery store. Mr. Johnny wasn't there yet, so we sat around talking with the patrons until he came to pick us up. I hoped Daddy would tell him about our treasure hunt, but he didn't. Maybe that was because Mama might overhear and put a stop to the plan. And I guess it was just as well, because Mr. Johnny seemed to be preoccupied with something himself.

All the way home I was restless and fidgety. I was *so* excited about the treasure hunt coming up. "What's the matter with you, Liz?" Mama asked. "Try to contain yourself, we'll be home soon and I'll make you some supper. You must be hungry."

Mr. Johnny had insisted that I sit up front in the cab because he was afraid I would fall out of the back, I was acting so excited. I calmed down some when Daddy caught my eye and stared at me with that *you'd better watch it* look he could get sometimes when I was acting stupid.

When we got to the house Mr. Johnny came in with us to help bring in the supplies and to visit. He was spending more and more time with us now. He and Daddy drank coffee and talked well into the evening, after Mama had put Bet and me to bed. I listened as long as I was able to stay awake.

I slept fitfully that night, dreaming about Blackbeard's treasure and the adventure coming up. My dreams were equally divided between finding great treasures to being chased by demons parading as ghosts of pirates from days clouded in a distant and dim past.

It seemed to me it took those two weeks about two months to pass. But pass it did and we met Captain Worthy at the bend in the road at five o'clock on Sunday morning. Mama thought we were going fishing. We didn't lie to her; just didn't tell her the whole truth. We were going to try and catch a few fish after the search. She'd never know. It wasn't that she would be that opposed to the idea; it was just that she didn't believe in doing anything that was apt to get Daddy in trouble with the law, or God.

Captain Worthy wasn't alone as we expected him to be, and from the look on Daddy's face I could tell he didn't like this new addition to our plan at all, but he didn't say anything. I didn't either, but I wanted to.

In the back seat of that car sat the most unusual looking creature I had ever seen. It was a scrawny black man with eyes that could look right through a person. I didn't want to get back there with him but thought Daddy might not let me go if I didn't. I climbed in and sat as close to my side as I could, clinging to the door handle in case I felt like jumping out. He and I just stared at each other. He vaguely resembled a dead man I had seen that night Mama had taken me to a wake at one of the black people's house. As he stared at me he stated in a low growling voice, "I didn't know you was gonna bring along a young'un, and a girl at that. I don't like it."

"You ain't got to worry about her none, she's quiet as a field mouse, just like her Mama," Daddy said.

"Okay, but you better keep an eye on her," the old man said as he squinted at me through his strange, bottomless black eyes.

Captain Worthy introduced the old black man as *Mr. Nathaniel.* Then he introduced us to him, and stated that Mr. Nathaniel was an expert in the field of treasure hunting. "He knows a great deal about this treasure hunting thing, and we can use that knowledge today, I think," the Captain said with some authority.

Within a few minutes, Captain Worthy had found a place where we could safely leave the car, and pulled off the road as far as he could. We got out and made our way through the woods toward the creek.

While we were walking, Mr. Nathaniel produced an object from his overall pocket that I couldn't see clearly. I moved ever so cautiously closer to the old man out of curiosity, and saw a six inch tall gallows with a doll resembling a man dangling from it by a rope around his neck. I knew what a gallows was, because I had seen men hung from them in cowboy movies.

"This here is a talisman, I can use if we needs to ward off evil spirits," Mr. Nathaniel explained to us in a calm voice.

I drew closer to Daddy. He instinctively reached down and picked me up, depositing me on his shoulders, sensing my need to feel safe, I think. I locked my legs under his arm pits, and got a death grip on his forehead, just above his eyes.

We walked to where our little skiff lay attached to its rope. After we got in, Daddy bailed the water out and we started toward Tar River. We must have looked a bit strange to the fisherman we passed that morning. They stared at us with unasked questions in their eyes. Some tipped their hats, scratched their heads and said nothing, although they usually did when they were near enough to be heard distinctly.

We were near Old Tabletop when Daddy said he thought we ought to stop, *right there*. He paddled up to the shore in a place that looked like we could get through the underbrush along the shoreline, and tied the skiff to a small sapling that reached out over the water.

When we were all safely on land, Mr. Nathaniel just naturally fell in at the front of the line. Daddy and I fell in at the rear with me riding his shoulders. Captain Worthy took up the center. Mr. Nathaniel reached under his shirt and pulled out a foot long, two pronged stick he had been concealing. We were all quiet, waiting to see what he would do with it, when I became aware that there were no sounds around us. All the animals of the woods seemed to have gone away. Even the pesky flies and mosquitoes that were usually present at any time of day in a thickly wooded area were absent. I had never seen a time when the swampland was so quiet.

It was an eerie kind of silence, and to make it even more dramatic, the trees over our heads were so thick that sunlight was barely getting through. It was as if twilight had come early. I clung to Daddy hoping he wouldn't drop me. The idea of being on my own two feet at that particular time was not pleasant, to put it mildly. I had visions of the underbrush swallowing me up. It was pretty evident that human beings had not traveled on that part of the river bank in quite a while.

After tramping through the woods for about half an hour at a snails pace, Mr. Nathaniel stopped dead in his tracks and stood still, as if listening. Then the stick in his hand suddenly turned to point downward, and he started talking.

"I  believes there's somethin' here, but I don't wants to be here when you try to git it out. Not specially if it's at night," he said. "It has a curse on it, Cap'n. I ain't never felt such a binding curse as this has on it. Who's gold you all trying to git out o' here anyhow?" he asked, turning quickly to look at Daddy.

"We think its Blackbeard's stuff," Daddy hastily responded. "I wasn't sure how to git at it but I guess you think it's too dangerous. I think I'll try it anyway, but maybe I'll wait until winter so the underbrush won't be so thick, and the snakes will back off."

"If I was you I'd wait a long time fo' I tried diggin' 'round here," Mr. Nathaniel said, absently scratching his head.

During this entire conversation, Captain Worthy had been silent. We were looking at him for his input; he was known to have nerves of steel. "I ain't going to let no ghost stop me from trying to come up with some extra spending money," he said. "I ain't going to wait until winter, either. I could use some money to get my boats in tip-top shape. You with me or against me, Andy?"

"I guess I'm with you, Cap'n," Daddy answered. Then turning toward Mr. Nathaniel he said, "You can come in with us for a share Nathaniel. I don't have no objection if that's what you want, but you got to do your share of the work, and keep your mouth shut. Personally, I ain't afraid of ghosts though, they can't hurt you."

"Yea, but they can make you hurt yo'self," Mr. Nathaniel said. Then he went on to say, "I'll think about it."

They spent the next fifteen minutes marking the place they planned to dig on our next trip and completed the task by carving a cross on a nearby tree.

"How did we get in here?" The Captain suddenly asked of no one particular. "I was so busy thinking about the treasure; I never bothered to look where we were going."

"Don't worry about that, Cap'n," Mr. Nathaniel stated, "I was watchin', I can git you out agin'."

"Well that does it, you'll have to come with us on our next trip, Nathaniel," Captain Worthy announced magnanimously. "We can't get in and out of here without you. How much are you going to charge us?"

"A ships ransom fo' sho' Cap'n," he said, without cracking a smile.

When we arrived back at the skiff we baited our hooks and fished long enough to catch a few small ones, which would hopefully satisfy Mama that we had indeed been fishing. Then we made our way back to the landing. I was glad to be hearing the birds singing again.

On our way home, it was decided to come back in two weeks just after daylight to dig. Mr. Nathaniel was recruited by telling him we would absolutely be out of there by dark. He thought that might be safe enough, because he said he thought the curse might be null and void during the day time, seeing as how most people hunted for treasure at night.

Captain Worthy left us off with our fish at the bend in the road. But, before we parted, we all held hands and solemnly swore to never tell a soul about what we had done that day.

Mama was a welcome sight to me that evening. I had really been frightened, although I would never have admitted it. But, I had always been fascinated by that feeling, and I wanted to go back with them.

Mama remarked about how quiet I was, and asked Daddy if anything had happened on our trip out of the ordinary. His reply was: "Now, what do you think, Elizabeth?" Then he went out to the back yard to smoke his pipe until she forgot. I, of course, went with him.

Daddy looked very thoughtful as we sat there listening to the frogs singing in the ditch behind the house.

I didn't feel he wanted me to say anything; he apparently needed to think about something. Then suddenly he looked at me and said, "We had better tell your Mama about this trip with Cap'n Worthy. She'll probably hear about it anyhow, seeing as the Cap'n brought that black man in on it. They ain't no good at keeping their mouth shut."

Mama listened without a word until Daddy stopped talking. Then she just burst out with side splitting laughter. "If that ain't the silliest thing I ever heard of you doing, Andy," she said, moping at the tears in her eyes with her starched white apron. "I can just see you and Captain Worthy, tramping around the woods with that young'un, looking for some old dead pirate's gold." Then she started laughing all over again.

Daddy got red-faced and sulked his way back out to the shed to sit with Jim and Jake, while he licked his wounded pride. Those old mules seemed to know when Daddy was upset, and something about being with them seemed to console him, when his feelings were hurt.

That night was another one of those when I was really happy to have Bet sleeping close by me, and even happier that Mama insisted on having a lamp lit. Thank God it didn't rain; I don't think I could have tolerated the sound of ghostly footsteps as well.

It was the second week of August when Captain Worthy showed up again. Daddy had sent him word that he had told Mama what we were up to and he could come on to the house. He brought Mama soft shelled crabs fresh off the boat as a kind of peace offering, I think. It did seem to help soften the hard look Mama had on her face when she saw him drive up. He had left Mr. Nathaniel in the back of the car so Mama wouldn't see him right away. I think Captain Worthy thought Mama might have objected had she seen that man who so closely resembled a warlock.

He didn't know if Daddy had told her about him. Of course Daddy had not.

"Come on in, Captain Worthy," Mama said. He was standing at the door with his hat in one hand and the soft shelled crabs in the other, looking rather sheepish. Had he known how much Mama liked crab meat, he would probably have been more forward.

Mama had just finished fixing breakfast and we were *kinda* waiting for him. He politely said he had already eaten and had someone waiting in the car, so we had better go as quickly as possible. Daddy and I grabbed a biscuit, quickly finished off our coffee, and headed out to the car to start a day of discovery.

In the car was a shovel, three pickaxes and a bucket. The Captain had brought a tarpaulin to cover everything up with until we were sure we were not being observed by people on the river that day.

As soon as we were out of Mama's sight, Captain Worthy and Daddy got to talking excitedly about the adventure ahead. Mr. Nathaniel and I were quietly eying each other in the back seat. We were not feeling good about being back there together. I don't believe we would have found anything to like about each other had we been forced to sit together for the next ten years.

When we arrived at the landing we spent a few minutes wrapping the tools up. Then we stowed the tarpaulin wrapped tools in the bottom of the skiff, and started up Tar River.

I felt something akin to fear as soon as we started out that day. The fog lay in drifts along the banks and we could barely see the few people on the water before being right on top of them.

I turned around on my seat so I would be facing Mr. Nathaniel. I felt better looking at him than I did with his cold stare boring a hole in my back. I noticed him being kinda uneasy at my gaze. He reached inside his overall pocket, pulled out a huge silver cross on a long chain, and hung it around his neck. We never spoke to each other. I noticed, however, the cross seemed to bring him some degree of security, because the look on his face softened. I had seen Mama's face do that when she was satisfied that things were going her way. I wondered what he might think was going his way today.

Nobody spoke as we traveled to the place in the river where we planned to get off the skiff and take to the swamp. I think everybody, even little ole me, was wondering what we were going to find. I couldn't help thinking about how strangely quiet it was becoming as we neared our destination. It was just as it had been on our last trip out there.

Our little skiff plowed through the water, surging forward a bit with each pull Daddy exerted on the paddles. I watched the quiet wake we were leaving behind us create its predictable pattern of tiny ripples, and observed them as they slowly fanned out and disappeared. My senses were alive and my attention was at a fever pitch. As we neared the place we had marked to get off, I noticed that indeed, just as before, every sound suddenly and mysteriously stopped, before we ever got off the skiff.

Mr. Nathaniel took up the lead position again. This time he was carefully watching the path he had marked to the spot he thought might be where the treasure was buried. Captain Worthy followed with Daddy and me close behind. Daddy had decided I could walk the distance this time on my own. I kept a firm grip on his hand. The sparse, damp swamp grass was up to my waist. I kept scanning the ground ahead of me to avoid stepping on snakes, or other varmints.

We found the tree with the cross on it, and Daddy told me to stay a few feet back while he and the captain started to dig, right where Mr. Nathaniel indicated would be a good place to look.

Every nerve in my body was on edge as I stood watching. My brain seemed to be silently admonishing me for being there.

Suddenly, Captain Worthy struck something with the shovel. "I think I found something boys," he said, "I hit something solid, it felt like wood."

Daddy went over to Captain Worthy and stood looking down into the hole that he had opened up and stated, "I don't see a thing."

Mr. Nathaniel moved forward from where he had been leaning against an ancient oak tree at a safe distance. "Let me see," he said. He leaned forward and peered into the hole. "I think you have dug into some poor souls grave," he stated in a loud whisper, "It may or may not house what we're looking fer. I think we had better dig somewheres else."

Captain Worthy wasn't happy with that observation, and said so. "I think we ought to open this up and see what we found for sure. It might be the old rascal buried his gold right where nobody would have the nerve to go digging, like in a grave."

"Well, you can count me out when it comes to disturbing the dead," Daddy said, leaving his pickaxe and coming over to stand by me.

Mr. Nathaniel indicated the same by backing up against the oak tree and crossing his arms securely over his chest. I don't think he was too into *this* treasure hunting trip anyway.

Captain Worthy dropped the shovel and grabbed the pickaxe. He swung it high above his head and brought it down hard. It struck something and the sound vibrated against the trees around us with the rumble of thunder. He bent over the site and began to pull up with all his strength.

He grunted as he struggled to lift the ax, and as it came up a horrifying sight met our eyes. Along with a huge chunk of wood came a human skull with a copperhead entwined throughout the sickly white orb!

I felt a silent scream rising at the back of my throat; silent because for all practical purposes, I was paralyzed. I couldn't have uttered a sound if my life had depended on it.

I've never seen anyone drop anything so fast. I stood there petrified and watched the skull and the pickaxe slide back into the grave with the snake writhing and squirming around it. Captain Worthy backed up until he was well out of sight of that opening in the ground, turned and walked over to the nearest tree, leaned on it and threw up any breakfast he might have had. His face was as white as the fog that continued to infiltrate that ghostly scene around us.

There were no words that needed saying. Daddy picked me up and Mr. Nathaniel and Captain Worthy followed us. We walked in silence, down that marked trail without looking back a single time. That should put an end to the treasure hunting, at least for a while around our house, or so I was thinking.

When we got home Mama just looked at us and never said a word. I guess she knew something happened that neither of us would ever talk about, so she didn't add to the misery; she wisely said nothing.

Daddy and I just wanted coffee for supper. Mama smiled at that and stayed quiet about the whole thing.

## Chapter 6

It was a good day. Mama had let Daddy and me off the hook with regards to the treasure hunt. As she had not questioned us thus far, we felt we were in the clear, at least for now. It was Friday, the last week of August, 1943; a hot summer day toward the end of harvesting season.

Three tenant farm families, plus Mr. Johnny and Miss Lillian, had gathered at our tobacco barn early that morning to help us bring the crop in. That was the custom of the times. Local farmers would take turns helping to bring in the neighbor's crop. They all took their turn at helping and being helped in that way, so that everything could be done in a timely, inexpensive manner. That was our day.

The time frame from the field to the auction warehouse was crucial to the amount of money you made for your crop. It was dependant on many factors. Timing had to be just right to get top dollar. You needed to have your tobacco on the auction floor as early as possible, before the major buyers had filled their quota. That fact didn't mean so much to us because we were more like migrant farmers, paid by the day, or the hour. But to the land owner, it was of dire importance.

A great deal of attention was paid to the weather. That too could make or break you. Weather reports were not all that easy to get, and disastrous storms could come up very quickly to destroy your money crop, which at the time was tobacco.

There was a part of the equation that dealt with how fast the tobacco matured in the field, which also depended to a great extent on the weather. Then there was the ever present problem of how to get the crops in ahead of the threat of hurricanes, which usually occurred at some point between July and September.

During those years tobacco was graded up to eight or ten grades. Sand-lugs were primed first and demanded the least money. They were the leaves at the bottom of the stalk, and were considered the bottom of the barrel as far as quality was concerned. It was used for snuff and chewing tobacco. The leaves were primed (removed from the stalk) by men walking between the rows and taking them off by hand from the ground up, as they matured. It usually took from five to six weeks to prime all the tobacco from the lugs to the tips.

The highest grade, or best quality, was about three fourths of the way up the stalk, including the top of the stalk which was called *tips*. Major buyers paid the highest price and went for the best grades. There was indeed a need to have your tobacco on the floor when those buyers were there to bid on it.

After priming, the tobacco was loaded onto flat bed trucks which were about two feet wide and five feet long, lined around all four sides with three foot tall burlap fabric. The trucks were pulled, by mules in our case, to the barn where the farm hands waited. They would tie it onto tobacco sticks which would be used to hang it in the barn by the men folk at the end of the day, or when you had enough pulled to fill a barn.

The handers, as they were called, consisted that day of Mama, Miss Lillian and two neighbor ladies. There were also two ladies called *loopers*, one on each side of the truck, handling the wooden *tie horses*. The handers bunched the leaves together, consisting of about three or four at a time. The leaves were then handed to the loopers. They tied the tobacco onto the sticks with thick twine. The twine would be quickly wrapped once around the stalks at the top of the leaves.   Then the leaves would be slid along the string to fit snuggly against the tobacco stick that was supported by the tie horses.  The next bunch of leaves would be done the same way except it would be flipped over to the other side of the stick.  The ladies could get very fast at doing this and seemed to enjoy it, or so *I* thought.

It seemed like everybody wanted to be a looper, including me.  It was the in fashion thing to do at the barn. Daddy had built a little tie horse adjusted to my height, so I could practice when I wanted to.  The ladies went along by handing me a few handfuls once in a while, when I was a'mind to try my hand.  I lost a lot of interest as soon as I figured out the twine would cut my fingers after a short while.  I also figured out, in record time, that Daddy got awfully angry if it wasn't tied just right at the end, and fell off the stick before it reached the men straddling the tiers at the top of the barn.

Some of the ladies were wearing aprons that covered as much of their clothes as possible to keep the sticky gum off.  Mama wasn't.  She said the darn things were too hot.  It left me wondering, though, why Mama, who was so meticulous about cleanliness, *really* never wore an apron.  The sticky gum could ruin your clothes and no one in that group had any to spare.  Getting it off your hands was another problem altogether.  Mama would spend lots of time at the pump in the evening, trying to get rid of the black, sticky stuff, before making supper.  She was never completely successful.

Barbara and I were watching Bet for Mama while we made mud pies in the dirt we had softened with a little water, snitched from the common water bucket.

"Liz, don't eat that mud, it'll make you sick!" Mama yelled in my general direction, as I was about to taste the mud pie I had just finished constructing.  I declare, I believe that woman had eyes in the back of her head! "If

I see you do that again, I'll make you take a tablespoon of castor oil tonight," she stated. That threat was enough for me.

Just before noon, Mr. Johnny and Daddy prepared to go to town to get the Pepsi's and the ice. It was expected that the tenant who was being helped out by his friends would supply this treat. Of course, Barbara and I went with them. Our first stop was the *Crystal Ice House* on the water front where we retrieved a large block of ice and left the proper change in the box. Mr. Johnny took the ice pick from the wall where it hung for that purpose, and chipped the block into small chunks which he placed in the galvanized tub.

Then we went to the grocery store and bought ten Pepsi's in those nice glass bottles, along with a few boxes of Nabisco Nabs. Daddy placed the drinks in the tub of ice for the trip back.

Mr. Williams had provided money for the treats earlier, as it was his crop. He knew how important it was to keep the workers happy and this treat was expected. Like all the other workers who had come to help, Daddy was working by the day. He didn't have the money, and really had no stock in the profits from the sale of the tobacco.

For lunch we had collard biscuits and molasses cake Mama had brought for us and anybody else who wanted it. Miss Lillian brought boiled eggs. She had several laying chickens, Rhode Island Reds, I believe. Lunch was *such* a treat like that, at the barn. The odor of honeysuckle mixed with a tantalizing odor of tobacco was a great appetite stimulant.

About thirty minutes later, the grownups went back to work. Barbara and I went back to watching Bet, playing in the dirt, and eating cherries from the tree behind the barn. We were told not to eat too many as they might make us sick, but of course we didn't listen. Barbara, who was a little older than I and wiser in worldly things, came up with a novel idea. We would say *cross my heart and hope to die* if we told any one that we ate all the cherries we wanted from that tree that afternoon, which of course we did.

By mid afternoon, we were rudely reminded of that solemn pledge by the severe diarrhea and cramps. Mama said we deserved it for not listening to our elders.

Jim and Jake kept pulling the trucks in, creaking slowly along, filled to the brim with the huge green leaves. The pile of tobacco was growing. Finally Daddy declared we had enough to fill the barn, so the men came in from the field to hang it up for curing.

Daddy was the first man in the barn and went up to the top like a monkey. He always liked to go up to the highest tier because of the danger; he said he liked to *test fate*. Or, perhaps it was because there was less tobacco to hang and the dirt didn't fall back into your eyes as much. I had my suspicions. The *tiers* were made up of small logs that spanned the barn from side to side allowing the hanging of the sticks, laden down with tobacco. This activity was not without danger. If your foot slipped off the wet logs that made up the tiers, which reached as high as fifteen feet, the fall could break your neck. That assumption is especially accurate, if you happened to hit the brick flue that served as a heating unit on your way down.

I was looking forward to that night. Daddy and I would stay up all night at the barn, keeping the heat at just the right temperature for the curing process. Mama said I could stay with him if he promised to watch over me. That included the understanding that he would make me take catnaps occasionally on one of the tobacco trucks. She would send an old quilt with us to cover the bed of the truck. I was always so excited about being able to stay up all night the first night; I was rarely able to sleep. And Daddy never kept me from doing anything I wanted, unless he felt it would be really dangerous. That wasn't often a thing we saw in advance, though! Daddy and I would watch the temperature gauge together, and he would tell ghost stories that would scare me half to death, but I loved to hear them anyway.

The mosquitoes were bearable if you stayed close enough to the fire Daddy would build with scattered debris consisting of twigs and leaves he had piled up. The smoke kept them at bay. I would come back to the house with a few itchy bumps. Daddy seemed immune to them, at least he never complained. If anyone talked about how bad they were, he would usually comment on how much worse they were at Cape Hatteras.

Around four-thirty that evening, before all the tobacco had been hung in the barn, storm clouds began to gather on the southwest horizon. We watched anxiously as it advanced to cover half the sky. Blinding streaks of lightening slithered from black clouds to touch the earth around us with a sharp hissing sound, too close for comfort at times.

When the rain started, Daddy brought Jim and Jake under the shed, tied them to a post and covered their eyes. It was better for them if they couldn't see what was going on. They seemed more frightened of the lightening than the thunder; at least that was what Daddy said. He must have been right, because they stayed put after he covered their eyes.

All the workers went inside the barn and shut the door against the storm, except us. Mama knew a man who had been killed when he was leaning against the flue in a barn when lightening struck it. Therefore, she would never let us stay in a barn during a storm, even if it meant we got soaked to the teeth standing outside.

The four of us sat on the ground, huddled together against the side of the barn, while the storm raged around us. The clouds were dropping so much water that it was difficult to see more than a few feet when a scrawny black kitten came running around the corner, and made a bee-line for me. I gathered it up and wrapped my skirt around it.

"Don't even think about keeping that cat," Mama said. "We ain't got enough food for ourselves. We don't need another mouth to feed."

I looked at Daddy and pulled the little thing up under my chin. It was shivering. I could feel its frail rib cage rise and fall with every breath. It felt as if I held it tightly it would break. After about a minute it started to purr contentedly. I wiped it as dry as I could and kept a firm grip on it, hoping Daddy would make Mama let me keep it.

Daddy finally spoke up and said, "Now don't be too hasty, Elizabeth, the little thing has probably been thrown away. It don't look like it has had nothin' to eat in a week. It'll starve if somebody don't take pity sake on it."

"Well, it ain't gonna be us!" Mama stated firmly.

I held onto him and waited for more discussion. His skinny little body lay quietly on my shoulder, curled up like he was with his Mama. His breath tickled my neck as he breathed softly in his sleep. With his hair mostly dried out, he didn't feel quite so skinny.

By the time the storm blew over and the men had finished hanging the tobacco in the barn, I knew Mama would say no more. Under all that sternness was a heart just as soft as Daddy's. She would let me keep the cat, and do her best to keep it fed.

It wasn't until we started home that we realized the heavy down pour had done its work well. The stream close to our place had swollen over its banks and spilled out over a low place in the roadway. I ran ahead under protest from

Mama, holding my kitten high over my head and plunged right into waist deep water. It felt cool and refreshing. I loved water and would have enjoyed a plunge into the nearest ditch if I hadn't had that horrible aversion to snakes. A group of ducks entered the water from the other side and proceeded to swim past us. I could have touched them, and would have if my hands had not been occupied with the kitten, which at the moment seemed absently resigned to its fate.

Right after we arrived home, Mama found a box for the cat and put him in it, with some clean rags for him to cuddle up in. "Don't touch it until I get supper ready and I'll get it some food," she said. Then, after looking it over with a keen eye, she stated, "It might have some disease, its mighty quiet."

I named him Blackie.

She got us cleaned up and made supper. "Liz, I expect you to keep that cat clean and fed or I promise you, out it goes!" That was her parting shot at my behavior. I knew I had won, that is, Daddy and me.

After supper I fed the kitten some bread crumbs softened with bean soup which he ate as if he was starving. Mama seemed to be satisfied that he would be able to survive after all, and was happy to see he wasn't finicky about food, and had a laid-back personality. "He probably won't be a problem to us," I heard her say to Daddy.

Mama cleaned the kitchen while Daddy and I prepared to go to the barn. We collected a big jar of strong, black coffee, some left over fried fish, and a couple of baked sweet potatoes. Mama gave us an old quilt and some mosquito netting to use for me if the mosquitoes got *too bad*. Then after a few concerned looks from Mama, who never wanted me to go on these outings, we set out for the barn.

The first thing Daddy did when we got there was to make a tent of the mosquito netting for me to hide under if need be. Then he sat down beside me on a bale of hay and filled his pipe with Prince Albert tobacco. He never was one to be in a hurry to get to a task like Mama was. I liked that about him. He didn't get upset or flustered much; he just did things in his own sweet time.

"Son," he said, "I want you to always remember these nights. There'll be troubles in your life, but if you can remember the good times they'll see you through. Look at that sky. There'll be times when you'll be so busy livin' you'll forgit how purty it is. And there'll be times when you'll be so wrapped up in life that you'll forgit that this earth is not the only thing in the universe. I believe there are lots of worlds out there, not just ours. If you were standin' on one of them stars right now, you wouldn't even be able to see us sittin' here. Think about that when the world gits too hard for you. It's a giant old universe God made. Don't git so big-headed that you think we're the only ones in it, we probably ain't."

We sat there for a long time with Daddy puffing smoke rings into the darkness, studying the blanket of stars that twinkled and shivered in the moonless night sky. It was as if a million little lights were winking at us from above, lights on a background of black velvet that filled in the spaces between and behind them.

Daddy told me again about The Evening Star, The Big Dipper, Orion, The Three Sisters, and other constellations. He said they would help me find my way home if I ever got lost at sea. I couldn't imagine being lost at sea, but I listened carefully, just in case.

Finally he got down to business and filled the external firebox that heated the flue inside the barn with hardwood, which was able to hold a more even temperature. The external firebox allowed the tobacco to be cured by indirect heat without exposing it to smoke. This created a smoother tobacco product. The entire process usually took about a week. An experienced tobacco farmer like Daddy could tell when the leaves were at the right stage by the smell and feel of it.

Once the fire had started, we watched the temperature gauge rise to the proper setting. Then he asked me if I wanted to hear a ghost story. Of course I did.

"There's a story about a slave and his master who lived in the foothills of western North Carolina a long time ago," he began. "Do you want me to tell you that one? I learned it when I was in that C.C.C. camp, up near Linville Falls. It tells about a light that people sees from time to time up there in the hills. I saw that light and I know ain't nobody knows what it is. It is referred to as: *The Brown Mountain Light*. A lot of very smart people from around the world have tried to figure out what it is, but to my knowledge, nobody knows to this day. So I guess the story I heard is as good as anybody's. It's real scary and some say it's the truth. You ain't gonna git so scared you want to go home to your Mama, *are you*?"

I replied *no.*

"A slave owner who once lived in the foothills of North Carolina had an old black slave that he loved very much. The slave loved him as well, and did all he could to see to it that his master's life was as comfortable as the old slave could make it for him. One day the master decided to go out huntin' a bear that had been seen threatenin' his livestock. He couldn't have that could he, so, even though he loved animals he had to git rid of that bear. The slave was terrified of bears, so the master told him he could stay at home that day and take care of things around the house. He would bring the bear home that evening. They would dress him out and the slave could have whatever meat was edible."

"So the plan was set and the master left with his shotgun slung over his right shoulder, and a big bowie knife hangin' from his belt. The old slave watched him out of sight and felt guilty about not goin' with him. Then he got busy and forgot about it until around sundown. The master had not returned and the slave became aware that he had not heard a gun being shot all day. No matter how far from the house the master was, the sound of his gun should have been heard echoing through the hills. When it was gittin' long about dark, he begun to really be afraid somethin' bad had happened. He went to the back door and asked the woman of the house if she knew when to expect her husband back. She said she didn't, and had thought the slave had gone with him. The slave got a lantern, lit it and went to find his master. He was destined to never return, either."

"They never found the master or his beloved slave. Some say the slave still looks for him nightly. A light that could be a lantern can be seen swingin' as if from somebody's hand, as it seems to search the mountain. Can't nobody explain it. I believe it's that slave, and even after all these years, for they've both been dead a long time now, he still walks that mountain in search of his master, and always will."

I moved in closer to the lantern and took a quick look around the circle of light. "When will the moon come up, Daddy?" I asked.

"Soon Son, soon," Daddy replied. He looked at me from the corner of his eye and smiled. He liked to scare me, I think. And I liked to be scared.

I stayed close to the lantern, which was swinging from the roof of the shed, until the moon rose over the field. It cast long shadows and bathed everything around us in its cold, silvery light. By then I was ready for another ghost story.

"Do you want to hear the one about the state hospital patient?" Daddy asked. Then he began to tell me the story I had heard before, but could have listened to a hundred more times and would never tire of it.

"These two young people were travelin' down a dirt road one night, near the state hospital for the insane. It was a night kinda like this, full moon shinin' overhead and all. They were takin' a shortcut to the nearest town, because they were almost out of gas. Then all of a sudden the car stopped. They were indeed out of gas."

"The young man told his girl friend he would go on ahead to a gas station, buy some gas, and come back for her. *Lock the door*, he said as he walked away, casting a worried look over his shoulder as he departed. After about an hour the girl got sleepy, and since the moon was up and it wasn't so dark out, she decided to take a nap for a few minutes. She curled up in the seat and went to sleep. It was well into the night when she awoke and realized she was still alone. Frightened she sat up suddenly and stared straight into the face of her boyfriend. A full harvest moon lit his face up like it was noon time. His head, minus his body, was sittin' on the hood of the car, starin' at her with huge eyes that had seen some powerful evil."

"The next day a passin' driver found her there, as crazy as a loon, the bulgin' eyes of her dead boyfriend still starin' at her. She babbled out what had happened and afterward never spoke another word. She spent the rest of her life in the very institution where the murderer that had beheaded her boyfriend lived. He had been recaptured that very next day, a little late for the two best friends."

Things got quiet for a while as I thought about that one, seriously.

All that night we watched over the curing process and Daddy told me several ghost stories. Needless to say I never slept. Daddy never dozed off that night either. He had promised Mama he would try and get a little sleep at the barn so he could work the next day, but she knew he couldn't. It was a hard job and would make almost any saint crabby, but not my Daddy. I never saw him crabby or hateful in any way. He was almost always cheerful and happy. He would say, when someone complained about the hard labor, that it beat the alternative, which meant having no work to do. It was the Roosevelt years and work was scarce, almost as scarce as welfare and hen's teeth.

At the break of dawn the next morning, the man who would take over that day and keep the heat up to par arrived. This would go on for about a week, or until the tobacco took on a certain golden color and texture that indicated it was at the right stage for the auction warehouse.

After I ate breakfast, Mama made me go to bed for a few hours. It was Saturday and there was no work to be done in the fields, plus Bet was not feeling well again.

Daddy went to help Mr. Williams with chores at the big house, trying to make enough money to buy supplies that next Saturday.

Time seemed to fly by until it was the day to bring the tobacco home from the curing barn and get it ready for the warehouse in Greenville. This would require a lot of preparation.

Daddy and the other men folk brought the tobacco to the barn where it would be tied in bundles again; then placed on grading sticks, allowing easy storage until time to take it to the warehouse. The stack of ready for market tobacco would stand about six feet high when we were through tying in the wee hours of the morning. Daddy had been told to spray each layer with a mixture of water and honey, so it would weigh more at the auction. I do believe that was against the law, but Daddy did as he was told. I thought it would make the tobacco taste better. Daddy used a hand held sprayer that we used to spray flies with. I think I remember him washing it out first.

That last night before taking the tobacco to the market was one of the best times of the whole year, usually. Everybody got together just as they did to bring it in from the field, using the same method as then. They took turns at each barn and worked well into the night until the grading and tying up was done. Then they would bring out the guitars, mandolins, violins, tambourines, spoons, washboards and anything else they could make a happy sound with, and commence to sing and dance the rest of the night away. The men folk would drink at least a gallon of moonshine on those nights.

Daddy usually brought the liquor for the occasions and would leave it out of Mama's sight. There was an unspoken rule between us from the start about Daddy's involvement in the liquor trade. Mama and I were never to get involved in the storing or sale of the *white lightening*, and Mama could pretend she didn't know anything about it. I knew to play along.

Of course the moonshine was not to be seen by any of the women folk. I remember following Daddy out to the truck parked behind the barn and watching him get a big swig of that stuff from the gallon jar that particular night. I made note of the fact that he felt much happier afterward. So I decided I would give it a try when nobody was around. I waited in the shadows until the coast was clear, then carefully crept up to the truck, opened the jar and smelled the sparkling clear liquid. It had the odor of oak wood burning in the stove on a cold winter evening. Well, anything that smelled that good had to taste good, I thought. I lifted that jar to my mouth and took a big drink from it, just like I had seen Daddy do. To say the least, it almost took my breath away. It burned all the way down! I couldn't get the top back on that jar fast enough!

In about two minutes, even before I could get myself back to the barn, I began to feel kinda funny. I felt like I was swimming, but there was no water! Just about that time Mama *would* miss me.

"Liz, where are you?" came that all too familiar voice.

Now, I knew where *I* was all right, but finding the door to the barn where Mama was, that was another story altogether. And when I did find it, that latch kept moving every time I tried to grab it.

I don't remember much more about that night. The next day, however, remains burned forever into my brain. The taste of the castor oil that I had not had time to turn into Karo syrup yet, was worse than I had remembered! The little house out back with the half moon over the door and I became great friends before it was over. That was the beginning and the end of my drinking career. From that day forward, I could hardly stand the thought of the stuff.

The following Monday, Daddy and I went with Mr. Williams to the auction warehouse in Greenville. It seemed unusually hot that day, partly because of the enormous crowd that was there to sell their tobacco. The air was thick with oxygen depriving tobacco smoke. It seemed there was a cigarette hanging from the lip's of every man in the place. It's a wonder they didn't burn the warehouse down before they got the tobacco sold.

The auctioneers were already busy with their chant when we arrived. We unloaded the truck and brought the tobacco to the auction floor. Daddy and I stayed with Mr. Williams and listened. I wasn't able to understand a word they said, but I knew it didn't sell that day because I saw Mr. Williams turn the tags on it. The bid was apparently not high enough to suit him. That meant another trip to Greenville which suited me just fine. I loved to watch the selling process. To me it was just a lot of fun.

I was one of a small group of children who were allowed to attend the auction, and as such was the object of much attention. Everybody seemed to think I wanted a drink or a candy bar, or something. I took everything they gave me until Daddy put a stop to the handouts, which he did as soon as he became aware of it.

"Don't give her anythin' else," he told the gentleman who was handing me my third Pepsi. "Her Mama will git mad at me if she gits sick, and she will, she's not used to such things." I didn't get any more treats that day as Daddy kept a close eye on me and prevented it.

On the way home, Mr. Williams stopped by Bill's hot dog establishment and we ate at his expense, standing at the back of the big truck that had hauled the tobacco in to the warehouse that morning. He told Daddy he had done a good job and asked him to stay on that winter and take care of the crop next year.

"I don't like to stay too long anywheres," Daddy stated, "I think you wear out your welcome if you do that, but I'll think about it."

We took Mama a couple of hot dogs and found her rocking Bet, waiting for us. She wasn't happy about the crop not selling, saying it was taking too much time. "There's more to sell," she said. "And I know you'll be up all night tonight to keep that barn hot. You can't keep this up, you'll make yourself sick."

Daddy promised he would try to sleep a few minutes at the barn, which we all knew he wouldn't be able to do.

It was a pleasant night, cool enough to tolerate the heat of the furnace. Daddy didn't have any trouble getting me to take a nap. I was exhausted. The sound of a familiar voice woke me up somewhere around two in the morning. It was Mr. Johnny.

I wasn't too surprised that Daddy was telling him about the walking we had heard on the porch. I didn't know how he had kept his mouth shut about it this long, especially since Mama had asked him to tell Mr. Johnny several times. Mr. Johnny seemed very interested.

I listened as Mr. Johnny said, "I wonder if that has something to do with my wife, I mean, if there is any such thing as ghosts. I've heard people say that if a soul is restless, it will stay around the last place it lived on earth, until it is satisfied that everything is alright. Then it goes on to be with the Lord. I know she was a good woman, and she's going to Heaven, in the end." It sounded to me like he was trying to convince himself. "Mama said she was no good, that she was wild and would make me really miserable. She told me that she had heard Katie ran around with anyone she could find that would show her a good time."

"I'm sure it ain't her, Johnny," Daddy said. "There ain't no such thing as ghosts. I think somebody is tryin' to get us to move out of the place. Do you have any idea who would want us out of there and why?"

"No one I know of, Andy," Mr. Johnny said. "I don't know anybody who wants to live there except you and your family. My wife Katie and I moved in there because she didn't want to move in with my parents, and I didn't have enough money to get us a nice place. She said my Mama would drive her crazy if she had to live with her, and that if I went away to the war, I could get enough money for a good place."

"Ain't no man understands a woman's way of thinkin'," Daddy said. "I don't understand my wife most of the time, I just let her have her way, she will anyway in the end."

It started to rain on the tin roof over the shelter, somewhat drowning out the voices. I drifted off to sleep again. When I awoke Mr. Johnny had gone. I never told Daddy I had heard them talking. It felt like a private conversation between the two of them.

Around four o'clock, Mr. Johnny showed up again, this time with his Martin acoustic guitar. For the next two hours, until the man came to relieve Daddy, we sang all the songs he could play and we could remember. I know he didn't sound as good as the singers on *The Grand Old Opry*, but it was good enough for me.

We walked home through a soft warm rain and lay down to sleep for about an hour. When we got up, Mama told Daddy she had heard walking on the porch while we were at the barn. She said she had been too scared to go to bed, so she had also been up all night.

Daddy just shrugged his shoulders and changed the subject, stating, "Mr. Williams offered me the crop next year, Elizabeth."

"I don't care if he did, Andy, I want to leave here as soon as we can," Mama said. "I don't like him or this place."

"There's no makin' you happy, is there?" Daddy asked. "You said last week you might want to stay put until Bet was bigger, now you want to move as soon as possible. Well, I don't know if we should. There's a lot of unfinished business here, and it's apparent to me that whatever that noise we hear is, it's not gonna to hurt us or it would have by now."

"If what you mean by unfinished business is that you're going treasure hunting again, or want to keep up business with that gang of bootleggers, I'll be darned if I don't find myself another place to live without you, Andy," Mama asserted.

I could see Daddy was in a pickle. I was anxious to see how he would get out of this one.

"I don't mean anythin' of the kind, Elizabeth," Daddy said. "I mean to plant and tend next year's crop as that is a job I can do, and feel I have to work where and when I can. You know how hard it is to find work now, and we're used to this place. If we move, the next place will have its own problems."

"Do you mean that you'd rather have the known problems here than to face new one's elsewhere?" Mama asked. "That's a new idea from you. You said you like to move. Is there any reason you want to stay here another year you're not telling me?"

"Well for one thing, Elizabeth, Mr. Williams ain't *too* bad as a boss-man, and we all like Johnny. I think he likes us too. For some reason I believe he needs us."

I noted that Daddy didn't tell Mama about the conversation last night at the barn. Well, I wouldn't either then.

We were listening to music on the *Grand Old Opry* when I fell asleep.

## Chapter 7

Summer was almost gone. It was finally time for the county agricultural fair, a favorite time of year for all the farm laborers. That is, entertainment for the masses that the masses could *almost* afford.

Mr. Johnny came to get us that Saturday evening. I listened while he and Daddy hatched a novel idea: If Mr. Johnny could manage to get in free; he would be financially able to afford more of the rides for us. He would also be able to buy more of the goodies from the concession stands that always inhabited the first section of the mid-way. That idea had been brought up by Mr. Johnny while Mama was busy getting Bet ready. He said he wanted to be certain that I was able to ride everything, and that seemed to be the only way, as none of us had much money to spend. He said he had been thinking about that for a day or so. I noted they never told Mama about the plan. I thought it a swell idea.

On our way to town, Mr. Johnny made the statement that he was going to make certain I rode every ride on the mid-way with him, and got everything I wanted to eat. Mama told him we didn't have enough money for all that. I would have to pick the two rides I wanted to ride the most, so our money would cover it. But his mind was made up. Mr. Johnny had already cased the grounds the day before. He had seen where he could get in under the fence without being observed. That way, he would have enough money to cover everything. It was obvious that he chose to ignore what Mama said.

We arrived at the fairgrounds just about twilight. Well before we got there, I could see the Ferris wheel and

hear loud music. The booming voices of barkers rang out
way beyond the fairgrounds as they brought attention to
their rides and concession stands. Excitement peaked with
the appearance of bright lights reflecting on low-lying
clouds above the mid-way.

All in all, it was going to be an exciting night. I
could tell. For obvious reasons, Mr. Johnny parked as far
away from the entrance gate as he could. While we walked
toward the gate to get our tickets, Mr. Johnny slinked his
way around to the back of the lot. He was to crawl under
the fence, between the buildings where the police had taken
up residence and the trailer that directed the business
affairs, then onto the mid-way. We would join him there.

"Where did Johnny get off to?" Mama asked as we
were pushed along by the people headed toward the ticket
booth.

"I think he has another plan, Elizabeth," Daddy
stated calmly.

Mama glared at him. She was beginning to
understand how Mr. Johnny was going to get the money for
us to ride everything.

We purchased our tickets, entered through the gate
and went directly to where Mr. Johnny would be coming
out, Daddy and I hoped. None of us had noticed the small
cloud just over our heads that had suddenly decided to rain
on the plan.

Mama said, "It's beginning to rain," as if the rest of
us hadn't noticed. "I know God is not happy with this. I
told you, Andy, when you do something dishonest, nothing
good ever comes of it!"

Daddy pretended not to hear her.

About that time, Mr. Johnny apparently stepped on
a live wire, which at the moment was wet. Sparks went
flying at about the height of Mr. Johnny's head, in the
darkness between the buildings. Lights all along the mid-

way blinked, and time stood still for me, I was *so* afraid
Mr. Johnny had hurt himself. That was apparently not the
case, because just then he yelled out loud enough to wake
the dead in the cemetery down the street.

Two policemen that a moment before had been
drinking coffee, watching people go by, tossed their coffee
on the ground and ran toward the space between the
buildings where the yelling was coming from. Nothing
could be seen.

We backed off to stand with the crowd and see what
would happen. Mama had that *I told you so* look on her
face.

It couldn't have been more than a couple of minutes
before Mr. Johnny came up behind us and tapped Daddy on
the shoulder. He had slipped beneath the building the
officers had been standing in front of and escaped by
crawling out from under the backside. He was standing
behind us, attempting to look like the rest of the crowd.
The whelps beginning to rise on his face and neck were
about to give him away, though.

The police kept looking for a few minutes, then
gave up on it and went to report the frayed wires they had
discovered.

"What in the world did you get into?" Mama asked
as we quietly slinked away.

"I think there was a yellow jacket's nest under that
building," Mr. Johnny stated. He was quickly taking on the
look of a man that had been in a fight with something. And
the something had won.

Mama handed Bet to Daddy, pulled Mr. Johnny to
the side of the mid-way and took her snuff box from her
pocket. She put some of the brown powder in her palm and
spit on it to make a little paste. Then she told Mr. Johnny
to bend over so she could reach his wounds, rubbed the
paste into them and said, "Now try to stay out of trouble;

that is if you can. I know it's ugly, but the snuff will take the sting out."

After we were sure Mr. Johnny's illegal activity hadn't been found out, we started our tour of the fair grounds. At that point, Mr. Johnny was on the receiving end of more than a few curious stares. Some people veered over to the side to avoid him. His face did kinda look like he had a contagious disease. We pretended we didn't notice, and went on having fun trying to decide what to do next.

Mama had enough money to get us in, and for us to ride the merry-go-round and Ferris wheel. It wouldn't go much further if we were going to eat hot dogs and cotton candy, she asserted.

We started with the merry-go-round. That was the thing Bet seemed to want to do. She clung to Mama and squealed as the thing turned round and round with its unique carousel music, prancing ponies, and multi-colored twinkling lights. Mr. Johnny, Daddy and I rode the ponies. Because of Bet, Mama chose one of the little seats that were easy to get into and out of.

We rode around several times more than we had paid for, waiting for the shower to pass over. The man didn't say anything; he just let us all ride until it stopped. Soft, warm rain sprayed over my face when the wind shifted and blew under the canopy. Children's laughter rose and fell in a symphony of pure happiness, creating a world apart for a time, just as the pony I was riding did, as he gentle rose and stooped, in his eternal, circular dance.

After we got off the merry-go-round, we walked along the mid-way to the Ferris wheel for our next ride. Mama had to just watch us, because every time she tried to get on with Bet, she set up such a wail you would have thought she was being murdered. Mama had to be satisfied with watching us after that.

From the lofty top of the Ferris wheel, the whole town of Washington spread out like a sparkling carpet at our feet. We paused at that dizzying height for a minute or so while people got on at the bottom. I was glad to be sitting between Mr. Johnny and Daddy. I closed my eyes and sat back as far as I could and tried not to let on that I was frightened. I wasn't usually afraid of anything. It was embarrassing. The seat was swaying way too much to suit me. They seemed to be enjoying it, but to me it felt like it might turn over and spill us out.

I was happy when we started to move again and opened my eyes. I wanted to see all the beauty around me before getting off. Lights of the town mingled with stars that had just begun to emerge from behind the soft white clouds, in an artist's inspiring panorama fit for that man Captain Worthy had told me about. He had shown me pictures in a book the man had drawn of a sky once, when he had taken me to the library. I think the Captain told me his name was *Van Gogh*. Funny name!

After that Mr. Johnny and I rode on a few more rides and ate all the cotton candy we wanted, with Mama looking at us as if we were criminals. I kept waiting for her to say something, and felt guilty. Perhaps that's what she wanted.

Along about eight o'clock, another attraction set up. It was what Mama loosely referred to as the hoochie-koochie show. That is to say, women, scantily clad, standing on a platform swinging their hips to seductive music, throwing kisses at the men, and in general ignoring the women. I was fascinated, so were Daddy and Mr. Johnny. Mama was not impressed. She stood there staring at Daddy for a minute or two, then she said, "I think it's time to go, Andy." That was that. We left the fair to people with fewer morals than my Mama and headed for the parking lot. The fair was over for us, that year.

I was so exhausted I fell asleep on the trip home.

Some time went by after that before I remembered Daddy and I had been invited to go on another fishing trip with Captain Worthy. Both of his boats were outfitted and ready. On long trips with his *Miss Fortune*, he would follow the Inland Waterway south and go out at the Morehead-Beaufort inlet. From there he would follow the Atlantic Coast down to Foley Rocks just south of Miami. Fishing was really good down there.

*Miss Fortune* was an ocean worthy, eighty foot shrimper with five berths and a fine galley on her. She had been built somewhere along the Pamlico River, near Belhaven, not more than two years earlier. She was powered by a Bridgeport automobile engine, which ran on gas of course, and was located under the pilot house on her bow. Two berths were located on each side of the engine, one above. She was capable of supporting up to a ton of shrimp, and enough stores to feed his crew for an extended length of time.

Captain Worthy would visit the Crystal Ice House on the waterfront in Washington, and fill the hold with ice before he left the docks. Then, if the fishing was going well, he would stay out there and sell to runner boats, saving time going back to the docks. That way he could stay out a long time. The runner boats would come out to meet the working boats at regular intervals with plenty of money on hand to buy. It was a good arrangement for all parties concerned.

He and his crew would be gone from their families for up to two months at a time. It was a hard life, but it made them enough money to live comfortably, even in the worst of economic times. People along the coast had to eat, were partial to seafood, and the river was full of it. And, luckily for the fisherman, the price was at a premium. In addition to that, the government was allowing them to take as much seafood as they wanted from the river at that time.

Captain Worthy also owned a thirty foot boat he generally used for netting shrimp along the smaller rivers of the coast. That would be his *Miss Catherine.* It was better suited to that type of fishing. It was one of those times.

Captain Worthy had been on a long haul down south and said he'd been homesick. He was going to fish the Pamlico for a while. Daddy had been asked if he wanted to come along for part of whatever they caught that next week. The crew would share the money for the catch. It was near the end of shrimping season. In a few more weeks they would be dragging for oysters. Of course Daddy wanted to go, if Mama would agree.

It was the first week of September, a few days before the fishing trip. We were busy cleaning up the front yard. Weeds stood three or four inches tall. Debris that had fallen during a storm the night before lay scattered around the house. Daddy was cutting the weeds with a swing-blade while Mama and I raked it up in a pile at the edge of the yard, along with the small limbs and twigs from around back. We would build a fire with it and bake some potatoes later that evening. That was Daddy's way of rewarding me for helping. He had brought the potatoes out in an iron kettle with the lid on top and had placed them near the center of where he would build a fire.

It was a good day for yard work, not too hot or windy. We had been working quietly for a couple of hours when the sheriff's deputy, James William Crowley, seemed to appear from out of nowhere.

He had been to see us earlier that month. Deputy Crowley had said then that he thought something bad might have happened to the woman who had lived there before us. He stated he would never rest until he found out what it

was. He had asked us questions about how long we had
been in the place, and if we had seen anything unusual, and
had *warned* us he would be back. Mama had told him
about the tinker man who had been out there trying to sell
her some enameled pots, since she didn't have any
aluminum ones that needed repair.

"Howdy," he said. "I didn't mean to sneak up on
you, just thought I would come by and see if you
remembered anything else about that tinker man. It's been
on my mind ever since I was here last. I've tried to find
somebody else who might have seen him. Nobody seems
to have outside of you, Misses." His small, close set,
beady eyes centered in on Mama as he slowly removed his
hat.

"Well, I ain't seen him since and don't expect I will,
seeing as I didn't use his services," Mama said. She kept
on raking leaves.

"Is there anything at all you remembered since I
was out here last time? Think carefully," the deputy
insisted.

Mama stopped, leaned on her rake and thought for a
second. Then she said, "There was one thing, he had a scar
across his left cheek. It looked like something had cut it to
the bone. Ugly thing as I remember. 'Course, I didn't say
nothing about it. I didn't know the man and it was none of
my business. That's all I remember." She went back to her
raking.

The deputy turned his attention on Daddy. "You
gonna stay around here this winter?" he asked.

"Yep," Daddy replied and kept on swinging the
blade.

"Hope you don't mind if I look around a bit, do
you?" he asked. "Sometimes things show up after a little
storm like we just had."

"No, help yourself," Daddy said. I noticed he kept a wary eye on the deputy though, as he went to the porch and looked at the stain; then around to the back and searched the edge of the woods.

About half an hour later, James Crowley said, "If you hear anything, let me know," and left.

He strutted down the path to where he had left his police car, chin up, chest out, like he knew he was somebody. Mama stopped raking and stared after him. Then she said aloud, "They must be plum out of money down at the station, those pants surely do belong to a man half his size."

"He is bound to find that tinker man, ain't he?" Daddy asked. "He must think for sure he had something to do with the King woman disappearing. Wonder what he was looking for at the edge of the yard?"

"Who knows what he was looking for, Andy, maybe he thinks we had something to do with it," Mama said. She pulled at the wisp of hair that had fallen and was blowing across her face, tucking it back into the bun she had created on the back of her head. Her forehead wrinkled and I noted that she was no longer smiling as she went back to her work.

Daddy built a fire around the potatoes like he promised at five o'clock, after we had cleaned the yard to Mama's satisfaction. About an hour later, he thought they might be done. He pulled the pot out of the center of the fire with the wire he had tied to the handle before building the fire around it, and opened it up. The potatoes were just right. We ate them for supper with the collards and molasses cake Mama had prepared.

After supper Mr. Johnny showed up with his guitar, and we all sang along to his music, well into the night. Around midnight, Mr. Johnny left and it started to rain. Mama told me I had better go to bed.

I fell asleep quickly, being tired out from the day's work in the yard. I almost always overdid everything because I was so high strung, Mama said. She never tried to stop me from doing whatever I wanted to do, however, saying I would slow down when I got ready.

A sound awakened me some time into the wee hours of the morning. I couldn't quite make it out. At first I thought it was Blackie wanting to get out, kinda like he was scratching on the door. I got up and went to the door to let him out, but he wasn't there. Looking around I found him asleep in the little bed Mama had made for him behind the kitchen stove. The scratching continued at the door. As I stood there trying to decide what to do, from somewhere outside there came a scream and a gurgling sound like someone being strangled. I made a run for Mama and jumped into the bed between her and Daddy and pulled the sheet over my head.

"What on God's green earth was that?" Mama asked.

Daddy never answered. He was busy pulling up his coveralls when something blew out the lamp Mama had just lit. She had relaxed enough lately to leave the window up at night, since we hadn't heard any sounds from the porch in a while, and it was up that night. There was no wind at all though, and the curtains Mama had pulled across the windows hung down perfectly straight and still in the moonlight.

Mama felt her way back to the lamp and tried to relight it. Each time she relit it, it would go out. "Close that window," she called out to Daddy who was getting the gun down from over the door. He did and the lamp stayed lit. Daddy went out the back door and around to the front of the house. I suppose he was trying to creep up on whatever it was. By that time the noise, which had changed to the sound of log chains being dragged across the porch, had stopped.

Daddy came back in the front door; he hadn't seen anything. We barricaded the windows and doors as best we could and sat up the remainder of the night. Daddy made a pot of coffee, and it helped to keep us awake. They talked about moving again, but common sense won out and before morning it was decided that we would stay at least through the winter. Daddy still believed someone was trying to scare us away. Mama still thought it was the ghost of the woman who had disappeared from there. She vowed anew to always keep the windows down, even if it got to hot to breathe.

"I'm not staying here alone while you and Liz go out fishing next week," she stated. "I'll go stay with Kathleen."

"I believe I'd take my chances with the ghost rather than stay overnight with your sister Kathleen," Daddy said, and laughed. That seemed to break the icy mantle of fear that gripped me. Daddy said I was just like my Mama, *the Indian*, when it came to seeing a ghost in every corner. He always related any peculiar trait or belief on Mama's part to her Indian heritage.

"That sound could have been a bob cat for all I know," he said. "Don't you remember when we came home that night and found one sittin' on the porch roof? When we frightened him he made a sound like that. They tend to sound like a woman screamin' when they get angry."

"Even if that were so, it leaves a body to wonder, then, where the sound of chains was coming from," Mama stated.

By the break of day they had talked themselves into believing the sounds came from a bob cat.

Captain Worthy showed up very early that next Saturday morning. He was ready to go fishing on the Pamlico. Daddy and I had been ready for an hour before he got there. Mama and Bet were ready too. She still maintained she wasn't going to stay in a haunted house while Daddy and I went on an overnight fishing trip. She did agree the money Daddy would get would be good to have, but it wasn't worth her being scared to death.

"Don't either of you tell Captain Worthy about no ghost, you hear?" she stated firmly before he came into the house. "I don't want him to think we're crazy. I feel stupid enough without somebody telling me what I already know. There is no such thing as ghosts, but I can't explain what those noises we hear are."

I enjoyed the ride to town. It was the first time I had been in the car with the Captain that Mr. Nathaniel hadn't been in the back seat with me. This time it was Mama and me back there.

As we passed over the Pamlico River, I spied *Miss Catherine* as she lay at dock. I knew and loved every inch of her. The prow of her wooden deck was rising and falling softly with the measured rolling waves created by a boat that had just passed. It was almost like she was breathing, slow and deep, with her nose pointed out toward the open water she was so much a part of. It felt to me as if she were resting between adventures, kind of lazy like. She was a trim, white wooden craft that held four fishermen comfortably. Beneath her decks were four bunks that could be slept in, not so comfortably, along with a small galley that was meant to be used to make meals in a hurry. Mostly I think it was used by Captain Worthy to make his coffee toddies. There was always an abundance of white lightening stowed away in a basket in the corner of his cabin. Daddy kept him a good supply.

The *Miss Catherine* was not a boat built for pleasure, although she was a beauty. She was very much a working boat, small enough to get up close to the shore and large enough to face the rough weather often encountered on the Pamlico Sound. She would ride cleanly up a six foot wave and slice down the back side, without jarring your teeth when it bottomed out on the other end, like some smaller boats would. She was especially steady if she were topped off with a good haul.

As we drove over the river, that familiar peaceful feeling engulfed me like a baby being rocked in its Mama's arms. That river and I belonged to each other. That's the way it had always been, or so it seemed to me that morning.

Captain Worthy took Mama and Bet to her sister's house first, then we went directly back to the docks. It was a warm, sultry beginning for our day on the river. Humidity hung in the air. It was so thick it felt like breathing in water. The short walk from the car to the boat had my clothes sticking to me.

Two of Captain Worthy's trusted crew, Luke and John-John, waited anxiously for us so we could get underway. It was obvious to me right off that those two didn't want *me* there. Luke openly stated, "It's bad luck to have a female on board a working boat, we'll not catch a thing on this trip!"

"She's not a female," Daddy said. "She's just a young'un." That was his usual remark when this subject was brought up. "She'll bring us good luck or my name ain't Andy."

Luke glared at me.

"Leave her alone," Captain Worthy ordered in his gruff old voice. "She comes along with Andy."

Right after that Luke had another problem to contend with, Mr. Nathaniel had arrived. He disliked black people as much as he did female children. The salty old fisherman backed off, but kept an eye on us as he weighed anchor. I felt his stare right down to my bone marrow. I didn't like him and I could tell he felt the same, although I didn't know why either of us felt that way.

Captain Worthy got me a barrel to sit on and placed it at the port side of the vessel, toward the stern. I soon lost interest in the grouchy old fellow and feasted my eyes on the love of my life at the moment, the river.

The gasoline that powered Captain Worthy's boat was expensive, but he somehow managed to get it in spite of it being carefully rationed by Uncle Sam. The fumes flowed across the back of the boat where I sat. I took a deep breath, filling my lungs with the odor. I really liked the smell of it.

I watched as the dock dropped away behind us and our wake grew taller and wider. I carefully searched Castle Island to see if there were any goats over there, but none could be seen. I asked Daddy about it and he said, "The alligators probably ate them a long time ago, Son."

We stopped temporarily at the railroad trestle and Captain Worthy sounded his fog horn signaling the bridge keeper to swing the railroad back so we could get through. The window of the little room the keeper resided in was open. It was close enough for a short conversation between Captain Worthy and him. It consisted of the same words each and every time we passed through. "How are you keeping, Captain Worthy?" on the part of the bridge keeper, followed by, "Same as usual," by the captain as he carefully maneuvered his boat through the narrow opening.

The river got wider as we passed through. Because of the sandbars, it was treacherous until we got past the sandy beach that was part of the Whichard farm. Then it got deep enough that the buoy markers were no longer needed if you knew the river well, and nobody knew that river like Captain Worthy.

As we passed the last marker, the water became a bit choppy. Frothy white foam, resembling fancy white lace, danced along the ridge of little wavelets which practically covered the surface of the water. A sparkling white egret stood motionlessly perched on the marker, posing on one foot with head held high, as if he knew how beautiful he was. A squadron of wild geese flew over, sounding like a group of beagles closing in on the fox. With their long skinny necks stretched out ahead of them, they were communicating with each other in their own difficult to describe language. A brilliant morning sun reflected off the lazy, occasional cloud, portraying a golden hue in the eastern sky.

Captain Worthy came over to where I was silently taking in the beauty and sat down beside me. He was from a family of wealthy land owners who had seen to it that he was well educated. However, graduating from college with a teacher's degree in history could not compete with the charm of the river; it had already claimed his soul, as it had mine. He taught me the history of it in a way that was impossible to forget.

While we plunged ahead toward the spot where the Captain would be playing out the test net to determine if putting out the big net was worth the effort, he decided to tell me more about the river. Story telling, he called it.

Leaning over the rail with his pipe clenched firmly between his teeth he started by asking if I wanted to hear a story.

"Yes, please tell me one about the river," I pleaded, even though I knew he was going to talk about things I didn't know much about. He always did, but I loved his stories anyway.

He clasped his big old weather-beaten hands together, effectively creating a giant fist, and leaned further over the rail. "See that strip of sandy beach over there?" he asked, puffing on his pipe, making smoke billows flow across my face. I was immediately downwind; it filled my lungs with the sweet odor of cigar smoke I liked so much. I breathed in deeply; then answered in the affirmative.

"That little piece of land, I believe, was named for a certain doctor who had an office in the settlement that is now Little Washington, when the Tuscarora Indians started that war with the white settlers. From the history I have, it was that doctor who left us the story I'm going to tell you now."

"The Indians had apparently decided they were tired of white settlers taking their land, stealing from them, raiding their camps and taking their people into captivity to be slaves. After all, they had helped the settlers survive those first desperate years by teaching them how to grow the crops that would save their lives. It seemed to the Indians that the settlers should have been more grateful than that."

He struck his pipe sharply against the side of his clenched fist, emptied the contents into the river and refilled it, stuffing the Prince Albert into the bowl with a deft movement of his thumb.

"Upon hearing about the threat he quickly closed his office and went home. He was not going to take a chance on the life of his family. He probably had a little girl just like you," he said with a twinkle in his eye.

"He wasted no time in getting back home to what was then referred to as Bath Town. Bath was surrounded with a palisade constructed for just such emergencies."

"Little Liz, there was a lot of killing over the next few days, on both sides. Not like what you see in the movies, slaughter of real people, like you and me. They say the creeks ran red with blood. I think that skirmish lasted three or four days."

"The first attacks came on September 22, 1711, and were directed against the planters along the Neuse and Trent Rivers, and Bath Town. Hundreds of settlers were killed, along with some Indians, I suppose."

"The Tuscaroras were defeated around 1713 after which most of them went up north to New York State, and joined up with their people, the Iroquois Nation. Later on they went against the Iroquois Confederacy by joining up with the Colonial government during the American Revolutionary War, and wound up mostly in Canada. In 1831, or thereabouts, they sold their remaining lands in North Carolina."

"You see, Liz, everything that glitters ain't gold," he said. "Think about the stories you hear carefully." Then he leaned back and blew out a long trail of smoke that washed over me and drifted behind the *Miss Catherine* in the wind. Being apparently finished with his story, he fell to thinking, shutting me out. I went back to watching the shoreline that was drifting lazily by, and deliberately put the story into my memory bank to look at later when I felt like it.

Around eleven o'clock, Captain Worthy pulled *Miss Catherine* in close to the shoreline and threw out the anchor. "This is as good a place as any to eat," he said. We were all in agreement. The river has a way of making you so hungry you can eat shoe soles and they will taste good if you can get them tender enough.

He went into the cabin and made a pot of his famous coffee. After that a long conversation ensued between him and Daddy about whose coffee tasted better. Daddy vowed coffee was not as good without chicory and egg shells while the Captain argued that that would ruin *real* coffee. They mellowed into a temporary agreement after two or three coffee toddies made with Daddy's corn liquor.

After a lunch of pork and beans with potted meat and crackers, it was decided to throw out the test net to see if there were enough shrimp to warrant the big nets. The captain had said he thought this to be where the shrimp were, due to the swirling muddy water seen in the area. The contents of the test net assured us it was not a good place, and we moved out nearer to the middle of the river to search for a more likely spot.

Captain Worthy was not in a rush as he was just enjoying his stay in harbor this week, and his outing with Daddy. "No hurry," he said, "We have all week and the river is full of shrimp."

"*We* ain't got all week," Daddy said, "I told Elizabeth that Liz and I would be back by tomorrow night. She'll worry if we ain't home on time." He never forgot about Mama. Captain Worthy, who had never been married and apparently didn't understand spouse loyalty, looked at him oddly.

Soon after that, they decided to wait until tomorrow morning to throw out the nets again. It seemed only Daddy was in a hurry. We found a little strip of sandy beach and dropped anchor. It was the middle of the afternoon. We jumped into the tepid water and made our way ashore. Daddy, Luke and John-John dug a pit for the fire they intended to build later on and we all took a swim. Mr. Nathaniel and the captain mostly just watched. The temperature usually drops around Labor Day in the south, and it was chilly for that time of year in eastern North Carolina. It was decidedly warmer in the water than out. We all lingered there for a little longer due to that fact. It was fun for me, splashing around with grown men acting like kids.

Daddy reminded me to be careful and avoid jellyfish as their sting carried with it an awful burn. There was a bottle of vinegar on board the boat just in case. The

water was so clear I could see my toes in the sand.   A little
school of minnows swirled around my skinny legs.  I could
have easily seen any jellyfish in time to move out of their
way.

It was altogether a wonderful day to be out on the
water. We sat on the side of the boat in the evening sun to
allow the breeze to dry our clothing. The crew had no
problem with the chill as they were warmed by white
lightening.  I was not so lucky.  To me it was *very* chilly,
but I wouldn't have complained if my life had depended on
it, being that much like Mama.  I ignored the chill bumps.
Daddy and I threw over a couple of lines to catch some fish
for supper.

As night with all its mysterious shadows crept
nearer, we made our way back to the sandy beach by way
of a small boat carried along for that purpose.   The men
built a roaring bonfire in the pit.  Daddy scaled the fish and
rinsed them in the river. We speared them with sturdy
green boughs collected from nearby trees, and held them
over the fire until they were golden brown.  They were
absolutely delicious.

Captain Worthy had brought a piece of hemp rope
from the boat.  He placed it in the edge of the fire.  The
smoke from hemp was supposed to keep mosquitoes at bay,
and something about the smell was very soothing to the
senses as well.

As the sun sank over the tree tops, tales about high
adventures at sea began; tall tales, or so they seemed to me.
By the time they were finished, the ghostly shadow of
ships, especially of Blackbeard's fleet, could almost be
seen slicing through the silent waters. They were still on
their way to visit some long forgotten resident up river.

A huge moon rose ever so slowly out of the Pamlico
River, or so it seemed to me.  It cast a silvery glow over our
little beach; creating what seemed to be a pathway from us

to it, over the still cool water. There was an unusual chill in the wind blowing steadily from the north as the fire died down.   That, along with the effects of the alcohol, had an effect on the men and they grew less verbal.

Around eleven o'clock, the mate named John-John doused the fire and we went back to the boat.  The wind had changed direction, and true to North Carolina's fickle weather patterns, the warm air left with it.

As soon as we got on board, Luke and John-John found a place to their liking on deck, identified their blankets and rolled up in them, falling asleep almost immediately with their heads cradled on folded arms.  Loud snoring attested to the amount of whiskey they had consumed.

Daddy, Captain Worthy and Mr. Nathaniel, who had been almost invisible so far, moved over toward the opposite side of the boat and started to talk, kinda low like. They were discussing another treasure hunt on the river. All the sea faring stories must have triggered that adventurous spirit residing in their souls.

"Perhaps he buried it along the river just below Bath," Daddy was saying.   "That would make sense.  His sister Susie would be more likely to go lookin' in a less swampy area.  Plus there is no concrete evidence that Blackbeard traveled up river further than Bath that last night, and I believe he knew he was not long for this earth. If he were gonna leave somethin' for her, he was probably aware that this was his last opportunity.  Besides, he had just recently returned from a trip to Florida where that Spanish ship had fallen prey to inclement weather and sunk off shore, with all that loot on board.  It was fair game for anybody willin' to risk the dive for it.  I'm bettin' Blackbeard didn't return home minus part of it that day, and by all accounts, none of it was retrieved by Maynard and his crew."

I grew tired of the talk and went below, fished around and found an old yellow sou'wester someone had left behind, covered myself with it and fell asleep on one of the bunks. It had been a long day. I sure hoped Daddy *would* go treasure hunting again, but not up Tranter's Creek. The memory of that skull lingered with me yet.

The next morning found Miss Catherine surrounded by a dense fog. On deck, you could hardly see your hand in front of your face. The crew gathered in the galley to drink coffee and wait out the white shroud that engulfed us.

The silence was eerie to put it mildly. It felt as if we were all alone in an alien world. My imagination soared as the conversation got around to stories about Blackbeard again. Luke started the telling of tall tales. He started with one he had heard from his youth.

"It was on a day just like this, my granddaddy told me, Blackbeard hisself came up river under the cover of a heavy fog to visit his sister and to take a rest. I can almost see him leaning over the gunnel, keeping his boat just behind the white dolphin that guided the ship around shoals. He must have been an awesome sight to behold, and as dangerous as he was striking to look upon. He feared no man, and nobody around here dared to face him down. They tell me he would just as soon kill you as look at you."

"That's a bunch of hog wash, Luke," John-John stated. "There ain't no such thing as Dolphin this fur up river. There may have been out in the Sound, but not up here. You're always telling something that don't ring true. I've no doubt that he came up here every time he was in this part of the country, but it wasn't as often as people say. No sir, he operated mostly on the open seas, stealing and plundering the ships of the English, the Spaniards and the Portuguese. That's the long and short of it."

John-John left the cabin in apparent disgust, and to check on the weather which was clearing up to a degree.

I followed him and noted that the little strip of sandy beach where we were last night could not be seen yet. I snuggled myself up tighter in the old yellowed Sou'wester, barring against the chill of the morning air. Within minutes my hair was wet from the fog. It still felt to me like an alien land. I went back inside to warm up and sat by the stove listening as the men set up their plans.

The fishing turned out to be good in spite of a female and a black person being aboard, a fact that Daddy was quick to point out at the end of the day. We went back to port with a hold full of shrimp that evening and sold them within an hour to local vendors. The men shared the proceeds evenly with a little extra to Captain Worthy because it was his boat. Then we went to get Mama, and Captain Worthy took us home. We had made enough money to buy all the staples we needed for a month, which was good because the work for Daddy had practically dried up, due to the season.

Mr. Johnny was sitting on the back steps waiting for us when we got home. He knew we had gone on a fishing trip with the Captain and knew about when we would get back. I ran to him and he grabbed my hands, swinging me around in a circle until we were both dizzy.

"Tell me all about the trip, Little Liz," he said. "I want to hear how much luck you brought to that motley crew of old salts."

We spent the rest of that evening happily relating the events in detail for him and Mama.

## Chapter 8

By the third week of September, 1943, Bet and I had contracted some sickness that was new to the area. I was almost never sick, so it came as a big surprise to me. It was the sorest throat I had ever had. My throat was swollen from the top of my chest wall to my chin. I couldn't look down or swallow. If I tried swallowing, even just water, it would come out of my nose.

That was one of the rare times Mama relented and said this was something she couldn't cure with home remedies. She asked Daddy to go get the doctor to come and see us. He took one look and declared us to have Diphtheria. He explained that there were gray colored plaques in our throats and he needed look no further. He said something about an "epidemic" in town. Then he said, "The public health nurse will be out early in the morning," and told Mama not to let us eat or drink right now as we might *aspirate* it. I didn't know what that meant, but I had better sense than try to eat or drink when I couldn't swallow. Bet was too sick to even try.

With a worried, sad face, the doctor went on to say that there was a new drug on the market that might help. It was called Penicillin. "It's only being used to treat wounded soldiers on the battlefield right now, as far as I know, but because of this epidemic, we have been able to get a batch of it to see if it will save some lives. It's expensive, but if you can get the girls to the hospital in town, I'll see to it that they get the drug. It's their only hope, as I see it." At that, he stood up, picked up his black bag and left.

Right on time, at the break of dawn, the public health nurse arrived. "There is an epidemic in town," she repeated, as if she were parroting the doctor to make certain we understood. Then recognizing we didn't know or care what an epidemic was, she continued, "The hospital is full of children with Diphtheria. There are no beds. Even the halls are filled with cots for the ones that can't go home. You will have to come to the hospital, get the treatment which consists of two shots daily, and then go home. We should know within a few days if the treatment will work." Her voice trailed off at that point as if to say, *you're doomed if it doesn't*.

"Every business in town except the grocery store and the hospital is closed. Mr. Olfson, you may go to town for supplies if need be, but you have to come directly back home. And, only you can leave this house except to go to the hospital for the treatments. Diphtheria is spread by contact and we will have to quarantine your house. There are to be no visitors in or out of this place, *do you understand?"*

At that point, without waiting for questions, the nurse walked outside to the pump, washed her hands with the piece of Octagon soap that lay there, and proceeded to nail the big red *Quarantined* sign on our front door.

By eight o'clock that next morning, Mr. Johnny had arrived and told us he would take us to town for the shots. He wasn't afraid of getting the disease, and if he did, *so what*, he would not let us suffer for lack of transportation.

He helped Mama get us ready as both Bet and I were very weak. I was not able to move as fast as I usually did. He helped me comb my hair and wash my face while Mama washed Bet up. It didn't matter how sick we were, Mama insisted that we be spotlessly clean when we visited the hospital. Daddy complained out loud that we were wasting time.

"Cleanliness is next to Godliness," Mama said, and continued to wash Bet.

When we arrived at the hospital that morning for our shots, we found the sidewalks outside, as well as the halls inside, crowded with sick and dying children. Parents were sitting all over the waiting room area, looking like death warmed over to me. I guess it was lucky that this outbreak was only affecting children. At least that left the parents to care for them, and in this small town, they usually did.

I watched while the nurse injected the white liquid into Bet's backside. The needle was almost the size of her little arm, or so it seemed. She put one shot in Bet's right hip; then proceeded to put one in the left, explaining to Mama that it was too much medicine to put in one hip. *Any fool could see that*, I thought.

Bet never cried, she just winced when the needle went in, nothing more; then quietly closed her pretty little blue eyes and accepted fate.

I didn't cry either; I was too much like Mama. I wouldn't have cried if it had killed me. There was that element of the stoic Indian Daddy talked about already securely ingrained in my soul.

The next two weeks went by in a whirlwind of trips to the hospital. I slowly created a certain tolerance for those awful shots. Eventually they did help and I found myself able to swallow again. Bet wasn't that lucky.

Mama would take catnaps in her rocker, taking care of us day and night. Daddy just, more or less, stood by helping where he could. He seemed to me to feel lost. He would wander around as if death hovered around our door constantly. It did, as I was to discover.

Bet's little heart was not able to bear the strain. She died about three weeks after she contracted the disease. Some of the women around the neighborhood, none of

whom had ever set foot in our house, came to help. They
had all been touched by this disease. They each had a child
who was fighting to live, who had miraculously survived,
or who had died of suffocation as a result of the swollen
throat. They seemed determined to do what they could.

I watched Mama sew up a little shroud made from
the cloth of a flour sack she had bleached to a snowy white.
Then noted how she ever so carefully ironed it, handling it
as if it were made of an element that might disappear at any
time. She seemed bent on getting the pleats exactly right,
and paid no attention to the women who had come to help.
She was in a world of her own. Her silence screamed into
the darkness of a pitiless void, suspended for a time
between the cares of this world and the agony of a loss felt
by a mother unable to show emotion. Her pretty face was
etched with bitterness, as cold and hard as steel.

Daddy picked me up from the bed where I lay
exhausted that morning, and we all followed Mama in a
little procession to a pretty place on the hill behind our
house. There they put Bet's little hand made coffin in the
ground and piled dirt about a foot above the site. Then we
all went back to the pain of trying to live through a great
tragedy thrust upon us by an unforgiving, unfeeling, natural
disaster. It left about everybody but Mama with questions
about a God that would allow such a thing to happen to
innocent children.

I felt as if the space that Bet's frail little body had
occupied for such a short time had been left suddenly as
empty and as far from me as the space between the earth
and the stars, never to be filled again. It left a strange
empty ache that simply wouldn't go away.

I slowly got physically better under the care of
Mama, who seemed determined that Bet's destiny was not
going to be mine. Her every waking moment seemed bent
on my survival.

For about two weeks after Bet's burial, Daddy worked on a project he was determined to finish. He and I would sit on the back porch steps in the late evening sun while he carved a cross for Bet's grave. I watched silently as he cut and trimmed the small limb he had removed from the big oak tree out back. When he was finally satisfied with it, it was quite beautiful. He showed it to Mama and asked what she wanted put on it. "Her name of course," she said without so much as a thank you. At that Daddy proceeded to carefully carve the name Bessie Mable Olfson into it, and then darkened the writing by burning the wood over the words.

We made our trip to the site and Daddy placed the marker over the grave while Mama and I watched. Then we left her, satisfied that she would be remembered whenever some one passed the grave in the future. Perhaps they would know she was *so* loved and leave her in peace.

We also visited Barbara's grave that day. It was down the road a'ways at the black cemetery where she had been laid to rest about the same time as Bet. That was when Mama told me about her death. She knew I loved Barbara and had been reluctant to tell me until I got better, or so she said. Barbara and I would have been going to school that year and I knew I would see her every day because the black school was just across the railroad tracks from the white school where I would be going. Maybe we could have played together at recess if allowed to.

School had been delayed because of the epidemic. I had been looking forward to going. I wanted to ride the big yellow bus that went by the end of our lane. That was to be a milestone for me.

The year before when Mama had tried to enroll me, they wouldn't take me because I was so small. Mama was told to bring me back when I could at least climb up on the chairs in the first grade.

Daddy had taught me the alphabet and the numbers up to one hundred by the time I was six. The idea that I was learning to read from the Bible in an old English brogue never dawned on me. That is until I started to read from school books in *proper* English.

My hopes were dashed when the doctor came by to check me out that day. He listened to my heart and hit my knee with his closed fist to see how far my foot would kick out. Then he said to Mama, "I believe she has some heart and nerve damage from Diphtheria. She should not be allowed to do any thing that would be a strain on her for the next year or so. That includes going to school."

That was that, Mama would not hear of me going that year. Daddy seemed down right happy about it. "We'll be able to go fishin' or huntin' everyday if we want to," he told me. Mama said we would not, if I wasn't able to go to school, I wouldn't be able to tramp around the woods either.

As time went by and I got better, I began to resent Mama's constant attention. She was spending a lot of time watching my every move. This led me to tell my first lie.

It happened one day when I went to sit in my favorite place, on the ground by the chimney, behind the kitchen. It was a chilly day toward the last of October. I was sitting with my back against the sun warmed bricks, digging a hole in the soft earth with a spoon I had *borrowed* from Mama's stash in the box by the stove. I was planning on making mud pies in memory of the times Barbara and I had made them that last summer. It was an attempt to remember better times. All my life I had purposefully saved happy moments to look at later when I needed them to fill up a lonesome period. That was one of those.

Mama, being dead set on knowing where I was at all times, came around the corner just as I decided to taste the concoction. She saw the dirt go in. There was no way out for me.

"If you don't stop putting that dirt in your mouth, the devil is going to get you," she boldly stated, in an apparent attempt to discourage the behavior.

I had to think of something fast or Mama was going to whip me. Without giving much thought to what I was saying I blurted out, "No he won't, I just ate him," and down went the dirt, choking me into a coughing spasm.

Mama just stood there shocked by the lie I had just told, then unexpectedly, she began to laugh. It was the first time either of us had heard laughter around our house since Bet died. She came over to where I sat, sank down on the ground beside me and gathered me up in her arms. We both laughed hysterically until we cried. Then we just sat there holding on to each other for the longest time. After that Mama seemed to me to be better in her mind.

Daddy had gone to the boss's house to do some cleaning in his yard that morning, so he never heard that laughter, but he surely did notice the change when he came home that evening. Mama had gone out to the woods, pulled some wild flowers that still grew there under the protection of the ancient trees, and put them in a jar on the table. She was humming one of her favorite hymns softly as she fixed supper. The house felt warm again. We would survive, somewhat due to Mama's faith, I think.

The next morning, I had followed Mama out to the woodpile and was picking up some of the light-wood chips to keep the fire going when I saw the man and his old Model- T. It was traveling slowly up the path which was just wide enough to accommodate it. The clatter of pots and pans could be heard as the vehicle lumbered toward the house. It was the tinker man again. Mama laid the load of wood down and stood staring at him.

The car came to a standstill right beside the house. The man got out and slowly walked over to where we were standing, looking around as if to see if there were anyone else around.

"Can I give you a hand with that wood, madam?" He asked, smiling widely, showing a row of grimy looking green teeth."

"No, we can get it," Mama said. "And we still don't need any pots or pans mended."

"I wonder if you've changed your mind then about the aluminum ones?" he continued. "They don't cost much, and I hear cooking in those iron pots and pans ain't good for your health, neither, too much iron in them, I've heard."

I could tell Mama was getting agitated by the way her eyes were flashing. They did that when she got angry. "I already told you when you were here before, we don't want anything you are selling," she stated firmly. "Now if you don't mind sir, I'll get back to my work."

The tinker man stood there for a minute looking at Mama kinda funny.

"Is your man at home?" he asked.

Mama never answered.

He asked again, a little louder this time.

That's when she looked up and stared him in the eye. Then she took me by the hand and we went straight to the house without another word. I didn't look back, but I could feel his eyes boring into the back of my head.

When we were safely inside, Mama told me to go to my room and not come out until she called. I peeped back around the corner in time to see her taking the squirrel gun down. I ran to my bed and jumped under the covers, head and all.

The next thing I heard was the sound of Daddy's gun going off. Just after that I heard the vehicle with pots

and pans clanging as it careened down the path. I ran out to
see if Mama was alright.  She was standing in the doorway
with the gun pointed at the backside of that old car, and just
about that time it went off again.  I watched as the back
glass shattered into a thousand fragments just as it
disappeared from view.  Mama was not afraid of anything
except God and ghosts, and she would, I found out that day,
take care of her own.

Without another word, Mama and I went back to the
woodpile, gathered up the wood and took it in the house.
She secured the doors and we stayed in there until Daddy
came home.

When she told him what had happened, he said he'd
better go to the boss's house and get him to call the sheriff.

"Do you think that tinker man had something to do
with the King woman, Andy?" Mama asked.

"What makes you think I would know that?" Daddy
asked.  "I ain't got no crystal ball, but I feel like we need to
let that William Crowley know the man came back here.
We said we would."

"I wish we had never moved here," Mama stated.

"You always say that when somethin' happens that
upsets you," Daddy said.

I watched from the window as Daddy walked off
down the road to the boss's house. Mama propped kitchen
chairs against the front and the back door. I noted she was
quietly listening as she kept an eye on her biscuits. She
wasn't singing like she usually did.  She kept going to the
window, looking for Daddy.

He was back in about an hour and told Mama the
deputy would be out the next morning.  He had insisted on
coming out to get the story firsthand.

Right on time, during breakfast, William Crowley
showed up apparently intent on getting every scrap of
information Mama could tell him about that man.

D. A. Lay

After she told him what happened, Deputy Crowley scratched his head and muttered, "Pervert, I knew it. We got our man I think; I'll bet he is up to his neck in the disappearance of that King woman. Can you tell me which way he went after he left here, misses?"

"No, I didn't see the car after he turned round the bend in the road down there, but from the sound of it, seemed like he went south on the main road. I hope you get him soon as I'm uneasy about being way out here in the woods with a little child. A body can't stay awake all the time."

## Chapter 9

November was a hard month. It always was with farm laborers. Mr. Johnny was our bright spot during those meager times. He came almost every evening with his bright smile, guitar and fun songs to sing.

Mama kept us fed the best she could with winter collards and the few meager jars of canned food left over from the summer. That and the rabbits Daddy killed from time to time was enough to keep a body alive, but certainly not fat!

Every time she opened a jar of tomatoes to put in the ever present dried beans to make them palatable, I would remember her bent over the iron wash pot, watching the boiling water around jars filled with the red fruit. Once in a while one would break and make a big mess, but she was always pleasant about starting over. "It's God's way," she would say, "to keep us from getting too lazy."

One day near the middle of December, we had managed to acquire enough money to buy staples and Mr. Johnny took us to town. We ate hot dogs at Bill's, after which Daddy was to take me to see the Christmas decorations. We made plans to meet back at the store in about an hour and Mr. Johnny headed out to see one of his friends. He said that the friend was preparing to return to the war. He was lucky to have made it home near Christmas, and it might be the last time Mr. Johnny would ever see him, he said.

I was interested in seeing toys in the store windows. Even though I was almost seven years old, I never tired of looking at the dolls and dreaming that one day I might be lucky enough to own one.

I most certainly never expected to get one from Santa for Christmas. Mama never introduced me to a belief in Santa Claus. She said if I was taught to believe in him, I might have a problem believing in God. I might think that if they told me a lie about that, I might believe they were lying about God also. After all, it was hard enough for a child to believe in something they couldn't see to begin with. There was no need to add another puzzle to an already difficult to understand situation.

But, oh, to see those beautiful doll babies. That was a treat. We passed the Salvation Army band on the corner of Main and Gladden streets singing a Christmas carol, accompanied by the drum and horn; turned left at the Candy Kitchen and headed down Main Street. Everything was so grand! All the store windows were dressed with holiday cheer in mind. Mama said it seemed every one wanted something to help them forget about the horrors of war for a while, and were going to use the holidays to do just that.

We passed window after window dressed out with beautiful things, but nothing to compare to that last one. It almost took my breath away. I stopped and pressed my hands and nose against the cold glass pane and just stared. In that window sat the most gorgeous doll I had ever seen. It's hair and eyes were *so* much like little Bet's. The jet black hair hung down in a tangle of curls and its blue eyes were looking straight at me. I was dumbfounded. Never had I wanted anything that badly. It was as if she were calling me.

Daddy stopped to see what I was looking at. "We can't afford that, Son," he said, with more than a little sadness in his voice. Then he stooped down and picked me up. "There's nothin' says we can't git a better look though." We went inside the store and right up to the doll in the window.

"Can I touch it Daddy? If I could just feel of her I'd be happy. She reminds me of Bet."

"No son, we can't touch it. That kind of thing is not for the likes of us, you know that."

He put me down and he and Mama were walking along the isle of toys with me to look, when I saw a man watching me. I drew closer to Mama and kept my eye on him. He was a strange sort. He had a beard like Mr. Johnny's except it was as white as snow. He was wearing a black suit and tie, kinda like the preacher had on that night at church. His face softened as he stared at me. A smile slowly turned up the edges of his mouth. Wrinkles appeared on his forehead and down his plump red cheeks. He looked positively ageless. Mama reached out, took me by the arm and pulled me along, averting my gaze. "Don't stare," she warned me. "You don't know that man."

I felt as if I did though. I could tell when a person had character, even before I was aware of what that was, and he had *character*. I turned to get one last look at this strange fellow to find him standing right behind me, holding that doll I wanted so much.

"Please, may I give her this?"

Mama just stared at him, but Daddy, who wanted me to have it as much as I did, had already said *yes* with his eyes. They, who had never taken so much as a free piece of bread from anyone, gave in this one time. Then, miracle of miracles, the man reached up to the top shelf, took down a big black-leather stroller, placed the doll in it and sat it down in front of me! And without another word, he walked over to the cashier, paid for it and walked away. I watched him leave the store dumbfounded. As he walked out onto the street, he looked back at me and smiled the biggest smile I had ever seen before disappearing into the crowd. I knew at that moment I would forever after believe in Santa Claus, no matter what anyone said.

D. A. Lay

Leaving the store pushing that doll and stroller, I held my head high. I had been visited by Santa Claus. I looked straight into the eyes of that little girl with her pretty dress and black patent leather shoes, holding to the white gloved hand of her well groomed mother. She would never compare to me in my homemade dress and the rags that kept my skinny legs warm that night. I was special!

Mr. Johnny was waiting when we returned to the grocery store. He had a drawn, tired look on his face, as if something had happened to drown his joy in the season. There it was again, that kinda *nobody's home* look. Like when we first met him. He didn't tell us what had happened, and we didn't ask.

"Look, Mr. Johnny," I said. "I met Santa Claus and he gave me this doll and baby carriage. Ain't they purty?"

He seemed to perk up a little and said, "I'm happy for you." His face and the sound of his voice didn't match his words, though. He lifted the carriage into the truck bed, me and the doll into the seat between him and Mama, and we started home. There was very little conversation on the part of Mr. Johnny as we drove along. It was as if he was with us in body only.

When we arrived home, he helped us get the groceries into the kitchen, said a hurried goodbye and left.

"What do you think happened to him, Andy?" Mama asked after he left. "I thought he was getting better from whatever happened to him as a soldier. Now I think he's right back where he started from. I don't think he's a danger to others, but I think he's a danger to himself. I am worried about what he might do. Why don't you go and talk to his folks and see what you can do for him."

Daddy said he would tomorrow. "Although," he said, "I think we ought to leave him alone to work it out, as whatever it is, he is the one who has to worry with it."

The next morning Daddy went to see about Mr. Johnny like Mama asked him to. He was gone about three hours, and when he came back he had a strange story to tell.

"When I got there, Johnny's Mama said he was asleep. I was invited in for coffee and found him sleepin' in a chair in the living room. He woke up about the time his daddy and me got to talkin' about his strange ways since he had come home from the war. I had just raised my cup to take a drink when he woke up and started yellin' that the bombs were fallin' and started tryin' to shove us into a corner. I spilled coffee all over the livin' room floor. He was screamin' and hollerin' like he was crazy. Finally his Mama slapped him hard across his face. Then he sort of wilted down to the floor and just lay there whimperin' like a whipped puppy."

"His Mama said he had trained as a bombardier and was on a mission to bomb a factory that was makin' materials for the war, or something like that, when it happened. The plane was flyin' too high and there was a cross wind. When Johnny opened the bay and dropped the bomb, it hit a school instead of the factory, killin' all the children in it. She said he never got over that. She said Johnny always loved children and he wanted some of his own. His wife refused, though, sayin' they didn't have enough money to raise a cat, much less a young'un. Knowin' Johnny like I do now, I'd say that was exactly right."

"What are his folks going to do with him?" Mama asked.

"I don't know Elizabeth. I ain't never seen nothin' like it. They said he acted that way every time one of his friends went back *over there*. They think he'll be alright in a few days."

"I tell you Elizabeth, if that is what bein' *shell shocked* means, I'm glad I decided to wait a while, rather than go on over there like I planned to do. I might git *shell shocked* too."

I felt sad about Mr. Johnny, thinking he must be sick like Bet and me when we had Diphtheria. I asked Mama if he was going to die. She said she didn't know, we'd just have to wait and see.

The next few days were spent mostly just trying to stay warm. The weather was doing its thing like it did every winter, Daddy said. It would be really cold in November and turn shirt sleeve weather by Christmas day. He was right. On Christmas day the temperature was sixty eight degrees and felt even warmer because there had been such a cold snap in late November and early December.

That was the day Daddy and I went out to the woods and found a beautiful baby cedar tree, about twelve inches tall. Daddy dug it up and put it in the bucket he had prepared with some black dirt from the edge of the field. He said we shouldn't kill it for our pleasure, but he wanted me to have a Christmas tree.

Mama had been saving the shiny, silver colored papers from cigarette packs. Daddy had collected them from his friends that smoked cigarettes. From them she had created tiny silver balls to decorate the tree. They shimmered like quick silver, picked up from the lamplight's glow, casting flowing, silvery bands of shadows against the walls. I placed my most cherished possessions, my doll and carriage beside it and watched it twinkle and shine until I fell asleep. The day after Christmas, Daddy replanted the tree next to the back door and thanked it for the favor.

It wasn't long before Mr. Johnny showed up again with his guitar, like nothing had happened. Daddy had told me not to talk to him about that day at his house. I didn't know what to say anyway, I didn't understand any of it.  I just enjoyed his company like I always did.

Along about dark the wind changed around to the north east and the temperature dropped dramatically.  It went from the low fifty's to the thirties in the space of two hours.  The rain shower rapidly turned to sleet.  Then the sleet turned to big fluffy flakes, quickly burying the landscape in a winter wonderland of white.  I watched in awe while there was still enough daylight outside.  The broad, naked branches of the oak tree next to my window became a bed to hold the snow.  I found myself wishing little Bet could be there to enjoy it with me.

Mama went out to the backyard, filled the dish pan with the white stuff and rushed back in to make us some snow cream, using all the sugar and canned milk we had left.

By dark the snow had gained a couple of inches and Daddy reminded Mr. Johnny he'd better be going if he planned to make it home before it got too late.

"I told Mother I was going to stay over here if the weather got bad," he said.

"Okay," Daddy said, "but we'd better git in some wood, it's gonna be a long, cold one."

Long cold nights and snow in this part of the country are not that frequent.  We were excited about it.  After we ate all the snow cream, Daddy and Mr. Johnny brought in two armloads of firewood each, enough to last all night.  Daddy built a roaring fire in the big tin heater, making the sides turn a cherry red.

While Mama made supper, Daddy started on one of his stories about the Vikings.  I believe he liked to tell stories more than anyone in the world, and was very good at it.  Mr. Johnny and I were hanging on every word when the sounds we had heard so often started up. Someone was walking on the porch!

For the space of a few seconds, everything was deathly quiet in the house. Then Mr. Johnny jumped up, knocked the chair he was sitting in over, and ran to the front door. He yanked it open and yelled, "*Katie*" into the white empty world that stared back at him.

Mama went over to him and put her hand gently on his arm, telling him nobody was there. She said, "Johnny, it isn't her, it's most likely the wind or something like that. Come back inside and close the door, its cold out there."

Mr. Johnny allowed himself to be led back into the kitchen, but the joy had gone out of him. He buried his face in his hands and sobbed like a small lost child until he fell asleep. Neither Mama nor Daddy spoke, they just let him cry.

After he went to sleep, Mama said, "Maybe you ought to go get his folks."

"No, he'll be alright, it's too dark and cold now to git very far from the house," Daddy said. "Just let him sleep, we'll decide what to do later."

Strangely enough, we never heard another sound that night.

Johnny awoke about an hour later and didn't seem to remember what had happened. The remainder of the evening was spent with frequent visits to the door to watch soft snow flakes drift and swirl around the house, while we sang with Mr. Johnny and drank coffee. Daddy would make another pot every time we ran out. It was one of those rare times when we happened to have enough to splurge.

I went to sleep thinking about the white mantle of snow slowly accumulating around the shack outside, listening to Daddy and Mr. Johnny talk excitedly about the weather. When I awoke the next morning, there was a warm fire burning in the heater. The snow was creating a brilliant shine in the morning sun light and Mr. Johnny had gone home.

## Chapter 10

It started out like any other; that cold January morning, 1944. Daddy had gone to cut wood for the stove. Mama was busy kneading dough for biscuits when a loud expletive cut the crisp air like a knife, and the sound of splitting wood ceased. Mama stopped dead in her tracks and stood perfectly still. She was staring out the window at something I wasn't able to see from where I sat at the table. Silence fell on the shack for what seemed like an eternity, a silence that was deafening.

Mama stood there motionless, as if frozen in time, until Daddy pulled the door open and stepped into the kitchen. Blood was streaming from his left, lower leg, below where the axe had dug in. His pants were sticking to his skinny leg with the bright red stuff.

Mama pulled a chair over to where he was standing and told him to sit down. He did so, looking dazed. She frantically ripped the pants leg down and found the axe had cut into the bone.

"I'll clean it up, and then we have to find a doctor, somehow," she said. I had never seen Mama that intense. Her eyes were as huge as the doe Daddy and I had almost bumped into one day a week before, when we had accidentally slipped up on it as it slept. I wanted her to tell me it would be alright, but she was taking no notice of me at the moment.

I watched as she held a clean dish rag firmly over the cut for a few minutes, before telling me to come hold it for her. "Press down hard," she said. I remember feeling sick to my stomach, but I closed my eyes and held it like she told me to, feeling the warm blood ooze between my fingers.

Mama poured Kerosene over the cut and bound it up tightly with clean rags she had torn into strips.

"I'm alright now, Elizabeth," Daddy said. "I'll go finish cuttin' the wood." When he stood up he staggered and almost fell.

"Yes. You're alright, that's a fact. Sit down; I'll go get the wood."

I watched Mama through the window. Her moccasin covered feet were slipping on the drifts of snow and half frozen mud around the wood pile. A cold north wind was blowing steadily, kicking up the powdery white stuff, making it swirl around her tiny frame like the proverbial smoke from hell. Her skirt whipped around her legs in a frenzy of contempt. I felt the cold of the window pane on my hands which were pressed against it at the moment, and my heart felt the cold my Mama was feeling.

When she came back into the house, she was shaking head to toe. Her skirt was stiff where the blowing snow had saturated her clothes, creating icicles that were clinging to her skirt tail. The south land doesn't have many winters that are bitterly cold. What it generally does have is considered ice storms rather than snow storms. And they are just as cold as the storms up north; they just don't last as long. That, combined with the fact that eastern North Carolinians are not equipped for them, makes it even worse when they do come, or so Mama told me.

We ate breakfast and Daddy went back to bed like Mama told him. Then she announced she was going to try and find a doctor.

"I'll go to the boss's house and see if they will call the hospital to tell us what to do," she said. Then she pulled Daddy's old coat around her shoulders and slipped the ugly rubber boots on, the one's Captain Worthy had loaned Daddy on the last fishing trip. She was getting ready to set out in the cold morning air against Daddy's objections.

"Elizabeth, I'm gonna be alright," Daddy called out from his bed. "There ain't no need to git so excited about everythin'. You always do that. You're just like your sister Kathleen, always makin' a mountain out of a mole hill!"

Mama didn't seem to be listening as she walked to the door. Then turning to me she said, "Liz, you keep that fire going and keep the door latched. Don't let nobody in until I get back." Then she stepped out the door under a barrage of protests.

I watched her tiny frame making its way down the snow covered path, arms folded across her chest, head bent low, staggering against the onslaught of a cruel north wind. Then I turned my attention to the task at hand, taking care of Daddy and the fire like she told me to.

After a couple of hours she came back with bad news. She hadn't seen Mr. Williams, but Mrs. Williams had tried to call the hospital to no avail. The phone lines were down, thanks to the storm, and the country back roads were impassable, or so Mama and Mrs. Williams had determined. We were on our own.

Daddy lay on the bed sleeping. Mama said that was best for the moment. She kept the house warm as she and I planned how we were going to take care of things until he got better.

"Johnny will probably come back sometime today," Mama said, partly to me and partly to the world in general. "We sure could use him. He might have some idea about what to do. He *was* in the war, so he must have learned something about caring for wounded people. There ain't nobody else I can think of."

After a while Mama stopped talking and I pulled my chair over to the window facing the front yard to watch for Mr. Johnny. I was not disappointed, he came up the path around eleven o'clock.

I ran out to meet him, bare feet plowing through the half frozen slush, jumping into his arms before he got to the porch. I knew he would carry me around to the back. He never came in the front door, and I knew why. He never wanted to see that stain again! And that stain wasn't going anywhere.

"Daddy got cut with the axe," I said as he made his way around the house, carrying me piggyback with my bare legs and feet dangling over his arms. "He was cutting wood and the axe slipped. He's hurt real bad. Mama is scared and said she hoped you would come over today and help us."

Daddy was still sleeping. Mama had coffee ready on the stove. She smiled up at Mr. Johnny, a benediction she seldom bestowed on anyone.

"He's gone and hurt himself, Johnny; cut his leg about half in two with the axe and lost a lot of blood. It has stopped bleeding now but we can't get him out to the doctor. Roads are impassable, thanks to the muddy slush left by the snow storm, and the telephone lines are down. I don't know what to do."

"Don't worry Miss Lizabeth," Mr. Johnny said. "We'll think of something, he looks kinda peaceful right now."

"Well I do know about herbs, at least what my Mama taught me. I checked out the place for healing herbs when we first moved in and found a patch down by the creek where yellow root grows. If you will stay with Andy and Liz, I'll go see if I can find it again."

"You don't need to be going out there in this weather, Miss Lizabeth, if you'll tell me what to look for, I'll go get it for you."

"No, this is something I have to do. I know where it was located last summer, before the snow covered it. I don't even know if it will help him, but it's worth a try."

I believed in it. I had watched her make a tea from the roots of that plant for a chest cold daddy had last winter, and he got well that time. I knew they didn't believe in doctors much anyway.

"I need you to stay here and keep the house warm until I get back. There's plenty of wood under the shelter if you need it. I'll be back soon."

"I reckon you know what you're doing, but please don't stay out there too long. It won't do your family any good if you get sick too," Mr. Johnny said.

After she left, he and I started singing songs from memory. Songs like *Big Rock Candy Mountain* and *She'll be Coming Round the Mountain When She Comes.* Later we played ring around the roses, chasing each other around the table. All the while he assured me Mama would be alright.

She came back with the yellow root and made tea. Then she woke Daddy up. He drank a cup of it and fell asleep again. It was getting dark outside and snow began to fall again in a soft, filmy white curtain. It made our little shack seem isolated in a world of its own. I was awfully glad Mr. Johnny was there.

"I'll make you a pallet on the kitchen floor," Mama said. It was taken for granted Mr. Johnny would stay with us all night.

They talked until the hour was late. I don't remember what brought it up, but the subject finally got around to the walking on the porch we had heard at intervals since we had been there.

"Now you understand I don't believe in ghosts, Johnny," Mama said. I just don't know what to make of it. It doesn't scare me much anymore. I'd just like to know what it is."

"I've heard that the spirit of a person who died a terrible death stays where that person dies until the mystery is solved," Mr. Johnny said. "I believe that is right, Miss Lizabeth. What about getting Miss Lillian over here one rainy night to see if she could shed light on it? I would like for you to do that. I think my wife was murdered here and it's her trying to get someone to listen to her. I don't believe she'll be able to rest until that happens."

"I admit I've been thinking about that myself, Johnny, but I can't get past where I think God wouldn't approve. Miss Lillian might not come anyway. She say's she's afraid of this place."

Daddy was still sleeping when Mama and Mr. Johnny gave up on what to do about the *ghost*, stoked the fire to make it easier to start in the morning, and we went to bed.

When I woke up, Daddy was sitting at the table waiting for his breakfast. He looked weak and pale. I went over and sat on the knee of his unaffected leg and hugged him. I didn't know what to say. I was happy that he was up.

Mr. Johnny was cutting wood and Mama was busy with breakfast. Even little Blackie, who was a grown cat now, seemed to sense that something was dreadfully wrong. He sat in his box staring at the scene as if he knew something we didn't know.

There was a hush over the atmosphere as we ate breakfast in almost total silence. When we had finished Daddy went back to his bed at Mama's insistence.

After breakfast, Mr. Johnny announced he had to go home to let his folks know he would be here for a few days.

He said they would understand. Then he and Mama talked a while about the dire circumstances.

"We have enough canned food to last a week or more. There are some of the Irish potatoes left in the ground and I know where the rabbit traps are set. That should keep us going for about three weeks. We can do without coffee, Andy won't feel like smoking, most likely, and I can do without snuff. That will save the little bit of money we have until he gets better."

"That sounds like a good plan to me," Mr. Johnny said as he prepared to leave for the day. "There's plenty of wood cut up under the shed. I'll be back late this afternoon."

About an hour after he left, Mr. Williams showed up. "My wife told me Andy got hurt and you all were trying to get a doctor to come out here," he said to Mama. "I came to see what happened. You know the ground will need to be turned by the middle of February. If you all can't get it done, I'll have to get some tenants in here who can. It's nothing against you, you understand. It's just business. Someone has to get the work done. I'm sorry for your misfortune and I'll see to it that Andy gets to a doctor when the weather gets better. That's the best I can do."

After he left, Mama just sat there staring out the window for a while, then she stoked the fire and started cleaning house like a woman possessed. I watched as she scrubbed the already spotless floors, washed windows and set the iron on the heater for pressing our meager supply of clothes, which didn't need it.

That now familiar sickening fear firmly wound itself around my heart and refused to leave, even when Blackie came to sit on my lap and started purring. He walked around and around, patting my lap until it felt like a good place to him, then curled up in a black ball of fur and fell asleep. Usually he made me feel happy, not that day.

Mama cleaned until she appeared exhausted and it was getting late. Then she fixed us something to eat for supper and woke Daddy up. His wound was now swollen and red looking. She applied some black salve she had purchased from a traveling salesman earlier that year when she had a little extra money for such things. Then she gave him a cup of the yellow root tea and asked him to go back to bed, a suggestion he offered no resistance to.

Mr. Johnny was back by then. He and Mama went to check the rabbit traps which were empty, and baited them with the only thing she had, collard leaves. "Rabbits don't particularly like'em," she said, "But if they are as desperate as we are they might be ready to try anything."

Apparently, they were not that desperate; we only got one rabbit that way. Mama did kill one with the shot gun, managing to tear it up until there wasn't much left to cook. That was the last of rabbit meat in our diet for a while.

Later that evening, Mama told Mr. Johnny about the visit from Mr. Williams that afternoon. He didn't say anything; there was nothing he could do. Mr. Williams owned the place and it was his decision as to whether we stayed or went.

Mr. Johnny had brought Mama some clean rags his folks had sent to help with wound care. Surprisingly, she had accepted them.

Daddy woke up and drank coffee with us but he was still quiet, a condition I had rarely seen him in. Blackie and I stayed as close to him as we could. Blackie had never been partial to Daddy, but that evening, upon occasion, he would reach out and place his little black foot on Daddy's foot as if to say, *we're here*. Daddy was so sick he never noticed, though.

By that time I guess Mr. Johnny had thought it over and decided he could do something after all; because he told Daddy he was going to stay until he could get around good again. Daddy thanked him and informed us he wasn't going to the doctor because we didn't have the money, and he knew he would get well just as fast under Mama's care. At heart, I think he had more confidence in the old remedies of Mama's than in the doctors anyway.

By the end of that first week, creek fishing had become very unfruitful for people using canes poles. Patches of ice reached out a'ways from the edge, making it necessary to break it up in order to fish from the bank. Neither Mr. Johnny nor Mama was willing to leave the shoreline in that dinky little skiff. And they didn't want to venture far from Daddy and me anyway, so that source of food dried up.

I began to feel real hunger for the first time. A hunger that hurts deep down inside, eating at your guts. Hunger that makes you feel sharp minded; the kind that speeds up your thinking and stirs up the fight or flight syndrome. At one point, Mr. Johnny had begged Mama to accept a handout from the neighbors. Mama stated, "If we starve, we'll do it on our own terms, Johnny, we'll not be beholden to nobody. But we thank you for thinking about us, you are a dear friend."

Mama kept finding something for us to eat from somewhere, and Mr. Johnny was able to catch a few fish. That's the way we survived.

By the first week of February, Daddy was having days when he felt better. That fact made me feel like things were going to be alright.

The snows had about dissipated. Here and there, where they were protected by tall pine and cedar trees, Daffodils poked their yellow heads up to see the sun and to announce the beginning of spring in the south. They were always a beautiful sight, but this year they were even more welcome because they inspired hope in us.

One evening just before it got dark, the tinker man showed up again. I saw him and a lady walking up the path and told Mama. I watched from the window as they came up on the porch. He knocked boldly on the door. The woman he had with him looked to be his senior by at least ten years. He seemed determined to keep her between himself and whoever answered the door. She was standing in front of him when Mama opened it.

"Please, madam, hear me out," he was saying over the head of the woman. "I would like to apologize for the misunderstanding that happened the last time I was here, for it was a misunderstanding. I'm not worried about the back glass window in my car. I understand why you did that, you misunderstood my intentions. Now, I don't want to lose any customers around here because of this thing. This here is my wife, she can tell you I am of good character."

He smiled broadly displaying his green teeth. Mama stepped back and took a deep breath.

The woman spoke up to say her husband was a good man and that she hoped Mama would allow him to come around on his working days to see if she might need something. She continued on to say that she didn't want her husband, Lester, to get a bad reputation in the community because of this *incident*.

"I've told him to stay away from here," Mama said. "I'm not going to tell him again, the next time I'm going to get the sheriff. I believe he found out the last time he was out here how I feel."

"We need to go, Lester, it's sure they don't want us around here," the woman stated, her voice changing from a begging sound to anger. "There is people who needs your wares; I don't know why you are bothering with this place in particular anyways."

"I don't know either, but it would be advisable to stay away from here," Mama said. She shut the door in their faces and went back to what she had been doing before they arrived.

I watched as they took their leave down the driveway and disappeared around the bend. I wondered what would happen to end this situation. I had a feeling it wasn't over yet.

It was late when Mr. Johnny got back that night. He said he had been helping his Father fix the pump in the kitchen. "The plunger attached to the bottom of the pump handle had broken off and fallen into the well. He ain't too good at fixing things. They depend on me for repairs like that."

Mama wasted no time in telling him about the tinker man whom she called Lester, as she knew his first name now. "I can't imagine why he keeps coming back here, Johnny. He knows he's not wanted. This time he brought a woman he called his wife. I reckon he thought that would get him into the house. It is true that if she had not been with him, the outcome might have been very different. I detest that man."

"Do you think we need to call the deputy? He told me to call if I saw that man again. I didn't tell you this before, but he really thinks that he might have had something to do with your wife's disappearance."

Mr. Johnny didn't say anything for the longest time. Then, slowly pulling himself up to his towering six foot plus frame, he said, "I sure do think we ought to tell William Crowley, Miss Lizabeth. I'll be on my way to do that right now. Don't open your door to him again, he could be dangerous. I'll be back as soon as I can"

Mr. Johnny left in a hurry, never even stopping to hug me like he always did. Mama told me she was kind of sorry she had said anything, she was afraid of what he might do. She woke Daddy up to ask him what he thought.

"Johnny knows what he is doin', Elizabeth," Daddy said. "That man has no business here. I pity his wife. I can't imagine any woman wantin' to live with him. I guess she has her reasons, though."

Early that next morning, Mr. Johnny came back to the house with the deputy and three other officers. Mama had to tell the story all over again. While she was talking I watched Mr. Johnny. He was very quiet, sitting there looking like a statue, so still it was like he was glued to the chair. His eyes had a strange gleam that frightened me. I wondered if Mama had noticed. If she had she didn't show it.

Right after the officers left, Mr. Johnny said a hurried goodbye and left also. It was as if he had forgotten that we needed him. When I asked Mama why he had left like that, she said not to worry he just had something on his mind. We could get by for a while without his help, she was just thankful he had stayed with us until now. "He didn't have to help us at all, you know," she said.

When he had not returned by nightfall, I could tell Mama was getting anxious. She made frequent trips over to the window, checking to see if he was coming up the lane. Blackie and I stayed out of her way. Daddy was asleep by dusk that afternoon when the rain started.

Mama had heated the radio battery up so we could listen to music. We were sitting by the stove listening to country music and trying to stay warm when we heard the now familiar sound of footsteps on the porch. Mama got up and checked to make certain the doors and windows were secure. Then she lit the lamp and turned the wick up as high as it would go without smoking the shade, to give us all the light we could get. Still the corners of the room remained dark and shadowy. Blackie and I cuddled up on

Mama's lap for safety. Daddy was still sleeping. Mama said she wouldn't wake him, it wouldn't do any good. She said she sure wished Mr. Johnny was there.

It was just at that point when we heard what we recognized as human voices shouting. Mama jumped up, dumping me and Blackie right on the floor. "My God!" she said, "What is that?"

We ran over to the door, opening it just wide enough to let the light shine on the front yard so we could see what was happening. There were several officers surrounding a man that we could see from the flashlight beam was the tinker man, Lester.

Deputy Crowley was shouting over the tumult. "What the hell are you doing, trying to scare these people to death? Did you have something to do with that woman disappearing?"

"What woman?" Lester was yelling back. "I don't know nothin' about no woman. I was just tryin' to get their attention! No, I mean, I was gettin' back at them for not buyin' my wares! They made such a big deal about my kind of business that I wanted to git back at them. That's all there is to it!"

About that time Mr. Lester had apparently taken all the pressure he could stand, because he broke and ran. The terrible sound of a gun discharging from somewhere close by rang out. The tinker man stumbled forward and started screaming, "I been shot!" and fell to the ground, grasping his right leg.

One of the flashlights caught the form of a man over at the corner of the yard. It was Mr. Johnny with a shotgun hanging loosely by his side, just standing there, staring at the scene.

Two of the officers slowly walked over to where he stood and reached out for the gun. It was handed to them without so much as a word.

Deputy Crowley came over to the porch where Mama and I were standing. He told us that when Mr. Johnny had informed them of the situation, they had staked the place out. Deputy Crowley had figured that the *ghost* was that very tinker man and thought he might show up tonight because it was supposed to rain. He said for some reason, he thought Lester had been trying to make us move. "He probably did have something to do with the King woman disappearing," he said. "We'll get to the bottom of it. I'm sorry Mr. Johnny shot him and he'll have to go to jail tonight, but I'll do what I can for him. There ain't a jury in the county that would convict him of anything, under the circumstances."

He went on to say that Mr. Johnny had been told to stay away from the stakeout. They knew he was already unbalanced in the head from something that happened while he was overseas, and that this might push him over the edge.

Mr. Johnny was handcuffed and taken away. Then they picked the tinker man up, not too gently, and carried him down the path, around the bend and out of sight. He was screaming like a wounded junk yard dog all the way.

The commotion had awakened Daddy. He was standing behind us in the doorway. His face was pale and he was leaning against the door jam.

After everybody left Daddy went to a chair and sank down in it. He told us he would be okay now. Not to worry about him.

"We're tough, Son, we have Viking blood flowin' through our veins," he said. "Ain't nothin' gonna happen to you and your Mama, and I will see to it that everythin' works out for Mr. Johnny if I can. He is a good man. Sometimes good people do the wrong thing, but that don't mean they have turned bad, just that they can't understand what's happenin'. It'll turn out alright. You'll see."

I could tell it was all he could do to just sit up in his chair. It was apparent to me that he was holding on for our sake. I never loved him more than I did at that moment.

We stayed up talking until around midnight. Then we went to bed. I don't know about Mama, but I felt better. The pain I felt in my heart for Mr. Johnny eased up a little, and the fact that Daddy was feeling better didn't hurt the situation none.

## Chapter 11

Those next few days were a flurry of activity. Mr. Johnny's Daddy came the following Monday to take us with him to bail Mr. Johnny out of jail.

Mr. Johnny came directly to our place that same day. So did the local police, all of them I think. With Mama's permission they searched the house, the yard and the woods nearby. They had brought hounds with them who sat up a wail as they scratched and sniffed their way around.

They looked inside and out of that old shack for anything that would, as they put it, connect Lester to a crime involving the missing Mrs. King. They came up empty handed again.

Mr. Johnny helped them look. I think he felt that he needed to know he had shot Lester for the right reason. He told us, while we were talking about the incident that might land him in jail for a long time, what had been going through his mind when he shot the man.

"I don't like guns at all," he stated. "But I thought I might need one if I saw that man. I knew he might try to get away and I wasn't going to let that happen. So I borrowed Daddy's gun on the way over here, just in case I needed it."

"I was thinking about the school I accidentally dropped that bomb on too, killing all those innocent children, and the horrible way they must have died. He swiped at the tears that came into his eyes with his sleeve as he talked, and his face seemed to age a great deal.

"Then I imagined how my wife might have died. All I could think of was what that sorry piece of human trash had done to her, and that he was probably going to get away with it."

"I've not been able to talk about what happened to me in the war until now, so I guess something good has come of my shooting Lester. At least that's what Mother thinks. I tried to rid the world of bad people in the war, and in the process managed to kill children. Now I've at least tried to rid the world of something that I don't think has a right to live; that is if he killed my wife. And if he doesn't pay dearly for it, I've failed there too.

We just listened quietly. Then Mama said, "Drink your coffee Johnny, and try not to think about things that hurt so much. Who knows, maybe she's alive somewhere and you may find her yet. And as far as you shooting him, he was trying to scare us to death, seemed like to me, and that's surely a crime. Any jury will take that into account."

"No, Miss Lizabeth," Mr. Johnny said. "I believe that he killed my wife. I've believed that ever since you all told me about him. I wanted him to be tried in court for his crime, and just shot him in the leg to stop him from getting away."

Right after that he left us for the night to check on his parents.

He was there the next morning when the officers came back to look again for evidence that Lester might be involved in Mrs. Kings disappearance. They told Mama they would probably have to give Lester a light sentence, because all they could pin on him was disturbing the peace. His court hearing for this would commence after he got out of the hospital, and they expected that would be in about a week, because he had not been seriously hurt.

They told Mr. Johnny his hearing would be right after the judge heard the case involving Lester. They wished Mr. Johnny the best. They said they believed

Lester to be guilty of at least knowing something about Mrs. King's disappearance.

Our attention would be diverted for a little while now, because it was time to plant the tobacco beds. Daddy was able to work most of the day without pain in his leg. Our daily routine went back to almost normal as he was able to take up care of the traps and the fishing. Food got less scarce for the moment, and fear lessened its cold, painful grip on my heart.

Lester got out of the hospital and stayed clear of us. The police had warned him to stay away. It would be nice to just enjoy the soothing sound of rain on the tin roof without expecting to hear the menacing sound of footsteps on the porch. We talked about how frightened we were and had a good laugh.

The next week, Lester went to court and was sentenced to five days in jail for trespassing and three months probation for disturbing the peace. Things would go back to normal for a while.

Right after we seeded the plant bed, a cold snap, complete with the last snow of the season made its ugly debut. It was the second week of March, a most unusual time for snow in the south. It had been sixty degrees a couple of days before. But it had the positive effect of giving Daddy another day of rest, which seemed to be exactly what he needed to get back to his old self. Mama said it was a blessing sent from God.

About a week later, Mr. Johnny had to go to a hearing at the court house. The police said they had to do it, it was the law. Nobody expected Lester to show up to press charges, and he didn't.

Mr. Johnny's parents and Daddy spoke about his strange behaviour since coming home from the war, and Mr. Johnny told the court what had actually happened the night he shot Lester.

"I wasn't laying wait for him in particular," he said. "I just happened to be there as a matter of chance. I had no preconceived notion of hurting him. When I heard the deputy talking it dawned on me that he was indeed trying to scare the Olfson's off. It was then I realized he probably did kill my wife. I didn't mean to shoot him, but I'm glad I did. If innocent people die in a war, I think guilty people should die for something like this. You may never get the proof, but I'm convinced of his guilt, and at least he's suffered a little for his crime."

The judge listened closely to what Mr. Johnny was saying, and then handed down his decision. Mr. Johnny would have to spend some time in the State Mental Institution for shooting Lester. He said Mr. Johnny's behavior had shown he needed help that could only be had there. He said his way of thinking wasn't quite right. Mr. Johnny just hung his head and accepted the verdict without comment.

I asked Daddy if he would be going to stay where the man who murdered the girl's boyfriend in the story he had told me lived, and he said yes. That made me think Mr. Johnny might get hurt, but Daddy said the people who worked there wouldn't let anyone hurt him. "Anyhow," he said, "The man who killed that girl's friend died many years ago."

I still worried.

We would be going to see him from time to time when we could ride with his folks. They told us they couldn't afford to go more than a few times a year, and really didn't know how long he would have to stay, but felt it was for the best. Everybody seemed to think that way except Mr. Johnny and me.

Within the week Mr. Johnny was taken away to *get help* as the judge put it.

One Saturday during the first week of April, we all crammed into Mr. King's Model-T and went to see him. It was a good three hour drive. Conversation was scarce as I think everybody was anticipating what we would see at the *crazy house.* That was what the local people called the State Mental Institution. We had no idea what to expect; none of us had ever seen the place.

As if on cue, it started to rain just before we got there. It was one of those brief, violent storms that come and go at the will of the Creator. It was impossible to see more than twenty feet ahead of the car, and we almost overran the drive that turned left off the main highway. It led up to the sprawling, three-storied gray stone building that was now Mr. Johnny's home.

As we drove up that lane through the downpour, the building rose before our eyes like a giant gothic rock, with barred windows as an adornment, adhering to a façade of stone. It appeared to me to be at least a thousand years old. It became more or less visible as the swish of the windshield wipers allowed. Well established English ivy grew up its walls. Where the stone was bare of ivy, it had taken on a dreary, gray look from the rain, sending cold shivers down my spine. There was not one sign of life anywhere. That old feeling of fear gripped my insides and came up to choke me as I sat quietly with my hands clenched into fists on my lap. A scene from an old horror movie Daddy had taken me to see revived itself in my memory.

We soon discovered that I was not old enough to go inside, and no amount of talk from Daddy would persuade the lady in the starched white uniform at the door otherwise. Finally she agreed to allow Mr. Johnny to come out onto the little stone porch to see me, with an escort. She said that he had not been there long enough to warrant trust.

And so we waited there in the shelter of a small overhang, just out of the pouring rain. I was surprised when I saw him. He had that strange look in his eyes of nobody being home, just like he had the first night he had visited us. He was flanked by two of the tallest men I had seen outside of the fishermen on Captain Worthy's boats. Daddy looked like a little boy next to them.

After what seemed like an eternity, Mr. Johnny recognized me and stooped down to my eye level to speak.

"I have missed you, Liz," he said. I noted how slow and full of effort his words sounded. It was as if he were speaking from a long way off and that it was *so* difficult for him. I reached out and touched his face. It felt cold and he recoiled from me.

The two men reached down and took him by his arms, one on each side. It was time to go back inside. He rose and followed as if on command, but kept his eyes on me until he disappeared behind the door.

One of his *keepers* had one last word just before the door closed. "He'll be better when you come again." It was almost like a promise.

I cried inside all the way back to the car. Just like Mama I was ashamed to show emotion, but it was there. I managed to keep it behind the façade that made up my visible to the world face.

Mr. Johnny's Mama cried out loud, off and on, all the way home. At one point she said, "I don't know if this was the right thing to do. It seems they have taken his soul away." His Daddy said that the way he was acting might be related to the medicine they were giving him.

Not long after that, we went to the big house to help with cleaning and Aunt Lillian was also there. She told us something that made Mama angry. She said she had heard Lester's wife had said Mr. Johnny had killed his own wife and she could prove it. She had told one of Aunt Lillian's friends, who in turn, had told her. She had also said that Lester was going to the police and prove it to them.

"She's trying to put it off on him because she knows he's in a mental institution and can't protect himself," Mama said. "I've a good mind to go to the police first and tell them what she's up to. But then I don't trust them either. They might think I'm just trying to protect Johnny."

That night after supper, Daddy started out the back door to go see about Jim and Jake, like he did every night about that time, with me right behind him. I almost ran into him when he suddenly stopped and stood staring for a second. Then he shut the door and turned around. His face had lost its color, taking on a sickly shade of white. He just walked back to his chair and sat down. Mama was busy and had not seen his face as I had.

"Did you change your mind?" she asked while continuing to dry the dishes.

"There's a woman dressed in white standing behind the well," Daddy said.

Mama turned around, still drying the iron frying pan she held in her hands, to stare at him. "What did you say?" she asked.

"There's a woman standing behind the well," Daddy said again. "And she don't look like she's really there, I can see the woods through her!"

Mama sat the pan down, wiped her hands on her apron and started toward the door.

"No, don't go out there!" Daddy yelled.

Mama calmly walked on over to the door and opened it. "There is nothing out there, Andy," she said. "You're imagining things; must be left over from your being so sick with that high fever. Come on over here and look for yourself."

Daddy crept slowly over to where she was standing and peeked around the door. "Maybe I am seeing things, Elizabeth," he said. "I'd sure like to think so."

We went on out the door and checked on the mules, but we didn't linger. We were back inside with the door shut within fifteen minutes.

Mama left the lamp burning as bright as it would again that night, for the first time since we found out about Lester.

## Chapter 12

The spring and summer of 1944 went by with its share of disasters and joys for us that were consistent with the nomad's way of life. Although we *had* stayed put, at least, for that short period of time.

Mama finally found a church that didn't look down on us for being poverty stricken, as about everybody there was in the same proverbial boat. And it was close enough for us to walk. Daddy still refused to go. Mama and I went every Sunday and prayed for Daddy and Mr. Johnny, along with an array of other requests from Mama.

I never saw any visible results from most of those requests, but I supposed it would eventually be done. I did make note of the fact that Mama always modified the prayer by saying: "If the Lord wills it." The trouble with that was that I couldn't see any reason to *ask* if He was going to do it or not at His will anyway.

"I do know you're a child of the devil!" Mama would always say with a shake of her pretty head, when I made a statement to that slant.

I was *so* excited about going to school that year. By the last of August I could hardly restrain myself. I asked Mama every morning if the day was near. Apparently she grew very tired of me asking. She finally told me if I asked one more time, she would tie me to a chair and gag me. I kinda *knew* she would, so I made every effort to only ask when she was in a good mood after that.

I was up and ready to go well before daylight that first morning. Mama had combed my long hair and tied it back with a twine string, creating a pony tail that hung down past my shoulders.

She helped me dress in my little white frock, and gave me the lard bucket with a couple of white, fluffy biscuits, filled with collards. Then she walked down to the end of the lane with me to wait for the big yellow bus.

We didn't have to wait long. Within a few short minutes it came lumbering up the dirt road, already half full of young students, some like me, headed for their first day of school. I watched Mama standing there waving until the bus was out of sight.

I wasn't the youngest child on the bus, but I was the smallest. That's the morning I found out that being the smallest meant to be abused, unless you could defend yourself.

As soon as Mama disappeared around the corner, the little boy in the seat directly behind me started in.

"Mama's little baby," he began, in a sing-song tone, and the other children took up the chant, "Mama's little baby." They were all looking at me.

I was bewildered by this attention. I just didn't understand. Why were they picking on me? I turned and stared out the window trying to pretend I hadn't noticed. They stopped when the bus driver finally told them to shut up.

I didn't know there would be so much to get used to. One of my biggest hurdles that day was to remember the number on the side of the bus that was to take me home. I hadn't counted on there being so many of those big yellow buses!

My life until that day had been spent with two loving parents who had, for the most part, kept me away from people who would hurt me. Usually, the only time I had come in contact with the outside world was while I was in the safety of their company. Today, I was to learn why Daddy had not wanted me to go to school. It would be a bitter lesson.

The dirty brick building loomed up in front of me. I didn't have a clue which door to go in. There were two on the side where I got off the bus. Grasping my little dinner bucket I went in the first door I came to. I remembered that was the one Mama and I had used when they had sent me home saying I was too small to attend. I solemnly wished that were the case that morning.

I found a room with a sign saying: ***Miss Hudson's First Grade*** up over the door. It was then I realized the advantage of being able to read, and silently thanked Daddy for teaching me. I was standing there wondering what to do next when I noticed I wasn't alone. Several other kids were slowly gathering around that door. They seemed as confused as I was. That apparent fact made me feel better, somehow.

A pretty young woman wearing a plaid wool skirt, a starched white blouse and a big smile, came to the door when the bell sounded and ushered us in. "Please sit down children," she directed, and I took a chair at a table in the back of the room, right next to a window I could gaze out of. "My name is Miss Hudson," she said. "I will be your teacher this year."

I didn't learn much that morning. I was too busy trying to remember the number on the side of that bus. Luckily I already knew the few things she was trying to get across. I think, mainly, she just wanted to get us acquainted with a routine and each other.

At recess I found out where the bathroom was. I knew about inside toilets because of the movie theater, Aunt Kathleen's house, and Captain Worthy's boat. But it was still kinda strange, using the bathroom inside, I mean. To me the little lean-to over by the woods with the half-moon carved out at the top of the door was more comfortable. It seemed more natural to go outside.

Recess was a lonely venture for me that day. I didn't seem to fit in with the other kids. All I wanted to do was go home. I found a place near the trees at the edge of the playground and sat down there by myself. The other children bunched up together to share their misery, I guess. I didn't have anything I wanted to share.

As I sat there I noticed a small path that led over the railroad tracks to the school for black children and I thought about my friend Barbara. I was glad recess was over about that time because the memory was too painful.

At precisely three o'clock the bell rang and the teacher dismissed us for the day. "See you children tomorrow. And oh, don't forget to tell your parents if they don't know, you need a dollar for books by the end of next week". I wondered where my parents would get that kind of money.

I had made up my mind that day that I wasn't going to just sit quietly if those kids started in on me that afternoon. And they did.

The little boy who started the chant that morning sat down in the seat next to me.

"How did the little baby do on its first day in school?"

I just stared at him.

"Does it want its bottle?" he asked, getting in my face and promptly sticking his dirty finger in my mouth. I bit it to the bone. The blood poured and he started screaming, "She bit me!"

The bus driver pulled over and stopped. He came back to inspect the situation. I was scared until I noticed he was holding back laughter. "You know I'll have to tell your Mama about this," he warned me.

Then he said, "You go sit with someone more your size young man, this little girl is too much for you. And if I catch you near her again I'll see to it that you are expelled from my bus this entire year. Do you understand me? I know your parents don't care what you do, but I drive this bus, and you will not terrioze this child again."

When I got off the bus Mama was standing there waiting for me, and true to his word the driver told her what had happened. We talked about it walking up the lane. She told me there were better ways to deal with problems, but was unable to tell me what they were at that moment. Finally she said, "If you bite him again, I'll have to tell your Daddy."

I had a question for Mama but didn't feel like it was the time to ask. It had occurred to me while I was sitting by myself at recess. I was thinking about how Barbara and I had planned to play together at recess if allowed, after we started to school. Eventually I'd ask her that question, that is, why all us kids didn't go to the same school. Our parents all worked the fields together during the week, why was there a difference?

I had taken for granted her explanation of, *that's just the way it is,* when I questioned why Barbara hadn't been allowed to go to the movies with us. I also wanted to know why she had not been allowed to drink from that fountain on Market Street where I drank water on a hot Saturday afternoon. The one with the sign that said *whites only.* Somehow her explanation didn't do it for me anymore.

That next Saturday we went to visit Bet's grave site like we always did. It was a little later than usual. We had gone just after dinner because Mama and I had helped Mrs. Williams with her cleaning that morning.

Mama had gathered wildflowers from the yard where they grew in beautiful profusion, as if they knew she loved them. She carried them carefully in her arms, and she and Daddy placed them in the ground just below Bet's little cross.

After we left the grave site, well before we reached the yard, we heard the mules making strange, frightened sounds. All of a sudden Daddy stopped and stood very still as if listening to something.

"There's a storm brewin', Elizabeth," he said. "Have you noticed there are no birds anywhere this mornin'? Let's go down to the creek and see if there are any down there."

The sky was gray and murky looking. Everything was still and quiet as we made our way to the creek. Daddy was right; there were no birds on the wing anywhere. There were no animals of any kind visible.

"This is gonna be a bad one; we'd better batten down the hatches."

It was September fourteenth, 1944.

When we got back to the house, Daddy turned the radio on. We had been saving the battery until Saturday night so we could listen to *The Grand Old Opry,* but we needed to hear the weather report if there was one.

For the longest time there was only country music, and then a man came on and said there was a storm coming. He said it would probably be hitting the coast early this evening with high winds with flooding in low lying areas.

As I've noted before, storms are frequent along the coast of North Carolina, and had been particularly active during the last decade. We knew what to do. Daddy took Jim and Jake up to the boss's house where they could get to higher ground and set them free. Then he and Mama picked up all the things in the yard that could be dangerous in a high wind and brought them inside. He propped the ladder up against the roof and secured it there so it couldn't blow away in case we needed it.

Mama stored everything she could up high, off the floor. I noted how carefully she stowed Bets little clothes.

She made sure they were as safe from the possibility of rising water as they could be. Daddy brought a full bucket of drinking water in and Mama started cooking a big pot of beans before the wind began showing what it could do to mere humans. Smoke from the chimney swirled downward and blew in at the windows. "That's the way it does when the heavens are in a tumult," Daddy remarked.

"Leave the radio on, Elizabeth, get all the information you can before it goes dead," he said, "I'm goin' over to Aunt Lillian's house to see if she needs help with gittin' ready. She might want to come over here and ride it out with us. I'm sure she don't want to be there by herself."

"She won't come Andy," Mama said, "You know how she feels about this place."

"Well, I'm gonna try anyway," Daddy said on his way out the door.

I watched him leave from the window. He paused at the edge of the yard, took his old straw hat off and held it up as high as his arm would stretch. I could tell the wind was coming from the northeast by the way it tilted. A sudden gust took it out of his hand and sent it sailing across the yard, with Daddy right behind it.

Before he could retrieve his hat and leave for Miss Lillian's, the wind was swirling through the tree tops like a giant hand playing tricks on Mother Nature. I stepped out on the porch and felt the air, suddenly cool and damp, as if it would go right through you if you stood still. The sky seemed muddier and closer to the earth than it had been earlier.

By three o'clock, Daddy was back without Aunt Lillian. I was not surprised. He said he had helped her to put things away safely and thought she would be okay. By then the wind was blowing steady from the east, bending trees sideways as easily as a smoker under pressure could bend a book of pocket matches.

"It sounds like a howlin' banshee," Daddy stated.

"That's an old wives tale Andy," Mama said. "You shouldn't talk like that, there's no such thing as a howling banshee." She nodded her head toward me, giving him that, *don't you dare be telling her those old stories,* look.

"It's a true thing, not an old wives tale Elizabeth," Daddy said. "The story comes from Ireland. They say that shortly before somebody dies, this ghost of a woman comes around and starts howlin' at that door. Before mornin', any sick person in the house passes away. They say it's the spirit of the death maiden come to take the soul and I believe it."

Mama just shrugged her shoulders and didn't say anything else.

Daddy said Aunt Lillian told him she had heard about this storm on the radio earlier. She said the storm was a hurricane, and it had first been detected three or four days ago, northeast of the Lesser Antilles. It was moving west-northwest and had become a major hurricane as of the twelfth of September.

She said the Miami Hurricane Warning Office had given that Hurricane a name. It was the first time that had been done. Up until then those monstrous storms were just known as hurricanes, nor'easters, or something like that. This one was to be named: *The Great Atlantic Hurricane*.

I sat by the window and watched as the wild wind grew to hurricane status. It was *screaming* around our little shack. I believe it would have blown it over, had it not been for the trees creating a buffer zone. You have to experience the sound and fury of that wind to say you know about hurricanes. Once heard, one can never forget.

I watched as some of the tops of the trees at the edge of the woods were cruelly twisted off and hurled through the air. Then the rains came in a blinding curtain of water. The big ditch in the back yard overflowed quickly. Within the hour an inch or two of water had spilled over its banks.

Mama used all the containers she had to catch the drips coming through the roof. As they filled up she would have Daddy open the back door so she could throw the water into the yard. At times the wind would almost tear the door out of his hands. Good thing it was blowing in a direction away from the back door; otherwise Mama might have been drowned in the backwash. It looked to me like they let more water in than they threw out anyway; it was raining so hard through the open door.

Blackie came over and crawled up on my lap. He curled into a ball and went to sleep. I cuddled him and got more worried as time passed. The wind just kept getting louder until it was useless to try and talk to each other. By four o'clock the old shack was trembling, threatening to come down around us. Mama had long since stopped trying to cook, letting the fire go out, saying she would start it up again when the storm broke.

I thought about Blackie and wondered what would happen to him if the house did blow down. It was then I got the idea. There was a place where he would be safe; in the oven of the cook stove. I put him in there and closed the door. Then I went back to the living room to watch the storm from the window where I had a ring side seat.

The storm lasted about four hours, including the lull that occurred when the eye went over. When the winds finally abated, Mama went back to the kitchen to finish cooking the beans. She built the fire up again. When it was getting right hot, she came to the living room door and asked Daddy if he knew where *that cat* was. "I do declare I can hear him and he sounds like he's in mortal danger, but I can't locate him." Then she turned to me and asked, "Where's that cat?"

It was then I remembered where he was! I half ran, half stumbled to the stove and opened it up. Blackie must have jumped ten feet, right past my head, and started climbing the curtains.

Mama sprang for the cat. He was busy at the moment trying his best to get out of a closed window. He was very intent, clinging to the curtains, scratching the glass, screeching, ears slanted back, eyes glittering.

Daddy was laughing so hard he was bent double and I was thinking about bolting for the door myself, storm or no storm, when Mama finally got a hold on Blackie. She held him with his eyes covered by her apron until he calmed down; then turned her attention on me.

I ran for Daddy, believing the only hope for my life at that point was in his hands. It was then I noticed she was laughing. With an amused expression on her face she asked me why I had put him in the oven. I remained on Daddy's knee while I told her. She gave Blackie to me to hold and told me to never do such a thing again.

Along about that time, Daddy seemed to feel the need to tell one of his stories. I knew by the tone of his voice it was to be a ghost story. I cuddled up on his lap with Blackie to listen.

"Son," he began, "There comes a time when a man must stand his ground. This story's about a man who did just that durin' a big storm on the Island. He was a rather young man and he and his wife didn't have no young'un. They lived in a rather isolated spot out there, and had weathered many storms the elements had thrown at them over the years. She died the day before of pneumonia, I believe. He had buried her where she wanted to be buried, in their yard."

"The next day a storm blew in, and all his neighbors tried to get him to leave, because by all accounts, this was to be a very big one. They told him his wife would want him to go to a safe place, and that he needed to save himself for his friend's sake. They even told him God wanted him to leave, to no avail. He wouldn't go."

He said, "I won't leave her here to face this storm alone. I'm stayin' with her as I always have, come hell or high water!"

"Then he sat down in her rockin' chair to wait. He sat there alone, rockin', with the wind howlin' and water beginnin' to seep through the cracks in the floor. He had accepted the fact that he would soon be back with his beautiful wife when he heard a knockin' sound at the door; *knock, knock, knock*... He thought to himself that a neighbor must have stayed behind to die with him. How foolish was that? Well, he would get rid of him in a hurry, before it was too late to get to higher ground. He rushed over to open the door with the words he would say ready to spill out. To his amazement, there was nobody there. Then his gaze went slowly to his feet where a casket was bumpin' into the threshold. *Knock, knock, knock*... It seemed to be quite new."

"*It's my wife*, he thought, and made an effort to move it back to where she was buried. He wasn't thinkin' too clearly, you see. The water level was already too high, reachin' to the man's waist. He stumbled and fell across her coffin. Then he shut his eyes and clutchin' the coffin with all his strength, waited to die. He was not afraid, just sad and lonely. He fell asleep that way."

"The next day he was found. He had washed up on the mainland, still huggin' that coffin. When he gained enough strength to speak, he insisted they open it. And guess who it was; his very own little wife, and there was a smile on her face! Oh, another thing, his graying hair had turned snow white overnight. Nobody ever knew just how that happened. By all accounts, he lived to be *very* old. All that knew him say he seemed happy all the rest of his life, and when he died, it was with a beautiful smile on his face."

"You see, Son, storms like this carry with them some miracles as well as the death and destruction they cause. Life is like that. The bad things that happen are always balanced with some good. Now go play with Blackie, and don't worry about things you can't do nothin' about."

Around five o'clock we were able to venture outside to see the damage. Daddy took some boards from the edge of the front porch and nailed them up over the places where the wind had torn the tar paper covering off. In those places there were cracks in the wall large enough to see through.

It was around five-thirty when we noticed water was beginning to spring up from the ground, like small fountains, and there was no place for it to drain. The ground was saturated and the ditches were full. It had started to rise! Within an hour it was five inches deep. Then it was up to the top step by the back door!

It wasn't until Mama saw a snake swimming toward the house that she decided it was time for us to go up higher. That was why Daddy had propped the ladder up to the roof. Thank God it had stopped raining.

Mama got the water bucket; Daddy brought Blackie and three blankets and we went up on the roof. We spent that night and until near noon the next day up there before the water receded below the floor of the shack.

The storm left its mark. Daddy had to use a shovel to get all the debris, snakes and bugs out. He and Mama spent most of that day cleaning before she would be satisfied that it was good enough for us to sleep in that night. We never even stopped to eat, we just fell into bed; I was so tired I don't even remember when.

## Chapter 13

We slowly recovered from the storm along with everybody else. There was no other choice. We were already accustomed to the survival way of life due to the economy at the time. Very few amenities were available in the form of comfortable living; surviving this disaster was just another link in the chain of misery we were all too familiar with. Things were looking pretty bleak to me until I remembered Captain Worthy and the long awaited, *last hunt*, for Blackbeard's treasure.

Daddy had been to town with Mr. Williams on business and had gone to see the Captain. They had renewed their desire to try hunting for treasure close to Springer's Point, near Ocracoke Island. The plan was to search around the old watering hole that had been a point of interest to treasure hunters for many years. That had been the last place Blackbeard and his crew had been seen, just before the fatal battle with Lieutenant Maynard.

The story goes that Blackbeard had not long before returned from a second trip to the coast of Florida. It was there he had forced his crew to dive for sunken treasure spilled from a Spanish galleon that had wrecked during a storm. As a matter of fact, a lot of vessels had taken up there to dive for the treasure. The ship lay in international waters and was therefore open to any vessel wanting to get in on the search for treasure on it.

It had been surmised, that one of his reasons for being again in North Carolina waters so late in the year, was to obtain a pardon offered by King George I. Ordinarily they would have been down south where the weather and the women were friendlier. Apparently he wanted to get *his* pardon from Governor Eden.

Captain Worthy thought the reason might have been partly due to a friendship between the secretary of the colony, Tobias Knight, Governor Eden and Blackbeard. And it may have been. Apparently, Blackbeard thought they might overlook the fact that he had been known to have continued his pirating ways since the deadline set for the pardon. According to law, the pardon had to be applied for prior to the first of January that year, in order to be effective. That deadline had already past.

Our final treasure hunt was to be in a place Captain Worthy thought Blackbeard might have hidden some of his loot from that ship. It was to be at the end of September, and I was to go with them. The exact details and who would go with us would be determined at a later date, Daddy said.

How to keep all this information from Mama was another story. He said we mustn't lie to her, so we simply told her we were going dredging for oysters along the Pamlico to the outer banks, for a little extra money. And we *were* going to dredge for oysters, as a way of covering the treasure hunting activity. We weren't really certain if it was legal or not. We did assume the law would probably take it away from us if we told them where we found the treasure, should we find any.

We went to town that next Saturday by train, as Daddy had secured a little money from helping Mr. Williams over the past week. Leaving Mama at the store picking out staples we could afford, we made a trip over to the boat to talk with Captain Worthy. We needed to decide who would go with us on our next great adventure.

Captain Worthy wanted to invite three of his trusted fisherman, and the now familiar *warlock*, Mr. Nathaniel. Daddy didn't want to take anybody with us but said he

realized we had to have a crew to handle the boat. And
having a crew was a good way to make it look like we were
indeed going out dredging for oysters.

I didn't like Mr. Nathaniel being in on it; but being
just a child I kept my mouth shut. I was pushing my luck
anyway; Daddy had already done something for me that
Mama didn't altogether agree with. He was going to lie
about me being sick, so I could stay out of school for the
next week, assuming that this trip might take at least that
long. He said the trip would be as educational as going to
school. Mama said she didn't think so, but for some reason
went along with the plan anyway. I was very grateful.

There were lots of preparations to make, as well as
some work around the farm to be done before the trip took
place. I had learned a little patience, but it was still all I
could do to keep from spilling the beans, so to speak,
before the time arrived. Mama seemed to take notice but
didn't say anything. I got on her nerves so badly at one
point that she ushered me out of *her* kitchen. I left with a
chip on my shoulder because she had just begun making
one of her molasses cakes, and I wanted to lick the spoon.

I went out behind the well and sat down on the
ground, staring into the woods behind the house, sulking.
It was then that I started scrapping away the dirt from a soft
place with my fingers. I was often fidgeting like that. All
of a sudden I saw something shiny and started digging with
both hands. I was rewarded with a small, shiny chain with
a locket attached. It surely was a pretty thing. I brushed
the dirt away and put it around my neck, under my collar,
assuming Mama would take it away from me if she saw it.
I knew it wasn't mine and I couldn't keep it, but I would
wear it for a while before I turned it over to her to find its
owner.

Daddy kept me as busy as he could to keep me from
accidentally telling Mama about the treasure hunt. When

he wasn't asking me to help him clean up the yard he was keeping me with him while he fed the mules, or walking over to the boss's house to see about any available jobs around the farm. I was with him at all times. That by itself was making Mama suspicious. I caught her looking at Daddy with a question in her eyes many times over the next few days.

On the day before the trip was scheduled, Daddy suggested we go to town with Mr. Williams, go to a movie, and spend the night with Mama's sister, Aunt Kathleen. He said we *really* needed the extra money this fishing trip would supply. Mama couldn't deny that fact.

As a rule, Daddy would have never set foot in Aunt Kathleen's house. They never saw eye to eye on anything. It was difficult for them to spend an hour with each other, much less a whole night. But that time it seemed there was no alternative.

Since Mr. Johnny had gone away to the hospital, we were at the mercy of whoever was going to town when we needed to go. This ride with Mr. Williams was the only one available at the time, so we made use of the opportunity and went to town with him on Friday.

To say the least, it was a memorable night. Along about ten o'clock we were preparing for bed when the shrill screaming of a siren blasted the air. It was a blackout. Mama had told me about them, but having always lived in the country I had not experienced it yet.

Since the war started, a patrol had been set up to protect the population. It was made up of a group of citizens. They were to conduct drills at regular intervals to prevent Washington, N.C. from being seen by enemy airplanes, I was told by Aunt Kathleen. Citizens were supposed to extinguish all lights so the town couldn't be seen from the air, making us a target for bombing. That happened to be one of those chosen nights. And there I was with my God awful fear of total darkness.

I knew about the war and the fact that we might be bombed at any time, as Mama had so eloquently put it, so I knew the drill was a necessary evil. That knowledge did nothing to quell my fear of the dark.

Aunt Kathleen went into action. "We have to turn off all the lights now," she said. "I know Liz is afraid of the dark. Put her under the table."

"You have to stay under there until I tell you to come out," she told me curtly as she shoved me under the table. Then she hurriedly placed a lamp under there with me. Mama covered the table with a couple of quilts to hide the light.

After a few minutes the sirens stopped and things got deathly quiet, except for the voices of the wardens as they traveled along the street outside our window. Mama said they were looking for any lights, and listening for airplanes. She reminded me that they would arrest us if they saw a light, whether I was afraid of the dark or not.

By the time they took me out, I was sweating profusely, and the odor of kerosene filled my lungs.

Needless to say, I didn't sleep much the remainder of that night.

Well before dawn Saturday morning, Daddy and I set out on foot, heading for the docks where we would embark on our *fishing trip* on the lovely *Miss Catherine*. A dense fog enveloped us as we made our way through town. Daddy took that opportunity to recall a story about Jack the Ripper, and likened the fog to that of England in his time. I closed the distance between us as we moved along, and kept looking behind me as I could almost discern the cold, dead breath of the Ripper down my neck.

It felt as if we were the only two people in the world. If it hadn't been for the ability to see the street directly under our feet, I don't believe we could have found the boat. We would have probably had to wait until after daybreak. Swirls of mists clouded everything, making the boat seem surreal, kinda like a ghost ship, when she finally appeared. Captain Worthy had hoisted a lantern on the stern so we could see her. The only sound we heard as she took shape before our eyes was the clanging of the bell on the channel buoy. On mornings like that the sound could be heard for miles. It seemed to carry better on air heavy with fog. It was speaking out a warning to the mariners brave enough to creep out onto the river under those conditions.

We encountered not a live soul on our way to the waterfront, until we got on board *Miss Catherine*. The pungent odor of coffee brewing felt like a good omen coming from the cabin where the crew waited for us. Mr. Nathaniel showed up shortly thereafter, and we were ready to depart.

After a hurried hello on all parts, we weighed anchor and so began our *final* treasure hunt, hopefully to find some of Blackbeard's plunder. We were headed for Springer's Point near Ocracoke Island.

I insisted on perching on the rail near the stern, so Captain Worthy found me an old sou'wester and threw it over my shoulders. The fog was so thick my hair was quickly saturated. It was hanging down my back in wet strings. Mama had not tied it up for me like she usually did. That served as testimony to her overall objection to this trip. The smelly old oil skin coat felt mighty good.

I sat there and drank black coffee, listening to the sound of fog horns, directing the path of those who had already ventured out. I was paying special attention to the crew. They were talking about the dangers of being out on the water on a morning like that. The river harbored many obstacles to travelers that early in the morning, in such foggy conditions. It would be difficult to avoid the shoals, and the occasional log that floated downriver, half submerged.

We moved ever so slowly through the water, not even fast enough to leave a visible wake, until we got through the opening at the railroad trestle. Getting through was very treacherous that morning. We were in that *darkest just before dawn* time of day. It was so precarious the gatekeeper and the Captain forgot to speak to each other. We were so close to the pilings under the railroad that I could have reached out and touched them as we passed by, had I wanted to.

After we past the Pamlico Point Shoal Lighthouse, and were entering the Pamlico Sound, Captain Worthy came and sat down beside me. He was in one of his story telling moods. This time, of course, it was about Blackbeard.

"Little Liz, there was a time when Blackbeard traveled these waters as a young man. I think that was well before he became a pirate, because I believe he lived here as a child. From the history I have heard, I believe his family were friends with Tobias Knight, and maybe with Governor Charles Eden, as well."

"You remember, I told you about a supposed sister of his named Susanna, who lived around here. I still believe he left some of his treasure buried for her. It may have been we missed it the last time because we were looking in the wrong place. At any rate, you remember what happened with that; we are not going back there again. The place we are going today is near the ocean where it is less likely that we'll get involved in nests of snakes when we dig. There will be, however, flying insects to pester us to death, so hang onto your hat child, we're in for an adventure this trip!"

I couldn't help but remember how the insects had ceased to be apparent, along with all the other creatures of

the swamp, at the time of our last treasure hunt.  Perhaps he
hadn't noticed, but I had.

Shortly after that, Captain Worthy asked the crew to
join him and Daddy in the wheel house, as he had
something to tell them.

"It's like this," he started out.  "For a long time
now, Andy, Mr. Nathaniel and I have been discussing
hunting for treasure out around Ocracoke Island.  That is
the main objective of this trip.  We need absolute secrecy.  I
would trust any one of you with my life, that's why I
brought you on this trip.  Anything we find we will share
equally, of course, but you must swear to never talk about
this trip to a single soul.  If we were to find anything, it
may not be exactly lawful for us to keep it. Do I have your
solemn promise on that?"

Mr. Nathaniel had hung back and was standing at
the door, smoking a cigarette, listening intently to the
conversation.  Luke, the surly old fisherman who always
had something to say against children and black people on
board a working boat, had been staring at him with a
questioning look.  Now he asked Captain Worthy right out
loud, "Why is *he* coming along on this trip?"

"Because I want him here and it's my boat," replied
Captain Worthy.

The old fisherman stopped staring and started
asking questions like why he and the other two fishermen
weren't told before we left the dock where we were headed.
"I thought we were going dredging for oysters, I'm not
certain I'd have come along if I'd know'd about this," he
said.  The other two men stood silent, listening like Mr.
Nathaniel.

"I knew you had a young wife and she has an eye
for pretty things," Captain Worthy said.  "And I knew if we
found something you would be in a much better position to
keep her.  I've heard the rumors as to how she's threatened

to leave you if you don't improve your position financially, Luke. I figured you would want to do this. You're a man of your word if I've ever known one, as are John-john and Steven here. Hell, man, we may all come out of this rich, you can't never tell! And, by the way, we *are* going dredging for oysters, as well."

Captain Worthy slapped Luke on his shoulder, in a *good old boy* way, and the tension eased a little. Luke said he would appreciate it if he were told the next time so he could make up his own mind. John-John and Steven were sworn to secrecy along with Luke, and all seemed to be okay for the moment.

It wasn't long before the sky had lightened up and we were ready to dredge for oysters. The hold was waiting, and so was I. We worked along the edge of the river, not because we couldn't dredge the center as there were oysters out there too, it was just the choice of the Captain at that particular time. I loved to watch them drop the wedges and pull them along the bottom to capture the oysters. I loved eating my fill of them too, and knew that was part of the rewards of the day. You always ate from the catch. That was part of the fisherman's life style.

We dredged until we had the cargo hold half full and the boat lay lower in the water.

Then it was time to eat and drink. The Captain found a nice spot and we dropped anchor. It was coffee for me and moonshine for the crew. Daddy helped me shuck my oysters and we ate them directly out of the shell with hot sauce poured over them. We tossed the empty shells back into the river.

The men mellowed out and began to talk excitedly about the week that lay ahead of us. Personal stories about Blackbeard and his exploits began to emerge. It seemed to me that about everybody claimed a special interest in the pirate. They all had their stories of gruesome deeds perpetrated by him and his crew on the high seas. I couldn't help but notice, though, that they were told with pride, almost as if they were talking about Robin Hood, or some other historical figure, who had robbed the rich and given to the poor. This crew had apparently decided that Blackbeard belonged to the Robin Hood group and was to be admired by poor people.

Eventually the conversation got around to some of the more nasty stories. Like the one about the silver plated cup. It was supposed to be the actual skull of Blackbeard himself, from which people of a certain cult were supposed to drink at scheduled meetings.

I listened until I got bored and started watching the shoreline drift back and forth, as *Miss Catherine* silently complained about being fettered by an anchor. I tuned the crew out and enjoyed the warmth of the sun, allowing my imagination to soar with the soft wind blowing across my face. The gentle rocking of the boat and seagulls soaring and dipping with the warm air currents lifted my consciousness from the mundane to the sublime. Time went by without meaning until the silence was broken by Daddy calling out to me.

"If you don't straighten up Son, you're gonna fall in the river," he was saying.

It was then I realized I was leaning precariously close to the point of no return. In another few seconds I would have tumbled head over heels overboard.

I often created stories from beginning to end in my sleep, and sometimes, like just then, I day dreamed during the day. It was my way of recreating circumstances to better fit my need for entertainment at the time.

Daddy went back to discussing the day's events with the crew, while I slowly returned to the situation at hand.

The cargo hold was as full of oysters as we wanted, and we couldn't eat another bite, so we weighed anchor and continued our trip at full speed, toward Ocracoke Island. We would sell the haul from the docks when we got back to Washington.

"That is if we don't have to empty it out so we can fill it with gold bullion," Daddy said with a laugh. I think he was just along for the ride, as usual. I don't believe he thought or even cared if we found anything. To him it was just another way to spend some happy time with his friends for a little while. It certainly was a good way to put the sad situation regarding the war off for a bit.

The dredge with the wire mesh net had been hoisted up and was swinging in the breeze as we picked up speed. The attention of the whole crew became fixed on our destination now.

We were well on our way down the Pamlico Sound when the conversation began to be centered on what each person would do with their share of the treasure, should they find any.

"I'm going to fix up *Miss Catherine* like she ain't never been fixed up before. She'll be the sleekest vessel in the fleet this coming year," Captain Worthy said. "She's been needing repairs for a while. Now she's going to get the fix up of her life."

Luke said he was going to buy his pretty wife a new dress that she had been wanting. "She's been wearing the same two dresses that she made herself for too long; it's time she got a new one from the store," he said, kinda wisfully.

"I'm gonna buy myself a gallon of good corn whiskey, and stay dead drunk for a solid week," John-John said.

Steven said it hadn't occurred to him what to do with his share yet. "I'll wait and see if we actually find something, I'm not counting my chickens before they hatch."

Then it was Daddy's turn to say what he was going to do with his share, but he didn't get to say it. *Miss Catherine*, which nobody was paying particular attention to at the moment, struck hard into the sand of the Middle Ground Shoal she had been skirting.

I lunged forward, fell and went sliding face down across the floor, with Daddy right behind me. The men, who had been so jovial just a moment before, started cursing and went into action. The craft lay still and was leaning slightly to port. I scrambled to my feet and stood clinging to the pole that held the tackle and boom which was swinging dangerously above my head.

For weathered seamen who had plied these waters for years, to run aground on *this* sand shoal, which had been known about for centuries, was an unforgivable embarrassment.

Captain Worthy and Daddy kicked off their shoes and jumped into the water at about the same time, one on each side of the boat. They went out of sight under *Miss Catherine* while the rest of the crew scrambled to see the damage on board. Daddy popped up first and reported the hull on the right side was okay, and then the Captain emerged to announce no damage that he could see on the left.

"She's leaning into the sand on her left side but I can't see any cracks. The old girl is built tough. When the tide comes in, maybe we can slide her off, if the wind is with us. There's nothing we can do but wait for now. It wouldn't be so much a problem if she wasn't half full of oysters, but I sure don't want to lose them," Captain Worthy stated.

The crew agreed that the loss of the catch would indeed be a disaster, so we decided to not try and lighten her by throwing over the oysters as Luke suggested.  No, we'd wait.

There wasn't much to do except eat and tell tall tales while we waited for high tide.  We'd had about all the oysters we could stand for one day, so we opened some cans of potted meat, Vienna sausage and crackers. While we ate we savored the telling of all the sea roving stories the men knew.

I entertained myself by feeding seagulls that were storming the boat, begging for crumbs.  I held up crackers, one at the time, and watched as they worked up the nerve to dive and snatch them out of my hand.

Luke suddenly stood up and made his way toward the cabin with a comment slung carelessly over his shoulder. "Who wants to play a game of poker?"

Everybody except Mr. Nathaniel and I took him up on the offer.   They followed Luke to sit around the table which at the moment was tilting dangerously at quite an angle.  The men, it seemed, were embarrassed enough already.  They certainly weren't going to say anything about having to sit lop-sided.  Seating themselves on the benches that were bolted to the floor, they pretended they didn't notice they were leaning a bit as the captain dealt the cards.

Mr. Nathaniel and I sat on opposite sides of the aft deck and tried to ignore each other as much as humanly possible.  Once when our eyes accidentally met, Mr. Nathaniel pointedly and with much ado, adjusted the cross that hung around his neck as he tried to stare me down with those deep set black eyes of his.  That was darned near impossible as I was really good at the stare down game myself.

The crew was playing the familiar old game of five card stud with the captain winning right along when the second streak of bad luck arrived.

Toward the east, a menacing cloud cover was showing its ugly face. Nor'easters did not usually follow on the tail of a hurricane, but that looked and felt, for all the world, like a nor'easter. It had wind with it and was coming from the east, advancing toward the west. Regular storms could pounce on you unawares, unlike this thing coming over the horizon. Nor'easters usually let you know they're coming, they don't sneak up on you, I mean.

Perhaps the wind tide that accompanied this one would help propel us off the shoal. In any case, we had no choice but to grit our teeth and wait.

"I hate to say it, but I believe you all know, females and blacks ain't got no business on a working vessel. All they do is bring bad luck. I ain't never seen it fail. Well, I hope you're satisfied," Luke stated, to no one in particular.

"Why don't you keep your fat mouth shut Luke," Captain Worthy said. "If *you* haven't brought us bad luck yet, I don't expect that young'un nor Mr. Nathaniel will, and that's a fact."

Luke did shut up, but he was sullen as we waited for the wind to do its job, maybe.

The Captain went to the wheel house while the rest of us huddled together in the corner of the cabin, watching the storm in the eastern sky approaching. It was rising like a dooms day holocaust, shadowing the world in darkness as it marched westward.

When we felt the craft shudder and begin to sway slightly, Captain Worthy started the engine and put it in reverse, helping the wind to pull her free. Or so we hoped. It did and we headed down the Pamlico Sound as fast as ever we could, hoping to get to a safe harbor before the big storm set in. We didn't make it. We found ourselves holding on for dear life, riding up one side and down the other of eight foot waves brought on by the wind tide on the edge of a nor'easter.

That's the way the Pamlico Sound is, sweet when she's sweet; a holy terror in the horrendous storms that arise from time to time.

*Miss Catherine* was riding the waves easy though, spewing salt spray over the craft after she crested the top of a wave and hit the bottom of the trough in between. Even though I was accustomed to riding the waves in a storm during fishing trips with the Captain, this time something about the rhythmic rise and fall was coming close to making me throw up. "Close your eyes, don't watch the water," Daddy warned. "It'll just make you feel sicker."

I clung to the table and tried to roll with the waves, keeping my eyes shut like Daddy said. I only opened them once when it felt like the boat was surely turning over.

"Don't worry Son," Daddy said with a laugh, "*Miss Catherine* was built for just such a gale as this, she's rode out a lot worse and come out of it smelling like a rose every time."

At the moment his words carried little comfort with them. As long as the boat seemed to be trying to throw me overboard, I wasn't satisfied that our lives were worth a plug nickel!

The storm only lasted about fifteen minutes, total, although it seemed a lot longer to me. When the rain abated and the sun came out, I felt that the bad luck streak had been broken.

The crew settled down to their usual shipboard chores afterward, leaving me and Mr. Nathaniel alone for a while. That is, back to treating us like we didn't exist. And so, the afternoon wore on.

We were hoping to arrive at Springer's Point under cover of darkness, not wanting to be seen in case we found anything of value. But not so dark as to render us incapable of landing at the precise place we wanted to be, near where the old watering hole was located.

We came in just past dusk, and a pretty sunset it was that day. In the west the sky had taken on a purple glow. The eastern sky was already dark enough to begin showing stars.

Meanwhile, the breeze was holding steady at a moderate gale, and was very cool to bare skin. I got out the sou'wester Captain Worthy had given me early that morning and pulled it around my shoulders. I also took time to give silent thanks for the little row boat that would be my taxi to shore. (a result of Mama's teaching, that is, to give God thanks for all the good things that happen to us every day, lest tomorrow we forget)

I didn't relish the thought of getting wet again in this temperature. I didn't even think the upcoming bonfire would be sufficient to warm me under those circumstances.

I scrambled into the skiff with the rest of the crew and we paddled ashore. The sand felt good between the toes of my bare feet as I stepped out. It was going to be an exciting night. My thoughts went briefly to Mr. Johnny. I wished desperately he were there, he would have enjoyed it as much as I did.

## Chapter 14

We built a roaring bonfire and warmed ourselves against the chill of the September air. Then we pitched our tents on the sand and began to consider trying to find the *well* before it got too dark to see. None of us had seen it, just heard about it, so we weren't certain we were in the right place. Daddy had been in this area when he worked with the CCC, and thought he remembered this as the place. The Captain thought it might be a little farther to the east. In any case, we needed to know before it got dark. Then, if need be, we could pull up stakes and try to find it elsewhere.

A gray gloom confronted us as we peered into a tangle of red cedars and live oaks. Some of their contorted limbs lay scattered across the little sandy beach in evidence of the recent hurricane. We thought the *well* might lie inside that tangle of brush. After searching for a few minutes, we discovered a path that led into the overgrowth laying just feet away from the shoreline. Daddy warned me to stay back as the place was perfectly capable of harboring snakes and poison ivy.

I didn't have to be told twice as I was equally allergic to both. My memory of the treatment with that awful concoction of coal tar and hog tallow, not too carefully applied to the blisters by Mama, were with me yet in a mighty big way.

And there was always present the image of the cottonmouth that haunted my dreams. Not that I had actually ever encountered one up close in real life. It was just the sight of the ones I had seen up Tranter's Creek, the way they slithered through the water as if they owned the place.

Just after the lantern disappeared from sight I heard a shout. "There it is, watch yourself; don't fall into that hole!"

They had found the well so I knew we were in the right place. I turned and ran back to the relative safety of the smoke from the fire, which was at that moment keeping mosquitoes and other flying insects away. I hovered around the camp site anxiously awaiting their return. The circle of light from the fire was denying access to the encroaching darkness that was quickly enveloping the little strip of sand.

"This must have been where the pirates had their ill gotten treasure laid out that day," I heard Captain Worthy say as they emerged from the wooded area. "According to history, the crew of the *Adventure* was waiting for the return of their captain from a trip up river to see Tobias Knight. That *business* being the pardon he had been expecting, probably."

"At the time I think they were more worried about the weather, and the need for the *Adventure* to be careened for vital repairs than anything else. They were probably also worried about all that loot. It lay on the sand, unprotected for the most part, where they had brought it from their French ship after it had gone aground upon arrival. They probably had an awful time getting it all to land and were anxious to get it back on board the *Adventure*. The sanity of their captain was probably also on their minds at this point, as he was not showing evidence of clear thinking at all."

"For instance," he said, "they could have stopped at several ports before they got here to get their coveted pardons, and some of the crew had done just that. Now the dozen or so men, who had been faithful to their captain found themselves on this God forsaken Island, stuck this far north at the beginning of winter. That was a most undesirable and undignified position for a weathered pirate of the high seas."

"As they awaited Blackbeard's return, I'm sure there were conversations regarding concern for his actions during that past few weeks. Worry about his ability to lead and his sanity at large wasn't exactly unfounded."

"Shortly after his return, early that Saturday morning, Lieutenant Maynard showed up and Blackbeard's crew made ready for what would be their last battle."

"I'm personally satisfied," Captain Worthy continued, "that at the time the battle ensued, they would not have all that booty from the French ship off the sand and back on board the *Adventure*. If Maynard and his crew didn't get it, who did? My supposition is that much of it was hurriedly dug into the sand or shoved up under scrub brush; anything to hide it from Maynard."

"If we can deduct this from theory, I know everybody else who has searched for his treasure here has had the same thoughts. So, we have to see if we can come up with a place to look that others haven't thought of, yet."

We decided to eat while we turned this over in our minds. Daddy filled the pot with fresh water from the supply on board *Miss Catherine*, as we didn't readily see a fresh water spring. Then he hung the pot to its frame and built a fire under it. We all helped with peeling potatoes and onions and placed them in the pot. When the water was at a rolling boil we threw in the fish we had caught earlier that day. The result was one of the best fish stews any of us could remember having. Maybe that was due to the place we were eating it, or perhaps it was because we were so hungry. There is something very unique about eating food around a campfire on a sandy beach that just cannot be found in any fine dining establishment.

After we ate we waded out into the surf a'ways and scrubbed the aluminum utensils clean in the salty water. Then the men put on their thinking caps. They were trying to reason out where the pirates might have hidden what they had time to hide on this little stretch of sand.

Captain Worthy took a long draw on his pipe and stated through the smoke escaping through his mouth and nose, "I think they might have seen that water well as a good hiding place. Time would have been limited after they realized the *Ranger* and the *Jane* harbored sailors from the British navy, and they would have known they could be seen by their enemy." He inhaled deeply again, propped his huge frame carelessly against the log behind him and made a sweeping gesture toward a sandy stretch of land with his pipe. "Therefore, they would not have been out there in plain view digging holes. The well would not have been in sight and didn't require so much time and effort. No one would have thought to look there. Bear in mind now, they had to be in a God awful hurry."

"Then the question would be how they expected to git it out agin'," Daddy said. "Does anybody have any idea how deep that well is?"

No one answered for the longest time, they just sat there thinking.

Then Luke said, "We can't see the well in the dark. Let's look around the edges of the woods and see if we can find any other places that could be used to quickly hide the loot."

"Where are you thinking we should look in the dark?" Steven asked, rather sarcastically.

"The moon will be up shortly and it's to be full tonight," Captain Worthy said as he scratched his back against the log he was propped against. He took another deep breath, puffed the smoke out and stared up into a starlit sky, seemingly contemplating the vast emptiness of space.

Things got quiet and kinda peaceful as we sat there inside that little circle of light, each person deep in his own thoughts, each taking his turn about, keeping the fire going.

Sparks, resembling fireflies, fluttered and skirted above our heads. White billowy smoke played havoc with my throat, and once in a while I'd have to walk away a few feet to get a breath of fresh air. It didn't seem to bother the others. I instinctively brushed a live spark from my hair.

Then the inevitable topic arose. That being, what if the pirates had done what they were reported to have done with the burying of treasure, killed someone and buried them with it to protect it?

"I don't think they had time to do all that, that particular day," Daddy said. "It all happened so fast, *but,* they might have buried it the night before. Then there was time. I'm wonderin' if the crew took it on themselves to put some of the loot outa sight of Blackbeard, so as to be sure to keep what they considered their fair share. It surely weren't beyond them to do such a thing, and Blackbeard was gone for a long time. I say we outa look right out here first."

I think that was what we had all been waiting for. Daddy and Luke went to the boat and collected shovels. Daddy remembered to bring back a pair of the smallest boots he could find on board for me, so I could go with them at daybreak to look in the well.

We decided on a pattern in which to dig and it wasn't long before the ground looked more like a bombing range than an innocent little beach, what with the pot marks and all.

We would dig until the hole filled with water, then move on to another spot. I helped until about half a dozen mosquito stings made me run for the protection of the campfire.

After about half an hour, John-John, who had been digging up around the wooded area suddenly yelled, "I found something!"

We quickly made our way over to where he stood in a hole, up to his knees in water, and watched as he reached down and tried to pull that *something* up. Daddy jumped in to help him, and after a few seconds they pulled up something alright. Something that looked for all the world to me to be a child's casket. I believe I was the only one who thought about the possibility of this being a shallow grave, and there just might be somebody's bones in there. I was remembering that last trip.

They heaved the chest up onto the sand and stood reverently for a couple of minutes before John-John stated, "Somebody needs to get an axe so we can open this thing."

Daddy scrambled for the boat and brought one back in the space of about a minute. It was the fastest I had seen him move in a long time.

The axe was handed to Captain Worthy as he was the person everybody accepted silently as *the boss*. Before he tried to split it open he stated, "Boys, this might be the mother load, we might be standing here as poor people for the last time in our sorry lives." He was apparently savoring the moment, unwilling to hurry it.

"Get on with it!" John-John shouted. "There ain't no time like the present to find out if we are rich, or are the butt of somebody's joke."

We all drew up close so we could get a look at what was in that old chest, apparently buried so long ago. The axe went up and came down in a swift second, splintering the wood into a thousand pieces.

Nobody spoke for what seemed to be ages. The only thing our eyes gazed upon was a few pieces of eight, and what appeared to be an age-yellowed letter. It was folded neatly; then stuffed into a bottle with a cork in it. Captain Worthy broke the bottle, unfolded the parchment and carried it over to the fire to get a better look. He stood staring for the longest time, then reported that it was unreadable, folded it carefully and deposited it in his pocket. I wondered why he would keep it if it were unreadable.

It wasn't long before John-John got his voice back and said, in a remarkable calm way for him, "Now listen up, this ain't the end of it, we might find something yet. We'll get to the well tomorrow, there may be something there. I vote we drown our sorrows in that good moonshine and get some rest before daybreak. We'll have to start early so as to not alert anybody who might be out fishing and come over for a howdy-do."

They decided to give me one of the pieces of eight and told me not to ever tell anyone where I got it. Daddy said he would punch a hole through it when we got home, so I could wear it like a necklace.

I remembered I already had a necklace and took it out to look at it. Daddy saw it and asked me where I got it. I told him as the men gathered around to look. Daddy took it from me and opened it up to discover an initial, *KK*, on the inside.

"This belongs to somebody, you know that Son. We'll have to see if we can find the owner when we get home. Your Mama will have an idea about it."

I put it back around my neck for the time being. I really liked it and was reluctant to give it up. After I crawled into my tent I took it out and stared at it for a while. It shivered, kinda like that quicksilver had, sparkling on the sand in my footprints earlier.

That night I dreamed about the pretty necklace I wanted so much to keep. Except for my doll and carriage, it was the only thing ever in my possession, up until that time, that was truly beautiful to look upon.

Excited chatter and the wonderful aroma of strong coffee brewing over an open fire brought me to a fully alert state. It took me a few minutes to remember where I was. I shrugged off the sweaty smelling coat I had wrapped myself in sometime during the night. As I crawled out of my tent I was confronted by a huge reddish orange sun, rising slowly out of the Atlantic. It was half in and half out of the water at the moment. I just stood there staring, mesmerized by the sight.

"Good mornin' sleepy head," Daddy said. "I do declare I thought you were gonna sleep past breakfast. We did keep somethin' for you to eat anyhow. It's time to go to the well, so hurry up if you want to go with us."

I didn't waste any time. I too, wanted to see what was in there.

It was still pretty dark once we got into the tree line. We followed the trail through the murky, soft darkness of the early dawn. It would be full daylight within a half hour.

I stood back a few feet and watched as they made ready to drop the hook into the well. It just kept dropping until the entire length of the chain played out, and still no bottom.

"I'll go get more chain," Daddy said, and called out to me over his shoulder, "Stay where you are, Son."

Just then a bright light flashed from the still dark western sky. I turned to look at the same time the others did to see what it was. *It* was a bright light, kinda like a round, full silver moon shining through the tree tops. It was surrounded by a cob-webby, twisty swirl of live oaks that had somehow managed to survive this hostile land. At the tree top level, something like a crown adorned its *head* surrounded by a rainbow of color. Its stick like legs and arms reached eerily downward to blend with the dark shadows near the ground. It wasn't moving, and for a second neither was I, being frozen to the spot. When I could move I made a mad dash for Captain Worthy who grabbed me up in his arms.

Nobody else moved. They just turned their heads and stood anchored in their tracks. By the time Daddy got back it was gone.

Daddy laughed at me when I blurted out what we had seen. Then Captain Worthy spoke up softy. "I know what it was, I've seen it before. It's known as a *Brocken Spectre*. Not many people have ever seen it, and nobody as I know of can tell you what it is. I suppose it's just the way the moon is caught shining through the trees at certain times of the early morning. Sure does look like a man with mighty long arms and legs staring down on you, though."

If ever I didn't know what terrors a man would confront for someone else's treasure, I did then. Not a man there was willing to turn and run, which I believe was at the foremost of everybody's mind at the moment. No sir, they would have stood their ground against the devil himself to get to the gold they thought might be there. You could cut the tension with a knife, it was so thick. Still, not a man was willing to give an inch until they could be certain if the gold was there or not.

They added the extra chain and tried again to get to the bottom of the well with success this time. Dragging it around and around for a while produced nothing, so they finally gave up in disgust. Not a fragment of anything was to be found, and by that time the sun was up a'ways in the sky, and enthusiasm had evaporated with the light of day.

Everybody was looking disappointed when Captain Worthy came up with another idea. "Why not give up the search today, go talk with the locals and come back after doing more research into the history and folklore of the place," he said.

"I agree," Luke stated. "We are all tired anyway and this is as good a time as any to talk with the people in the area and see what we can discover. I'm sure they must have some thoughts about the matter."

I seemed to be the only one suspicious about Captain Worthy giving up so easily and wondered if his decision had anything to do with that note in his pocket. I made up my mind I would try and sneak a look at it at the first opportunity.

We packed up and left the site. Our next destination was the little village on the Island where Captain Worthy knew some people. We were disappointed to find that most of the locals knew less than we did about the last days of Blackbeard. So, after spending a fruitless morning, we gave up completely and began our trip back home as poor as when we left. The whole crew looked disappointed and somewhat angry to me.

Captain Worthy was again the one who was willing to give up the search, as far as I was concerned, too easily.

It was a beautiful day. We had the wind at our backs and made good speed through the sound and up the Pamlico River. The men grumbled under their breath all the way. That is until the Captain got tired of it and told them to shut up.

Mr. Nathaniel was his usual quiet self until Luke started in on him as a reason we didn't find any gold. It was at that point he showed a side I hadn't seen before. He pulled out a knife, wiped it ever so slowly, one side and then the other, on his right trouser leg. Then he began to clean his nails with it, all the while keeping a close eye on Luke, who wisely took it as a threat and shut up.

Back at the docks, we sold the oysters to a local restaurant owner and the crew split up, going their separate ways with their share of the money. Daddy and the Captain lingered around for a while, and I saw the Captain pull out that little slip of age-yellowed paper. They read it together with great interest. Daddy didn't tell me what was there and I didn't ask, I was altogether too tired out to care right then. I just wanted to go home.

Mama was glad to see us and was happy Daddy had made a little money. We went to the store, and for once Mama bought everything she wanted, even some of those big red sausages she loved so much for supper.

Captain Worthy took us home with our treasure and stayed just long enough to drink about half a pot of Daddy's coffee. He admitted that day, finally, that egg shells did indeed help the taste of the Luzianne coffee Daddy was so fond of.

Just as Captain Worthy's car disappeared around the bend in the pathway a knock came at the back door. Mama looked at Daddy with a question written all over her face. *Who on earth could that be?*

Daddy had been leery of the back yard ever since he said he had seen that shadowy form of a woman beyond the well. He pulled down the squirrel gun and checked the chamber for a bullet, slamming the bolt forward before he *very* slowly opened the door.

Mama looked like she was going to fall down. She gripped the edge of the table with both hands and drew in a deep breath. Standing there looking like death warmed over was no other than, *Mr. Johnny*!

## Chapter 15

"I didn't know where else to go," Mr. Johnny muttered. He was staring at the floor. His shoulders were slumped over so much he looked as if he had lost several inches in height. "They'll be looking for me at Mother's house. I've been staying in the shed out back. I knew you all would come home sometime."

Mama slowly regained her composure and I saw pity soften the terrified look on her face. I took that as an answer to my question and ran to him, jumped into his arms and hugged his neck as hard as I could. He was home, that was all that mattered to me.

He went down on his knees and held onto me as if his life depended on it.

"Are you hungry, Johnny?" Mama asked gently as she took him by his arm and assisted him to stand, with me still clinging to him, and led him to the table. Daddy sat down beside him and started talking in a slow even tone. I couldn't tell if they were afraid of him or if they were sorry for him. It didn't matter at the moment. Mr. Johnny was home!

What had happened slowly began to emerge. He had found an opportunity and escaped from the institution. He couldn't tell us how he had found his way home. He said he didn't know.

His clothes were tattered and he had scratches all over his arms. Without another word, Mama went right to work. She cleaned his wounds and wrapped the deep cuts with clean rags. Then she started supper.

"Now we'll have someone to share my favorite food with," she said as she began frying sausage.

Soon, the kitchen was full of the tantalizing odor of food cooking and warm laughter. Even Mr. Johnny's expression came alive and the harsh look on his face softened a little in the soft glow of the lamp. Within an hour of eating, he fell asleep at the table with his head on his arms. Around nine o'clock, Mama woke him enough to stumble over to the pallet she had prepared for him on the kitchen floor. He fell into a deep sleep almost immediately.

"What are we supposed to do about this?" she asked Daddy.

"Why are you askin' me?" Daddy said. "I don't think we ought to tell anybody he's here. He ran away for some reason and he came to us for help. I don't think us turnin' him in is gonna help anythin'. Let's wait until he gits rested up and ask him what he wants to do."

Mr. Johnny didn't wake up until noon the next day. Even then it took him a while to remember where he was. Once he did, he seemed to be his old self again, at least to me.

Mama asked him what he wanted to do and he said he wanted to stay with us until he felt better. It was agreed that we would keep his whereabouts secret for now.

Late that afternoon, while Mama and Daddy were busy with building a fire and getting supper ready, I decided to show Mr. Johnny my necklace. I wasn't prepared for his response. He took it in his big hands and turned it over and over, as if trying to remember something. Then, all of a sudden he seemed to recognize it and snapped the lock open.

"Oh, my God," he muttered. "This is the necklace I gave my Katie just before I left to go overseas. Where did you get it, Liz?"

Mama was all ears by that time. Then she seemed to put things together. "Liz, tell Mr. Johnny where you found it," she said, followed closely by, "Why didn't you tell me about this?"

I took them out to the well and showed them where I had found it. Then I explained to Mama that I had wanted to keep it for a while because it was so pretty. "Daddy knew about it," I said. "He was going to tell you so we could find its owner when we got back from the fishing trip. I guess he forgot."

We gathered in the kitchen to decide what to do. It was decided that Daddy would go tell Deputy Crowley about it that very afternoon. We were not going to tell anybody about Mr. Johnny; he stayed with Mama and me while Daddy went on this trip alone. We knew he would probably be taken back to the institute if he were found there.

It was well past dark when Daddy returned with Deputy Sheriff Crowley. Mr. Johnny stayed out of sight when they came into the kitchen. Mama brought out the lantern so they could go look around the well as requested by the deputy. They scoured every inch of space between the house and the well. Finally the deputy leaned over the bricks surrounding the well and stared down into the water. "I think we better get somebody out to look in here. I'll be back tomorrow. Don't tell nobody about this Mr. Olfson, we don't want no amateurs poking around," he said.

The next morning the entire sheriff's department was at our house with chains and ropes. They placed a hook on the end of a log chain and dropped it over the side of the well. It went down until it stopped of its own accord. They slowly drug it around and brought it up again. I watched in horror as what was attached to the end of that hook came over the brick wall. A sickly looking white skeleton with some of its flesh still adhering to it, attached neatly around a shoulder bone to the metal hook, crept slowly over the rim of the bricks to fall in a heap at the

Deputy's feet. The rotted skin and bones clung to a remnant of material which looked as if at some point it had been a dress. Time stood still for me for a few seconds. Everybody's eyes were glued on those remains.

It wasn't long before I saw Mama go back into the house, apparently to look for Mr. Johnny. I followed her and was there when she found him in the corner of my bedroom with his hands clutched over his ears. His huge brown eyes were staring into space. The muscles in his face were contorted into an unreal torture, looking as if they saw things we weren't able to see. Apparently he thought those bones belonged to his precious Katie. I don't believe there was any doubt in any of our minds about that. I couldn't imagine what had happened to her or why, though. I was stuck in the present, trying to make sense of it all.

Mama went back out to the well to prevent the deputy coming into the house and discovering Mr. Johnny. I stayed with him. I didn't know what I could do for him; I just wanted to stay close. He was my friend.

After a while a black truck came and a man placed the bones carefully on a mattress in the back and drove away. Deputy Crowley lingered a long time in the yard talking to Daddy. He seemed to be trying to get an invite in but that wasn't going to happen. Mama took him a cup of coffee and told him that after seeing that body, she felt I needed peace and quiet, which wasn't far from the truth. I was more worried about Mr. Johnny than I was about my own feelings, though.

We managed to keep Mr. Johnny hidden until December, during which time Deputy Crowley and the King family came to see us several times to ask if we had heard from him. Mrs. King said he had escaped from the institution and thought he might come to us first for help. At each visit they told us they thought he was a danger to himself and others. Daddy always told them we hadn't seen him, because Mama wouldn't tell a lie. Daddy saw to it that she wasn't asked directly. We thought he was getting better as he had started to eat and drink enough to keep body and soul together, and had started to talk more.

"Do you think that tinker man, Lester, killed her?" He asked Daddy one day right out of the blue.

"I don't know, Johnny," Daddy said. "It might be or it could have been somebody else. Ain't nobody will ever know probably. I think it's better if you can let go of it."

By Christmas Mr. Johnny was making his own decisions again. He had said he was going to go see his parents on Christmas day whether they locked him up again or not.

"And I want to see if I can find that tinker man," he had said with a pitch to his voice that frightened me.

In any case Christmas Day, 1944, came at last. I was glad to have Mr. Johnny there to help us find a tree and to sing carols with. He said he was going home a little while after our celebration, to let his parents know he was alright. He said he wasn't going to tell anyone where he had been hiding out as that might get us in trouble, but he felt he was ready to begin a new life, without his precious Katie.

Daddy told him he was always welcome to come back here at any time he wanted, and Mama told him she felt like he was family. And so he left us that evening in clean clothes with his hair combed and beard trimmed, heading home. I watched his back until his long lanky frame reached the bend in the pathway. He turned and waved to me. I think he was smiling. I felt sad because I had become dependant on him being with us, but something in me felt happy for him. The feeling was kinda like the time I had brought home that Sparrow with the

broken wing.  Mama had fixed it up so it could fly away
on its own.  I was happy for the bird, but it hurt like the
dickens to let it go!

We didn't hear from Mr. Johnny again until the first
part of January, 1945.  We thought he was safely home
with his family.  It was on a cold, windy morning that Mr.
King and his wife drove into our front yard, got out of the
car and ever so slowly walked up to the door.  Mama
opened it and we knew something was wrong as soon as we
saw Mrs. Kings face.  She looked so tired and old.  They
had come to tell us that Mr. Johnny was dead.  They said
they thought they had convinced him to go back to the
institute for more care, and he had agreed.

"Last night around midnight we were awakened by
a gunshot coming from his room," Mr. King said.  "When
we got to him he was already dead.  He had put the end of
my double barrel shotgun in his mouth and pulled the
trigger, blowing the top of his head off.  He apparently
really wanted to die.  I will never understand.  Anyway, we
knew he loved you all and we came to tell you.  He will be
given a military funeral at the Oakdale Cemetery in
Washington.  We'll come and get you to go with us."

The next Thursday we rode in the car with the
Kings, following close behind the vehicle carrying the
coffin of my dearest friend at the time, to that lonely old
cemetery on the hill. The little procession turned in at the
gate and traveled about half a mile to where an ugly hole in
the dirt stood ready to take in Mr. Johnny.   It would hide
him forever from a cruel world; a world to which I felt he
had never really belonged, a society that never really
understood him.

Several men in uniform were there already, and
standing a little ways off was a man in a short skirt.  I
couldn't understand why a man would be wearing what
appeared to be a woman's plaid skirt out here in this cold

wind on purpose. He was holding some type of instrument
I had never seen before. I asked Daddy about it and he said
the instrument was a *bagpipe*. He said Mrs. King's family
was from Scotland; said the men always wore skirts like
that and played the *pipes* at a funeral.

The preacher from Mr. Johnny's church finally
finished speaking. I was glad because the man he was
talking about couldn't have been that gentle giant I knew so
well. He was talking about a brave soldier fighting a battle
in a land far away. He asked for a moment of silent prayer
for the deceased, and everybody except me bowed their
head. Just then, as if on cue a swirl of wind made the trees
around us shudder bringing with it a shower of dead leaves.
Women were holding onto their hats, in an effort to keep
them on their heads. I studied their faces and wondered if
they had really known Mr. Johnny like I did.

Then, for a time, it was so quiet you could hear
people breathe. Until, as if to break the silence, the
mournful wail of a train whistle announced its arrival as it
slowly made its way across the Pamlico. I was painfully
aware of a cold north wind biting at my cheeks.

Suddenly, as if from another world, the wail of the
train whistle was taken up by the bagpipes. The sound
filled the space around us with unspeakable sorrow,
mingled magically with joy and peace. I felt as if a weight
was being lifted from my shoulders as the sound made
chills run down my spine, and goose pimples rise on my
arms. Slowly the little group picked up the song and began
to sing, louder and louder, until the graveyard seemed filled
with the sound. I think it was the most beautiful rendition
of Amazing Grace I had ever heard. It was Mr. Johnny's
favorite song. It seemed to me to be giving us permission
to leave him there to rest, like we had left little Bet that
day.

After the service was over, the men in uniform
ended it by shooting their rifles up into the air. Daddy said
that was their way of saying goodbye. Then everybody
took turns telling Mr. Johnny's folks how sorry they were,
and a man in a uniform gave Mrs. King a folded flag in
remembrance. But there was yet a custom to be observed.
The little group split up and each went to view the sites
where family was buried. They always did that after a
funeral at that graveyard.

We went to see Mama's people, who were for the
most part all buried there. I asked her why we didn't bury
Bet there, but she never answered me.

Daddy paused for a second; then spoke up. "Your
Mama didn't want people to wander by her grave, stare at it
and wonder who she was. She wants little Bet to rest in
peace in that pretty place in the woods." That was all that
was ever said about it, but I always thought there was more
to it than that.

We visited several family plots before Daddy took
me again to see the graves of famous people who were
buried there. Two of those were the parents of Cecil B.
Demille, who was born when the family had been on
vacation in Ashfield, Massachusetts. Their home was in
Washington, North Carolina. He was raised to his teenage
years here. Daddy was an avid movie fan and knew his
work well. He was proud of the fact that so many poets,
writers and movie stars were from Washington, and had
wanted to come back home to be buried. He said we had a
lot of history to live up to.

After everybody grew tired of poking around
among the dead, we met at the gravesite to ride home with
the Kings. The sky was gray and angry looking. Most of
the trees around us were bare of foliage, exposing naked
skeletons to the uncaring dead. The ride home was quiet

and subdued. The whole world seemed to cry over the loss of Mr. Johnny.

It isn't often that so tender a spirit visits this earth, much less stays so long. It leaves us with a taste of what it's like to really care about and trust your fellow man. Mama said that Mr. Johnny just wasn't able to cope with the ways of the world. She said he simply cared too much for his own good.

As soon as we returned home we went to visit Bet's grave, and sat there with her for an hour or two. There wasn't much to say. We just took in the peace of the place. It was dark before we got home and built a fire to cook supper. A quiet supper it was, to be sure. I felt as if Mr. Johnny would come to the door at any time with his guitar and ask Mama if the coffee was ready.

After supper Daddy turned the radio on so we could perhaps get news about the war. Today seemed to make him think more about that battle going on so far away, and yet, the way he was talking, it felt very close. He told Mama again that if she would take me and Blackie and go stay with her sister in town, he would enlist and try to do his duty, in honor of Mr. Johnny. Mama said she'd think about it.

When I said my prayers that night, I asked God to take care of Mr. Johnny for me until I saw him again. I knew I didn't have to ask, Mr. Johnny was such a good man, but Mama's way of praying had made its way into my heart. I just felt like it was the thing to do.

## Chapter 16

I awoke the next morning to hear Daddy saying, "Come on in, Mr. Williams. There's coffee on the stove."

Then from Mr. Williams I heard, "I don't have time for coffee and this ain't no social call. I have noticed that you all are still doing everything but taking care of the farm business. How many times do I have to come out here to talk with you about it? I was here twice this past week to get you to help with clearing that piece of land down by the north pasture and here it is Saturday before I can even find you. I know you have been busy with other things, but you need to be here when I need you. I thought you all understood that!"

"I know we ain't been home all the time, but there have been some really bad things happen to our friends and us as you know, Mr. Williams," Mama said. "Andy and I work awfully hard on this farm, so I don't think you ought to be talking this way to us."

"Then you all need to stop using excuses for laziness!" Mr. Williams shouted in her face. "You are no better than that whore that got herself killed out here. She was always up to no good. I didn't put up with that high and mighty slut, and I'm not going to put up with you all and your lazy ways either!"

His words trailed off when he caught Daddy's eye. I could tell Daddy was *not* happy, his face was a bright red color, like it got when he was *really* mad. Nobody could talk to my Mama around Daddy like that. I knew we were in a tough spot though, because of being farm hands working by the day on his farm. I was frightened about the possible outcome of this conversation. We didn't have any place to go that I knew of. I backed up into the corner of the kitchen and stood there quietly, waiting to see what would happen. The way Mr. Williams was talking made me feel ashamed for us, but I didn't know why. As far as I knew we hadn't done anything wrong.

"I'll work for you Mr. Williams, and I'll do the best I can, but you will not talk to my wife that way," Daddy said. "If you want us out of here, we'll git out as soon as we can git another place."

"You won't find a place where you can come and go at will Andy," Mr. Williams stated. "I don't know of any place where you can live free of responsibility. I need my workers where I can find them at any time I want, and the other farm owner's around here do also. I can see that you are mad about what I said to your wife, but I can't allow anyone to stay here that can't be productive. You know about the last people who lived here. They paid rent until Johnny went away, then that wife of his quit paying. And I know Johnny helped you out a while back, but he's dead now and no longer able to help you."

"The last time I came out here to get my rent money from that whore, she told me to get off *her* porch. She said she would get me the money when she could, and wasn't willing to work it out on the farm. She was less than dirt in my opinion. You workers live here for free; all you have to do is take care of things on the farm. I expect that of you. If you can't do the job, get out and I'll find someone who can!" I've told you that before, don't you all hear well!"

He stormed out and slammed the door, leaving us to think over what he had said. We more or less knew we were at his mercy. Mama sank down in her chair, white faced. Daddy looked as if he could kill somebody. I'd never seen him look that way. It frightened me.

"You know we have to take the insults and not talk back Andy," Mama said. "We have to depend on people like him to survive. We don't own nothing and we've no place to go. There are no jobs for people without education or training that I know of, except farm work."

She and Daddy sat at the table for an hour trying to decide what to do now. I watched helplessly. That old familiar sickening fear tightened its grip on my heart. It felt like a strong hand squeezing the breath out of me. I knew we would probably be moving, but I had grown to like this place and felt almost at home here. Blackie crept up to stand idly at my feet. I reached down instinctively and picked him up, cuddling him under my chin. His warm little body set up a purr that brought me comfort, somehow.

I could see how Daddy had been humiliated and wondered how one person could do another that way. When Daddy left the house to go and sit with Jim and Jake, Blackie and I went with him. There was no need for words. We thought about things quietly for a while; then went back to the kitchen where Mama was humming an old familiar country song while she cooked supper. Nothing else was said about our situation that day.

At breakfast the next morning, Daddy announced he was going to find us another place to live. He said we had been there too long anyway, and it being January, we had time to find a place before farm work began in earnest.

Mama said we had better think about it a while longer. She said we had too much to lose to make a decision overnight. She told Daddy he needed to go with hat in hand to Mr. Williams and ask to stay at least through the planting season. That would give us time to find another place, maybe. Daddy reluctantly agreed.

That next morning he set out to see Mr. Williams like Mama had asked him to do. He was to ask if we could stay a while longer because of the things that had been happening that we had no control over. Mama said he was to say that we would be there each and every time Mr.

Williams needed help from now on. She said that if Mrs. Williams was home, she might be able to get Mr. Williams to listen.

When Daddy got back he said that Mr. Williams seemed to be in a better mood. He had agreed. He told Daddy he wasn't going to throw us off his land, in any case, not right now. He said that had not been his intention when he had visited the night before.

I knew I didn't have a say in the decision, but I was glad we might be there a little longer, because I didn't want to leave Barbara and Bet behind. I asked Mama if we would ever come back to visit them. She said the devil himself couldn't keep her away from little Bet's grave. I felt reassured.

Deputy Crowley came the next day to tell us that the police department had some new information and was looking for Lester to question him again about Mr. Johnny's wife. He asked if we saw him to let the department know right away. Mama said she would, but that we would be leaving this place as soon as we found another. When he asked her why we were leaving, she told him.

"I'm not surprised, I've heard there's more to Mr. Williams than meets the eye for sure," Deputy Crowley stated with emphasis.

"What do you mean?" Daddy asked

"I just meant he's a hard man to please. His wife has been seen in town a time or two staying at that hotel up on Main Street. I am told she was noted to have bruises on her arms and face sometimes, like she had been beaten up. I wouldn't be surprised if Mr. Williams didn't do it. They say he demands total control over all his possessions, including his wife. I guess that's his business, unless she complains."

Mama and Daddy looked at each other like they wanted to say something, but the only thing that came out was Mama asking, "Would you like another cup of coffee?"

"Don't mind if I do," Deputy Crowley said, settling back in Mama's chair as if he had a right.

After he and Daddy drank up all the coffee, Deputy Crowley stood up, tipped his hat to Mama and said he'd better be going. "You all let me know if you find out anything about that Lester fellow again, you hear?"

I watched until he disappeared around the bend in the path. Then I turned my attention to Mama and moved closer to the warmth of the kitchen stove. She was baking a molasses cake, and it smelled like heaven.

That weekend Captain Worthy showed up at our door. "I heard you all lost a friend, couple of weeks back," he stated. "I heard that Mr. Johnny was a good man but that he had a lot of problems. Also heard they found his wife's remains out in your well. That must have been an awful thing to see."

"It was," Daddy said, and offered Captain Worthy his chair while he took Mama's.

I went to the living room to watch Mama working on a dress for me to wear to school. She tried to make my homemade dresses look as much like the other girls as she could, and asked me to tell her if I liked the one she was working on. While we worked at getting it just right, we were half listening to the conversation going on between Daddy and the Captain.

"I've got Mr. Nathaniel in the back of the car, Andy," the Captain was saying. "You remember that note. I told him about it and he thinks we ought to check it out. This time there will be absolutely nobody there but us three and Liz, if she wants to go."

"Go where?" Mama asked right out loud, stopping the machine until she got an answer.

"Well, we were going to take a little trip down river next week and thought Liz might like to go with us, if we go on a Saturday. We had a note that the fishing is going well down that way, Miss Elizabeth," Captain Worthy blurted out.

"She ain't going nowhere, Mama stated emphatically. She needs to start putting more of her attention on book learning, and that's the final answer."

I wished they had not been talking so loudly. I knew Mama would never let me go now, and I knew they were going treasure hunting again. The fact that Mr. Nathaniel was there attested to that fact.

Daddy told the captain that he could ask Mr. Nathaniel in and he went to do that. Meanwhile, Mama told Daddy she didn't want that man in her house because she thought he looked like a warlock. "I've seen him in the back of the car before when Captain Worthy was out here, and I do believe he has a connection with the devil. In any case, you'd better get rid of him fast!"

Captain Worthy came back alone and said, "He won't come in, says he has a strange feeling about this place. Says the feeling is evidence of something that ain't quite right. I don't know what to make of him sometimes. He's been a friend of mine for a long time, and I know better than to try and force him to do anything. I'm not really sure why he agrees to come along on some of my excursions."

"We can pick this up at a later date. That's not the major reason I'm here. I might be able to shed some light on Johnny's wife's death. If somebody doesn't come up with a suspect other than that elusive tinker man, I'm afraid people will start believing the story that the tinker man's wife is spreading.  Have you all heard what she's been telling in town?  That Mr. Johnny killed his own wife!"

At that Mama got up and we joined the men in the kitchen.  "Yes, I've heard it but I still can't believe she's that crazy!  Ain't nobody ever loved a woman more than Johnny loved his wife.  She's just trying to get the pressure off Lester."

"Well, you know what they say, Miss Elizabeth, that love is just a breath away from hate.  I loved a woman once, but when I found out she loved anybody who had money, and was partial to the one with the most, I gave up on that emotion.  Ain't never been down that road again, and ain't never going to again.  Like they say; once burned twice shy."

"I hope you don't mean that, Captain Worthy," Mama said.  "There ain't nothing like having a person to talk your troubles over with.   It's so nice to have someone to help carry the load when you're too tired or sad to go on."

"It's been my experience from observation Miss Elizabeth; that the problem wouldn't have been there in the first place if the man had let well enough alone.  There's a lot to be said about having the freedom to travel where you want to and not be encumbered by a wife and kids."

"You're hopeless," Mama said with a hardy laugh, and we went back to sewing my dress for school.

I could tell Mama was happy that Mr. Nathaniel had remained in the car.  I understood what she was feeling more than I was willing to admit at the moment.

The Captain asked Daddy if he wanted a job with him on the shrimp boats and Daddy said he would think about it and thanked him for the offer.

"The answer to that is no too!" Mama called out over the steady hum of the sewing machine.  "I know how long you all stay out there, facing danger from the elements daily. And I know about your wanderings down around the Gulf of Mexico, where you ain't got no business either."

"See, I told you having a wife is like having a millstone around your neck," Captain Worthy said with laughter in his voice. Well, I didn't think she would let you go work with me now anymore than she did when I asked you the last time. Maybe sometime Mama will let you go."

"No I won't," Mama said, "I prefer a live *poor* husband to a dead *rich* fisherman, thank you."

The Captain left the house after that exchange. Mama had asked him to stay for supper, but he said he couldn't leave Mr. Nathaniel in the car much longer.

I followed them out the door and climbed into the back seat with the dreaded Mr. Nathaniel. He stared at me suspiciously and I stared right back. It was obvious that no love had grown between us since the last time we met.

Daddy and the Captain ignored both of us and talked about how they were going to get together at some point in the near future and try to follow some *directions* Daddy said was on that piece of paper he and the captain were looking at. I asked if I could look at it, but they both said *"no"* at the same time. Daddy continued with, "it's best that this be kept between the three of us grown-ups for now, Son."

Then they started talking about Lester. "I think he has some knowledge of the crime, but I don't know if he has the nerve about him to kill anybody," Daddy said. "After all, Elizabeth scared him off from this place right by herself one day. 'Course, she does have a right pointed way of lettin' folks know how she feels about a thing."

"I say, if I was the law I'd look in the direction of Mr. Williams," Captain Worthy said. "I have a sickly feeling that man could kill anybody standing in his way Andy, he's certainly mean enough, I hear tell."

"I believe Deputy Crowley thinks Mr. Williams might have the ability to kill somebody too, Cap'n. He said almost as much to us. She's so high and mighty though, nobody wants to get involved unless she asks, and she ain't," Daddy said.

"He's pretty good as a boss man most of the time and I just can't believe he's a killer," Daddy went on to say. "As for the trouble we've had with him, we knew when we moved here what he expected out of us. Our agreement wasn't any better or worse with him than one we could have had elsewhere. Life is rough on a poor man no matter where he chooses to hang his hat. We've been here longer than I expected to stay anyhow, and findin' out we had a body down there in that well was more that I want to deal with. I still don't believe it was Johnny's wife, somehow. I guess I just don't want to."

"As for this place, I've had a bad feelin' about it ever since we moved in here Cap'n. And to tell you the truth, we've heard and seen things here that there ain't no accountin' for. Now, I ain't sayin' they are ghosts, but I can't rightly say they ain't, neither, especially that woman I saw behind the well that night. Elizabeth said it was my imagination, because I'd been sick with such a high fever in the not too distant past, but that wasn't it. Whatever it was, I could see right through it, and I ain't never seen through a live human bein'!"

"The sounds we heard might be explained by Lester tryin' to make us move away from here for some reason I ain't got a grip on yet, but that woman in the long white dress can't never be explained to my satisfaction. And Lester was out of the picture that time anyhow."

"Maybe Nathaniel might be able to shine some light on it, Andy. He's into that kind of thing."

"No I ain't, Cap'n," Mr. Nathaniel spoke up from the back seat. "Some things I am too smart to touch, and that's one of 'em. No sirree, whatever is goin' on around this place ain't no business 'o mine, and I ain't gonna make it none, neither!"

"I sure don't understand why you're willing to go on treasure hunts with us, but you're afraid to mess with a little problem like this," Captain Worthy muttered in the general direction of Mr. Nathaniel

"'Cause there's a possibility of treasure at the end of one of those trips, and an endin' you don't want to know about at the other, Cap'n. I been messin' round with black magic long enough to know when to let a thing alone."

After that conversation died away, Daddy and I went back to the warmth of Mama's kitchen; Captain Worthy and Mr. Nathaniel took their leave. The Captain's last words before leaving had been to the effect that he would be back when Mama might be in a better frame of mind to talk about Daddy working with him.

We listened to music for a while before going to bed, and heard a short news brief about the war. Daddy said it reminded him of Mr. Johnny and asked Mama again if she had thought any more about staying with her sister in town so he could enlist.

"No!" was her only response at that moment. We went to bed.

The fire died down and a quiet darkness fell on the room, punctuated by a pool of light flowing from Mama's lamp. I kept my eyes on that small area. It seemed to shelter me from the ghosts I felt were hanging out in the corners of my bedroom. Never had I missed little Bet as much as I did that night. I remembered the soft sound of her breathing and the rustle of sheets as she turned in her sleep. My heart hurt like the devil.

Outside a cold wind was blowing around the eaves of the old shack and was creeping through the cracks around the windows. I became acutely aware of a stiff chill

that filled the room, and pulled the quilt up over my face to
let my breath warm the air I was breathing.

## Chapter 17

It was late February, 1945. An uneasy alliance had emerged between Mr. Williams and Daddy. Daddy seemed to me to be working like a puppet. Mama and I watched him every morning as he trudged stoically out to help with clearing the land Mr. Williams had asked him to clear, and assisting with whatever else he could do. He was quieter than usual too. I could tell the joy had gone from his duties, and I knew he was just waiting to hear from a man he had talked to that past week, to see if we could move to his farm a little to the south.

"I think Mr. Williams is finding it harder to replace me than he thought," I had heard him telling Mama just that morning.

"You are a hard working man Andy, there's few who could do what you do every day, I'm right proud of you sir," she had stated without a smile. She was saying it from her heart, and I could tell Daddy recognized that fact.

It was a cool, crisp morning that week while I was preparing to catch the school bus, and Mama was fixing food for us for the day when Deputy Crowley came strolling up to the porch. We hadn't heard him coming and Mama looked startled when she saw him. I guess that was because he had sneaked up on us. Seems he had a habit of doing that. He said he had left the squad car down at the end of the lane. Said it was because he had just had it washed by the prisoners up at the county jail. He didn't want it to get dirty underneath from scrubbing on the ground where the ruts were so deep in the lane.

Daddy had put more wood on the fire and started another pot of coffee before the Deputy got around to telling us why he was there. I noted he had that smug look of someone with gossip on his mind. I wanted to stay and listen, but Mama reminded me the bus would be there any minute, and if I wanted to catch it I'd better hurry. It was a long walk to the school house, she had pointed out.

Of course, I dawdled hoping to hear a word or two. On my way out the door I heard the Deputy saying they had caught the elusive Lester, and had him in jail with no bond seeing as he was suspected of murder. I paused long enough to hear him say Mama and Daddy would be required to attend the trial, if such occurred, to testify about the culprit's actions toward them since they moved in here.

I couldn't wait for more if I was to catch the bus. I arrived at the end of the lane just in the nick of time. The rest of that day was a blur for me. I couldn't wait to get home that evening to hear the rest of the story.

As soon as the bus dropped me off that afternoon; I took off running like the devil was on my heels. I couldn't wait to get Mama to tell me what was going to happen now. I found her cooking supper and started right in with my questions.

"Hold on Liz," Mama said with a smile. "I know you want to hear everything. I believe down deep in my soul that you are the most inquisitive child I've ever seen. But first I have something else to tell you. Since there's no school tomorrow, we're to go to the big house to help Mrs. Williams tidy up for the weekend. She say's if you help she will give you a nickel. Isn't that nice? You can buy candy with it the next time we're in town. It'll be your own money. Miss Lillian will be there. I can't wait to see her, it's been so long."

"Sit down here and I'll fix you a biscuit with syrup, it will be a while before supper. Now, what was that you wanted to hear?"

She was teasing me; she knew very well what I wanted to hear. I played along, telling her I wanted to know what the Deputy said about the arrest of Lester.

"Well, if you must know," she said. "The police think they now have enough evidence to charge Lester with the murder of Katie King. Now that they have her bones, they have decided he was trying to scare us away before we found them. They are going to charge him with murder and want your Daddy and me to go testify at the trial. That's all I know right now, but I'll be darned sure to inform you of anything I hear, *Miss Inquisitive*," she said with a twinkle in her eye.

"Can I go with you to the trial?" I asked.

"Now, whatever made me think you were going to ask that?" Mama said. If school is out maybe you can go, but not out of curiosity, no madam. And another thing, don't ask your Daddy, his answer is no too."

I knew there was no point in pursuing the subject right now, but we both knew it wasn't over. Daddy would definitely be on my side. He always was.

Just after dawn the next morning, Daddy left to meet Mr. Williams and the other men to finish clearing a section of new ground, and Mama and I were off to the big house. It was one of those cold winter mornings when you can see your breath hanging on the air after you breathe out; when all five of your senses are attuned with nature; when you can almost visualize your thoughts. We walked without talking, there was nothing needing to be said.

Mama had cut some branches from the red berry evergreen tree in our yard for Bet's grave. We had to go close by it on the way to the boss's house, and she always stopped if we passed that way. We spent a few minutes tidying up the site. She bent down and scrubbed roughly with her skirt tail at the moss that was trying to grow over

Bet's name. "I don't mind the moss, Liz; just don't want it covering her name," she said.

When we got to the big house, it seemed darker than usual. I looked at Mama and saw a worried face. We both knew Mrs. Williams spared no lights when she was cleaning. She always said you needed light to see what you were doing, and it was still not full daylight. The house would have been ablaze with light, usually. Neither of us said anything.

Miss Lillian was waiting for us on the veranda. She said she had not seen Mrs. Williams, and there had been no answer to her call. She had been waiting for Mama to knock.

Mama knocked loudly several times before Mrs. Williams came to answer it. She was wearing a scarf around her head and kept her face down and slightly to the right.

"Are we here on the wrong day, Mrs. Williams?" Mama asked.

"No, the house needs cleaning while Mr. Williams is out. He was talking this morning at breakfast, about how dusty it had become. I just won't be helping you. I fell down the stairs last night and got a few bumps and bruises. You all know what to do and I expect Liz wants her money, so go ahead and don't mind me. I'll sit over by the window out of the way while you're working."

She walked slowly over to her favorite chair and sat down to stare forlornly out into the front yard. You could tell by the way she moved that she had more than a few bumps and bruises, but it was not our place to inquire into the boss lady's business. We just started cleaning without saying anything more; but I noted Mama looking at Mrs. Williams like she wanted to say something. I did too, because I sure wanted to know what made her fall down those stairs.

We were finished with the work by lunch time. Mrs. Williams paid us and we prepared to leave. Just before we closed the door she called out, "Don't tell anybody about my bruises, will you? They might get the wrong idea. You know how people are."

"We won't," Mama called back and we left.

When we were out of hearing range, Mama asked Miss Lillian if she thought Mrs. Williams had fallen down the stairs.

"You ain't been 'round here long enough to know a lot about these people, Miss Lizabeth," she said. "No, she ain't fell down no stairs. That man o'hers is back at it agin'. He gits a mean streak every once in a while, and takes it out on his wife. I guess she don't have nowheres to go, and that's maybe the reason she don't leave him, I don't know. I do know she winds up at the hotel where my sister works at sometimes. Mary, that's my sister, she says they hears her a'cryin' in the night, but ain't nobody says nothin' to her. They feels it ain't their right. They say a man's home is his castle. Sometimes I can't help wonderin' what it is to his wife, in a case like Mrs. Williams."

The remainder of the walk home was more or less silent. Miss Lillian left us at the fork in the road and went her way and we went ours. Mama started cooking beans and opened the last jar of tomatoes she had put up last summer to put in them. It seemed she was so preoccupied in thought that she had forgotten to make my flour-bread man. When I mentioned it, she said I was too old now to be catered to in that way. That really hurt. I didn't think I would ever be too old for that flour bread man.

Daddy had gotten in touch with Captain Worthy to ask if he would take us to town to testify at the trial, and he had agreed.

Just past daybreak on the morning of the trial for Lester, I asked Daddy if I could go and he said, "Ask your Mama."

"I have and she said no."

"Well, why ask me?" he questioned.

"I want to know how the court works," I said, although that wasn't the real reason.

Daddy went out back to where Mama was hanging clothes on the line and said, "Elizabeth, I think we ought to let Liz go see what a trial is all about. That's somethin' she ain't gonna learn in a classroom."

"There's a lot about the court room that I don't want her to learn, either," she said as she shook out a sheet she was getting ready to hang.

Seeing Daddy was on my side I started to nag at Mama. "Please let me go. I loved Mr. Johnny and want to see what they're going to do about his wife's killer."

"You see Andy; she's already decided that Lester is the killer. You don't need a court of law and twelve honest men if you've already decided. I'm afraid that's what she's going to learn. Most folks around are of the same opinion. It ain't right."

"Then she needs to learn what not to do," Daddy said "And besides, how do we know we'll be home by the time the bus gits here this evenin'. She'd be alone 'til we got home. I don't want her to be by herself out here, do you?"

That got Mama's attention. She reluctantly agreed. Apparently she hadn't considered that. Neither had I. I was glad Daddy thought of it.

About that time Captain Worthy drove up. He was wearing semi-dress clothes. This was something I hadn't seen before. He looked too rugged to be wearing those kinda clothes. He seemed to be walking a little stiffly as he ambled up to the porch. His wrinkles were ever the more pronounced. I liked him better in his own clothes.

"Mighty dressed up there ain't you?" Daddy asked Captain Worthy.

"It ain't every day one goes to view a murder trial, Andy. I thought I'd dress for the occasion."

"If my clothes ain't good enough for them, I'll come home and they can do the trial without me, regardless of that thing they call a subpoena," Daddy said.

"You ain't got no fancy clothes, Andy," Mama said. "If you did you probably wouldn't wear them. You are as stubborn in your ways as those mules out there are." She gestured toward where Jim and Jake were standing staring at us like they wanted to know what was going on.

"What are you looking at?" Daddy called out. At that they turned around and walked away quickly, as if they were naughty boys caught with a hand in the cookie jar.

We left shortly after that, and the Captain turned the car toward town. It was a quiet ride as I believe we were all thinking about the outcome of this trial. Mama still maintained that she would make up her mind about Lester's guilt once she had heard all the evidence. The rest of us had made up our minds already. Mama said we were too quick to convict a person, and hoped Lester had a fair trial regardless of how she felt about him, personally.

When things got quiet I had time to think about our many trips to town with Mr. Johnny, and that familiar ache in my heart started up against my will. It stayed with me all the way to the court house. I kept thinking about how he used to let me sit on that bale of hay in the bed of his old truck and an involuntary tear slid down my cheek. I remembered how he had kept such a close eye on me to be certain I wouldn't put myself in jeopardy of falling out, by making me keep my seat until we reached our destination.

As we pulled into the parking lot at the courthouse, it became apparent we weren't the only people interested in that trial. I didn't know there were that many people in the entire county. We had to push our way through the crowd. Deputy Crowley had told Daddy to go straight to the District Attorney and talk with him before the trial started.

Daddy asked the lady who was sitting in a chair up next to where the judge would be seated, what we were to do. She told us to have a seat, *right over there,* pointing toward the area next to where the jury would be seated and to *wait*. She said the District Attorney would be along any time; that he had been looking for us.

He was there within ten minutes and escorted us to a little room behind Judge Hatcher's seat. There he questioned both Daddy and Mama about all they knew of that Lester fellow. They told all they knew and Mama concluded with, "Now we don't have any idea that he killed that woman, we're just giving you the answer to your questions as honestly as we can. You do understand that *don't you*?"

"Yes of course, that's what we want you to do. Only answer the questions, nothing more, nothing less, while you're on that stand."

I couldn't help but wonder how Daddy would be able to do that, he did so love to take a bone and run with it. I knew Mama would have no trouble. They'd be lucky if they got more than a *yes* or *no* to most of their questions of her.

We were told to go out and sit in *those seats* near the witness stand, and to come up when called upon. So we did that. Mama tried to interest me in going to sit with the spectators, but I managed to change the subject each time she started up. Daddy didn't seem to care one way or the other where I chose to sit.

I was watching the people cram in through the door at the back of the court room until the bailiff apparently noticed it too. He was making his way over there to stop anyone else from entering when who should push her way passed him but Mrs. Williams. A hush fell on the room. Whispers filled the air. About everybody turned to look. Mrs. Williams never lowered herself to show up at the courthouse for anything except business for the farm. What was she doing here? That question appeared to be on every busybody's lips in the room as they whispered to each other. The atmosphere was positively charged with anticipation.

Mama punched me in the side and stated, "Turn your attention somewhere else, Liz."

At precisely ten o'clock, Judge Hatcher came through the little door behind his chair, and the room suddenly became so quiet you could have heard a pin drop.

He was an awe inspiring figure of a man. He stood about six foot three and weighed in at about two hundred twenty pounds. His black hair was as white as cotton around the temples and his beard showed some thinning. But he could still calm a rowdy crowd with a steady gaze from his cold as steel, blue eyes. Some say he could talk his way out of hell with a pocket full of matches and never strike a one. Daddy had told me he spent time in the boxing ring in his younger days. He was well past fifty now, but was still in his prime according to Daddy, who had told me all that when he was telling me what to expect today.

Mama had stopped that conversation by saying that Daddy always exaggerated everything and was too easily impressed. I think for once Mama might have been a little wrong this time.

Finally, everybody was asked to stand while the Judge was being introduced, and then everybody was allowed to sit, after he sat down.  It was so regimented I felt like I was in church.  I thought even more about that as the witnesses were sworn in while touching a Bible.  That is everybody except, *Mama*.  When it came her turn, she stated quite clearly that she would not swear on the Bible, as she thought that would be a sin.  If people couldn't believe her, she would simple not testify.  "I have always told the truth," she said.   "I shall not compromise my values to be a witness in this trial or any other."

As if to punctuate Mama's words, thunder rumbled off in the distance.  It was to be another one of those rare storms that hit the coast without warning at this time of the year, keeping the weather men busy trying to predict.  There is a saying around Eastern North Carolina that goes this way:  If you want to know what the weather is going to be on any given day, take a look outside.

Rain started to spatter against the huge windows behind us and I turned around just in time to see a streak of lightening emerge from a cloud. It looked like a strange, arthritic finger stretching forth to touch the earth on some gruesome business.  I have always loved storms.  Mama told me once that rain drops were the tears of angels crying over the way human beings behaved toward each other.  Sometimes I believe that.

The Bailiff started to argue with Mama, whose jaw was thrust up and out in defiance.  Her stance said there would be no compromise on this issue, but Judge Hatcher came through with a plan.  Mama would state she would tell the truth on her dead mother's reputation.  The court would accept that as Mama's swearing in.  It was a deal, and everything got going again.

They called for Lester and he came in flanked by two officers, one on each side, as if he could have gone anywhere in those shackles if he had gotten away. His sockless feet below the restraints were housed in a pair of those brogans that were supplied to all prisoners in the county jail. Something about those sad looking shoes made me feel kinda sorry for the man.

He pleaded not guilty after being elbowed in the side by his attorney a couple of times. It was apparent to anyone looking on that Lester had no rapport with his lawyer who had apparently been appointed by the state as Lester had no money. The lawyer seemed to me to be more interested in what the District Attorney was saying than in protecting his client. When Lester tried to speak up a time or two, his lawyer told him he couldn't say anything in his defense until the District Attorney got through speaking.

Daddy was called, and after that, Mama. They told all they knew about Lester's strange behavior.

While they talked I noted that Lester's wife was on the edge of her seat, listening intently. At one point she tried to say something, but got cut off almost immediately by the Judge.

When he finally did get to speak in his own defense, Lester told a story that seemed to have a ring of truth in it to me. He said he had known the King woman, and had tried to sell his wares to her to no avail.

"She was a good lookin' woman, and she was very accommodating, for the right kind of money. I know what I did was wrong, and I've made peace with my wife over it a long time ago. Now I'm gonna tell you somethin' even my wife don't know. The last time I went to that place to see the King woman, I found out she was gone. I just sat down there in the woods and cried like a baby. No woman should have such power over a man. I couldn't help myself; I just kept goin' back agin' and agin' to see if she had returned. I tell you, she bewitched me!"

"When they, (he pointed at us) moved in that house, the thought came into my head that if I could make them go away, maybe the King woman would come back! I was like a slave to that woman. A lot of men around here were. I would have killed for her. I just couldn't believe she had gone away from me!"

"At first I thought she (he pointed at Mama) might be accommodatin' like the King woman. That's the reason I kept goin' there after they moved in. She's a good lookin' woman, as anyone can see, but she wasn't like the King woman at all. So I went back to tryin' to get rid of them, so the King woman might return. I didn't think her husband would come back from the war so soon, and thought we might have a long time to be together. That's my whole story, and I guess I've lost my wife because of it, but I ain't killed nobody!"

It was duly pointed out by the District Attorney that the jury had to look at the evidence, and that the evidence pointed to Lester being as guilty as sin.

It took over three hours to complete the trial. Apparently the jury thought Lester was lying, because it took them just thirty minutes to find him guilty of first degree murder in the case of Mrs. Katie King.

It was just as the verdict was being read by the jury that we were all startled by the sound of a voice from the back of the room. It was Mrs. Williams. I looked around to see her standing up talking loudly.

"Stop this sham of a trial," she was saying. "That man did not kill the King woman, my husband, Mr. Josiah Williams did! I will supply all the details when you want me to, in the meantime I need police protection. I believe he will try to kill me for this, but I can't see an innocent man go to prison for something he didn't do!"

The courthouse exploded in confused whispers. The judge called for order and told the Bailiff to get everybody out of there except Mrs. Williams, and the people directly involved in the trial. We stayed, of course. Wild horses couldn't have dragged me away at that point.

After the courtroom had been cleared, Judge Hatcher took Mrs. Williams, Lester and us into his chambers where Mrs. Williams told all.

"Ever since the day I married that man, I have been told how to do everything, from my housework to the length of the dresses I wear," she said. "I know that's the way it is with most married women, but I have always resented it. And he's like a lot of other men around here, too, as far as fidelity is concerned. He has always had women on the side and has told me about them, throwing in my face how much better looking they are than I am. Once he said he would never have married me if it had not been for the land my Daddy threw into the bargain. He has told me he didn't love me more times than I can count and I put up with it, but this is more than I can tolerate."

"He told me one night he was having an affair with that King woman, and was going to continue to have an affair with her. He fancied that he was *in love* with her.

"He also told me he thought she was having an affair with someone else. Now I know it was that fellow Lester, and God knows who else. He said if she didn't stop he would stop her, once and for all."

"He talks in his sleep when he's drinking, and I overheard him one night talking about how he had killed her. He indicated he had dumped her lifeless body down a well. I asked him about it when he woke up and he said if I ever told anybody that hogwash, he'd see to it that I was tarred, feathered and rode out of town on a rail. Said he'd always wanted to do that anyway, and since my father died there was no reason not to. Said nobody would believe me if I told it, and that's probably the truth."

After Mrs. Williams stopped talking, we were all silent for the longest time. It seemed nobody knew just what to say. Judge Hatcher rose from his seat and went over to Mrs. Williams. He put his hand on her shoulder and said, "Thank you for your testimony. You know you will probably be required to repeat it in the open courtroom. That is, unless your husband confesses. The court will put you up at the hotel with a guard at your door until it's over."

Then he called all interested parties back into the courtroom and declared a mistrial. He apologized to Lester for the court, and told him that he should take this as a warning that the kind of games he had been playing could actually cost him everything.

At that point he dismissed the court and told the sheriff's deputy, Crowley, to go pick up Mr. Josiah Williams and hold him without bail, charged with the murder of Mrs. Katie King.

I watched as Lester and his wife left the courtroom. They were holding hands and she was crying.

"There's no accounting for taste," was Captain Worthy's remark as we drove away from the parking lot.

The ride home was unusually quiet. It was as if no one had anything to say until Mama said right out of the blue, "I told you, you shouldn't find someone guilty until it was a certainty, Andy. Will you admit I was right this time?"

"Well, it sure looked like he was guilty, and I kinda wished he was as I don't like anythin' about that man," was Daddy's reply and things fell silent again.

Captain Worthy came in when we got home and he and Daddy had a long conversation about the day's happenings. They went through three pots of coffee before growing tired of talking about it.

Then the subject was brought up about what would happen to us and the farm now that the boss man was going to jail and his wife was at the hotel in town under witness protection.

"I don't know who will be runnin' the place," Daddy said. "I guess this is the time when we have to make a move somewhere. We don't have no choice."

"The offer of a job on my fishing boat still stands Andy," Captain Worthy said. "Any time you and Miss Elizabeth want the job it's yours. As a matter of fact, I've been thinking lately that I wouldn't mind staying close to home now. I've put in a lot of years on those boats running up and down the east coast and I'm getting old and tired. I know I could make a living fishing the Pamlico. Would you be interested in that?"

"Only if Elizabeth is," Daddy said; they both looked at Mama.

"Well, it sure looks like we've got to do something Andy," Mama said. "I'll think about if you will stay inside the continental waters and close enough to come home at least every two or three days. Now, don't think I'm saying yes. I'll think about it."

I went to bed that night feeling happier than I had in a long time. I'd always had a deep seated love for that river and could picture going out on it often, if Daddy was a fisherman. The feeling of pure joy had returned in spite of my fear that I would never be happy again after losing Bet, Barbara and Mr. Johnny. After all, the river would always be there. It would not leave me.

## Chapter 18

With Mr. Williams in jail, Mrs. Williams felt safe
enough to come home.  She came to see us right away to
tell Daddy she didn't know how long she could keep the
farm.  She said she didn't know much about the business
side of the place.  She was thinking about selling out if she
could manage to get a clear deed. "My sister has offered
me a place to stay with her up north," she said.

Daddy told her he would help her with the crop that
year, and then we were going to leave for sure anyway.  He
told her what Mama had done.  She had agreed to him
becoming a fisherman, as long as he promised to stay
within the Pamlico Sound area.   The agreement also
included the promise that he would not stay out more than
three days at a time.

I do believe Captain Worthy was one of the
happiest men I'd ever seen the day Daddy told him he
would take him up on the job offer.  He immediately
reminded Daddy of the house he had inherited down by the
Pamlico, the one that would be convenient once he started
working with him.  He said that since the house was right
on the banks of the river,  he could pick him up right there
on the way out, and not have to drive all over creation to
get him. "Furthermore," he added, "It will be rent free for
as long as you all live there and work for me."

Out of Mama's range of hearing, Captain Worthy
had a little more to say.  He told Daddy and me the house
was isolated enough to accommodate a liquor still in an old
run down shed about two miles behind the place.  It was up
in the woods a'ways where it was swampy enough to
discourage the revenuers.  He said that he sure would

appreciate it if Daddy would start making whiskey for him and his crew; said he would finance the operation. Of course Daddy was agreeable to that offer and told me not to mention it to Mama, as if I would. I was smart enough to know that would be the death of Daddy's work with the Captain.

We went to see the house that next Saturday. Mama was happy with it. It was in fairly good shape and even had a new outhouse right next to the woods in the back yard. There were screens on all the windows, and a wide screened porch reaching around two sides. The front of the place faced the river where there would be a good breeze in the summer. There was plenty of wood available, and a big space for a garden. Daddy took one look and said we were coming up in the world. He was so proud of the fact that, at long last, he could supply his family with a halfway decent place to live. His face was just beaming.

We were to move, just as soon as Daddy got the tobacco crop in for Mrs. Williams. The Captain said the house and the job would be there when we were ready.

Daddy didn't want to stay and work out that year, but Mama said she would not move until he did, because he had promised Mrs. Williams.

Our lives were better for a while, with new hope in our hearts. The only fly in the ointment was when President Roosevelt died. It was April 12th 1945 when we heard it on the radio. Daddy was very fond of President Roosevelt, and had a fear that Vice President Truman might not be able to make the right decisions about the war. He and Mama talked about it for several days, until Mama finally said there wasn't any need to worry about it anymore, a thing was what it was. We couldn't do anything about it anyway.

We did the usual farm work: planting, transplanting, weeding and bringing in the tobacco crop with one major difference, Mrs. Williams seemed unusually grateful. That was a roundabout way of thanking Daddy, I think, as he didn't have to stay there. He had a better job waiting; a job where he had high hopes of being treated as an equal.

Captain Worthy came to the house in a great hurry one afternoon, slamming on the brakes so fast that a curl of dust flew up all around the car. He wasted no time in telling us about the news in town. The day was August tenth, 1945.

He was so excited. "You don't have to worry about going to war now, Andy," he said. "I hear in town that there have been two bombs, called *atomic* bombs, dropped on Japan. One called Little Boy on the town of Hiroshima on the sixth, and one called Fat Boy on Nagasaki yesterday! They say there is no doubt that the Japs will have to surrender now or be annihilated! Thank God, the war is over!"

They both thought that called for a drink. He and Daddy went out back and proceeded to have two or three from the jug Daddy kept for such important happenings, out of Mama's sight of course. Their excitement was contagious. I couldn't help but feel it, although I didn't fully understand the implications of the thing. Even Mama seemed to be excited.

Summer storms had come and gone, but nothing catastrophic like the last hurricane. So far, it had been a pretty good year. Hope for a better future hung in the air and permeated everything we did. If the work got too hard or the day too long, either Mama or Daddy would say, "It'll be better next year for sure," and somehow that got us through.

That evening was spent talking about the little house we would be living in once we left this place. I was really excited about it, but leaving Bet up there on that lonely hillside kept quietly tugging at my heartstrings.

Mama seemed to be aware of what I was feeling, because she came to sit at my bedside one night, in the wee hours of the morning. All was quiet and as still as death. I could hear Daddy snoring.

"Liz," she said, "Out of total sorrow, grief and poverty, a garden grows. It is a beautiful garden that feeds strength and character. So, cherish the moments spent there, for they temper the soul."

"I don't understand Mama," I said.

"You will someday," she whispered softly and went back to bed without another word on the subject.

The following Saturday we all went to the new place to let Mama clean it up to her satisfaction before we moved in. It was close to the time when we would be leaving the place I had begun to feel at home in. Mrs. Williams, who had finally managed to get clear ownership of her home, had finally decided for sure to move up north to be with her sister. The place would be sold if a buyer could be found. Daddy said it felt like he was getting out of jail.

"That's just like you Andy," Mama said. "You always will like to move on I guess." That was the last comment Mama made on the subject. The next two weeks were a flurry of activity. Captain Worthy had borrowed an old truck from Mrs. Williams for us to use.

Mama had piled everything up in the corner of her bedroom that wasn't being used to work with at the moment, on that final day. We were just getting ready to go take some flowers to Bet's grave and tell her goodbye when Mrs. Williams' car pulled up. She came to the porch where I was standing with something in her hand.

"The Kings wanted me to bring this to you Liz," she said. "It's the locket you found that helped solve the mystery about Katie King. They are grateful, as I am, to have that behind us now and we all want you to have this

from Mr. Johnny. He would have wanted you to have it.
He was very fond of you. They said to tell you that if they
could, they would have brought it themselves, but they
can't bear to come out here yet. We all wish you well." I
thanked her and she smiled. Then she turned away,
brushing at a lonely tear making a trail down her weathered
face.

I pulled the chain holding the beautiful piece of
jewelry over my head to hang around my neck, thinking I
would never remove it as long as I lived. It shared a place
with the shiny, golden piece of eight. I made note of how
beautiful they were together. Then I closed my eyes and
said a silent thank you to my friend, Mr. Johnny.

"She seems to have aged ten years since we came
here," Mama was saying as Mrs. Williams car disappeared
around the bend in the road.

"Well, she's had a lot of trouble since then," Daddy
said

"And a lot before we moved here, apparently,"
Mama said as we set out on our journey to visit the little
grave that awaited us behind the house.

We found it just the way it was when we saw it two
days before. Mama quietly removed the old foliage and
replaced it with what we had brought. The way she
lovingly arranged the bouquet, one would have thought it
was being done by an expert in the business. She had a
good hand with the beautiful things God had created for
poor people to decorate their grave sites with.

After we left Bet's grave, we went to Barbara's to
find that Aunt Lillian had it decorated too, with the same
loving care Mama had taken with her child. We bid her
goodbye just as we had little Bet, and made our way back
home to wait for Captain Worthy and the truck. We didn't
have to wait long. Around nine o'clock that morning the

old truck came around the bend and up into the yard. It was time to go.

"You all ready?" Captain Worthy asked in his loud booming voice.

"As ready as we'll ever be," Daddy stated.

I clutched Blackie who was stuffed up to his neck in the pillow case Mama had placed him in for the ride. His head was the only thing sticking out. He was quiet and still, but his huge green eyes stared at me with a great deal of anxiety. I watched as the open back end of the truck was loaded with our meager belongings. It was amazing how little space they actually took up. Then it was time to leave. I climbed into the cab and looked out the back window for the last time. As we neared the bend in the lane I turned my head away, closed my eyes and tried to tuck away a picture of the place in my memory bank. With a little concentration I brought up the faces of Mr. Johnny, Bet and Barbara. They looked back at me with a smile, and I felt somehow like everything would be alright now.

I had found myself doing that more often after Bet died. It seemed that I could keep the things I loved with me always like that.

After we turned the corner and the little house died away into the past, I opened my eyes and looked forward to perhaps a better future. At least I knew it couldn't be any worse. Like Daddy said, as long as the river had fish and the woods had rabbits and squirrels, we would survive. And there was always that one last, hopefully fruitful trip to the outer banks to hunt for treasure. That brought the map Captain Worthy had kept to mind. Maybe when Mama forgot, we might go.

A quiet, thoughtful atmosphere permeated the air in the cab of that truck as we all looked forward to this new world we were entering.

Blackie curled up his now rather huge, five pound body in my arms and laid his head in the crook of my elbow, seeming to quietly give in to whatever awaited us. It was as if he knew he and I had very little choice. He trusted me, though, and I knew life would go on no matter what. I had learned a lesson worth keeping while living at that little shack. This life we live here isn't Heaven or hell, just more or less what we make it, day to day.

I had certainly learned that ghosts probably did not exist, but I sure do wonder what Daddy saw that night; that lady in the long white dress that he said he could see the woods through??? That one is worrisome.


My coffee is cold. God I hate cold coffee! The rain has stopped and the sun is out. The sweet aroma of honeysuckle clinging to the white picket fence below is blowing ever so softly through the window. I Pull the little blanket with B E T so carefully cross-stitched over the upper left hand corner around my cold, stiff shoulders with my left hand. I feel the warmth it has always afforded me. My right hand lies limp in my lap as it has since the stroke that had made this move to a nursing home necessary for me a few years ago.

I close my eyes and softly kiss the initials that decorate it. The doll on the shelf, the one with the curly black hair, is looking down on me as it has these many years. I close my eyes and tuck the memories away for another time and place, when they would be needed again.

I am waiting for my treat. A Bill's hot dog with extra chili and a Pepsi is on its way.

Its five o'clock in the afternoon and the nurses will be busy with their medication rounds. My favorite nurse, Rose, should be sneaking it down the hallway right about now.  If the charge nurse catches her, Rose will probably be fired.

Oh well, if they ever catch me eating it, they'll never get me to tell who brought it.  Rose is my best friend here.  Wild elephants could never pull that information out of me!  I close my eyes and wait patiently for the contraband, knowing it will taste as good as ever it did. They say my old digestive system can't tolerate junk food! Don't they know a Bill's hot dog will cure any stomach problem?

Made in the USA
Columbia, SC
03 June 2021